Day After Night

Day After Night

ANITA DIAMANT

London · New York · Sydney · Toronto

A CBS COMPANY

First published in the USA by Scribner, 2009
A division of Simon & Schuster Inc.
First published in Great Britain by Simon & Schuster UK Ltd, 2009
A CBS COMPANY

1 3 5 7 9 10 8 6 4 2

Simon & Schuster UK Ltd
1st Floor
222 Gray's Inn Road
London WC1X 8HB

www.simonandschuster.co.uk

Simon & Schuster Australia
Sydney

A CIP catalogue record for this book is available from the British Library

ISBN 978-1-84737-707-4

Designed by Carla Jayne Jones

Printed in the UK by CPI Mackays, Chatham ME5 8TD

In memory
of my grandfather Abe Mordechai Ejbuszyc
and my uncle Henri Roger Ejbuszyc,
victims of the Holocaust

Know that every human being must cross a very narrow bridge. What is most important is not to be overcome by fear.

Rebbe Nachman of Bratslav, 1772–1810

Prologue

1945, August

The nightmares made their rounds hours ago. The tossing and whimpering are over. Even the insomniacs have settled down. The twenty restless bodies rest, and faces aged by hunger, grief, and doubt relax to reveal the beauty and the pity of their youth. Not one of the women in Barrack C is twenty-one, but all of them are orphans.

Their cheeks press against small, military-issue pillows that smell of disinfectant. Lumpy and flat from long service under heavier heads, they bear no resemblance to the goose-down clouds that many of them enjoyed in childhood. And yet, the girls burrow into them with perfect contentment, embracing them like teddy bears. There were no pillows for them in the other barracks. No one gives a pillow to an animal.

The British built Atlit in 1938 to house their own troops. It was one in a group of bases, garages, and storage units set up on the coastal plains a few miles south of Haifa. But at the end of the world war, as European Jews began making their way to the ancestral homeland in violation of international political agreements, the mandate in Palestine became ever messier. Which is how it came to pass that Atlit was turned into a prison or, in the language of command, a "detention center" for refugees without permissory papers. The English arrested thousands as illegal immigrants, sent most of them to Atlit, but quickly set them free, like fish too small to fry.

It was a perfectly forgettable compound of wooden barracks and buildings set out in rows on a scant square acre surrounded by weeds and potato fields. But the place offered a grim welcome to the exhausted remnant of the Final Solution, who could barely see past its barbwire fences, three of them, in fact, concentric lines that scrawled a crabbed and painful hieroglyphic across the sky.

Not half a mile to the west of Atlit, the Mediterranean breaks against a rocky shore. When the surf is high, you can hear the stones hiss and sigh in the tidal wash. On the eastern horizon, the foothills of the Carmel reach heavenward, in keeping with their name, kerem-el, "the vineyard of God." Sometimes, the candles of a village are visible in the high distance, but not at this hour. The night is too old for that now.

It is cool in the mountains but hot and damp in Atlit. The overhead lights throb and buzz in the moist air, heavy as a blanket. Nothing moves. Even the sentries in the guard towers are snoring, lulled by the stillness and sapped, like their prisoners, by the cumulative weight of the heat.

There are no politics in this waning hour of the night, no regret, no delay, no waiting. All of that will return with the sun. The waiting is worse than the heat. Everyone who is locked up in Atlit waits for an answer to the same questions: When will I get out of here? When will the past be over?

There are only 170 prisoners in Atlit tonight, and fewer than seventy women in all. It is the same lopsided ratio on the chaotic roads of Poland and Germany, France and Italy; the same in the train stations and the Displaced Persons camps, in queues for water, identification cards, shoes, information. The same quotient, too, in the creaking, leaky boats that secretly ferry survivors into Palestine.

There is no mystery to this arithmetic. According to Nazi calculation, males produced more value alive than dead—if only marginally, if only temporarily. So they killed the women faster.

In Barrack C, the corrugated roof releases the last degrees of yesterday's sun, warming the blouses and skirts that hang like ghosts from the rafters. There are burlap sacks suspended there as well, lumpy with random, rescued treasures: photograph albums, books, candlesticks, wooden bowls, broken toys, tablecloths, precious debris.

The narrow cots are lined up unevenly against the naked wood walls. The floor is littered with thin wool blankets kicked aside in the heat. A baby crib stands empty in the corner.

In Haifa, the lights are burning in the bakeries where the bread rises, and the workers pour coffee and light cigarettes. On the kibbutz among the pine trees high in the Carmel, dairymen are rubbing their eyes and pulling on their boots.

In Atlit, the women sleep. Nothing disturbs them. No one notices the soft stirring of a breeze, the blessing of the last, gentlest chapter of the day.

It would be a kindness to prolong this peace and let them rest a bit longer. But the darkness is already heavy with the gathering light. The birds have no choice but to announce the dawn. Eyes begin to open.

I

Waiting

Tedi

Tedi woke to the smell of brine. It reached her from beyond the dunes and past the latrines, confounding the stale breath and sour bodies of the other nineteen girls in her barrack. She sat up on her cot, inhaled the sharp salt fragrance, and smiled.

Tedi Pastore had lost her sense of smell during the war. With too little to eat, she had lost her period, too. Her heavy blonde hair had grown dull, her fingernails brittle and broken. But everything was coming back to her in Palestine.

In the two weeks since she'd been in Atlit, Tedi's nose had become as keen as a dog's. She could identify people with her eyes closed, not only who they were but also what they had been up to and sometimes even what they were feeling. She caught the overwhelming scent of sex on a girl she passed in the compound, and gagged on the strange choking tang of burning hair that rose from Zorah Weitz, who slept on the far side of her barrack—an angry little Pole with flashing brown eyes and a crooked front tooth.

At first, Tedi thought she was going crazy, but once she realized that no one suspected her secret, she stopped worrying about it and fixed her attention on the future.

Her plan was to live on a kibbutz where everyone smelled of oranges and milk and to forget everything that had come before. For Tedi, memory was the enemy of happiness. She had already forgotten the name of the ship that had brought her to Palestine and of the stocky Greek boy who had held her shoulders while she retched, seasick, into a bucket. She wondered if she could fill her head with enough Hebrew to crowd out her native Dutch.

Tedi promised herself that the moment she walked away from Atlit, she would forget everything about it as well: the ugly, parched-dirt compound, the long days, the heat, and the girls from all over Europe—the nice ones as well as the obnoxious ones. She would forget the cool blue mirage of mountains in the distance, too, and the eccentric volunteers from the Yishuv, which is what they called the Jewish settlement here.

She would start all over, like a baby, and she toyed with the idea of putting a new name—a Hebrew name—on her next identity card. She would become like the pioneer boys and girls—the ones who had grown up in Poland and Romania singing about the land of Israel and dreaming of a life filled with farmwork and folk dancing. Sons and daughters of shopkeepers and teachers, their Zionist summer camps had given them a taste for physical labor. All they talked about was how they wanted to plow and dig and fight and build a state. They seemed to face the future without a single backward glance. She thought they were wonderful.

The Zionist kids liked her, too, though she knew it was mostly because of her blonde hair and her height. They could be arrogant and rude; one boy called Tedi "a fine specimen" to her face. And while she knew they said such things without malice, she was self-conscious among them. In Amsterdam, she had been one of many Jewish girls with blue eyes, narrow hips, and broad shoulders. Like her, most of Tedi's friends had had at least one Lutheran parent or grandparent, and it was considered bad taste to take note of anyone's mixed parentage until 1940, when non-Jewish relatives became assets.

Tedi yawned and stretched. She was the barrack's champion sleeper, out like a light as soon as her head touched the pillow, and so slow to wake that she sometimes missed breakfast. When she finally put her feet on the cool cement floor, she realized that she was alone and quickly pulled on the washed-out blue dress that showed a bit too much thigh, though it was not as revealing as the short pants some of the girls wore.

On her way out, Tedi noticed Zorah curled in a tight ball on her cot near the door, which Tedi closed as quietly as she could. Then she ran toward the latrine, telling herself not to worry; there really was no danger of going hungry in Atlit. Even when the kitchen ran out of tea or sugar, there was always plenty of bread and the cucumber and tomato salad the locals seemed to think was a fit dish for breakfast. Sitting on the toilet, she tried to remember the word for tomato.

"*Agvaniya!*" she said.

"What?" came a voice from behind the partition.

"I didn't know anyone was here," said Tedi.

"If you want *agvaniya,* you'd better get to the mess in a hurry. They're going to close the door."

Tedi decided she would ask Nurit, one of the Hebrew teachers, to tell her the word for cucumber, but then she remembered that there was no class that morning. One of the political parties had called a strike against the British, and the teachers would be taking part in the demonstration. No Hebrew, no calisthenics, nothing to break the monotony.

Suddenly, the day loomed before her, long and empty, with nothing to do among people to whom she could barely speak. Unlike most everyone else in Atlit, Yiddish was not Tedi's mother tongue. "That uncouth jargon" had been forbidden in her mother's house, although she had heard her grandfather speak it and learned some in the Displaced Persons camps and on the journey to Palestine. She understood more Hebrew every day, but it was still hard getting her mouth around the words, which often seemed like anagrams to her, random groups of letters that needed to be puzzled together before making sense.

"*Ag-va-ni-ya,*" she whispered, as she splashed water on her face. A pretty word, it would make a nice name for a cat. She had always longed for a calico cat. Were there any calicos in *Palestina*? she wondered. I will have to ask someone about cats, Tedi thought. And cucumbers.

The sound of a train whistle in the distance shook Tedi out of her reverie and lifted her spirits. The arrival of new immigrants meant the day would pass quickly now, and she would be spared the problem of having too much time to think.

She joined the crowd that was moving toward the southwestern corner of the camp, close to where the train would arrive. A few of the other girls said hello to her, and a couple of the boys tried to catch her eye. Hannah, a cheerful, moon-faced girl who seemed to know everyone's name, rushed over and handed her an apple. "I saw that you weren't at breakfast," she said.

"Thank you very much," Tedi answered carefully.

"Your Hebrew gets better every day," said Hannah. She already dressed like a kibbutznik, in shorts and a camp shirt with her hair in pigtails. "Isn't it wonderful?" she said, gazing at the train. "We need more settlers. More and more."

Tedi nodded furiously, ashamed at having thought of their arrival as a diversion. She followed Hannah, who pushed her way through until they were in front, looking out through the strands of barbwire.

There was no station or even a wooden platform at the end of the track; the rails just came to an end in an empty field surrounded by tall grass and wildflowers. Thousands of feet had trampled the weeds and packed the earth into a clearing and then a path that ran parallel to the Atlit fence and down to the road that fronted the camp. It was a long five-minute walk to the gate for the tired, frightened people who arrived carrying battered valises and the last of their hopes.

As the engine chuffed to a halt, British soldiers opened the doors to the three boxcars. Someone behind Tedi gasped. "How can they do that? They brought me here on a bus with the windows painted black and that was awful. But this?" Tedi turned and caught the faint but unsettling odor of camphor on the woman who had spoken. She was very pale, a sign that she was a recent arrival. "Surely these people know what it means for Jews to be forced into cattle cars. I do not understand the English. They fought Hitler. Why do they do this?"

"It's a terror tactic," said a stern Bulgarian girl who wore a black neck scarf, which signaled membership in one of the many political movements Tedi couldn't keep straight. "They put us in trains to frighten us and keep us weak, but it won't work." The new arrivals squinted as they staggered into the blazing sunlight, clutching at their belongings.

"Shalom, friends, shalom," the Bulgarian girl cried, cupping her hands around her mouth. "Shalom. Welcome." Others joined her, calling out greetings in Hebrew and Yiddish, German, Romanian, French, Polish, Italian, and Greek.

As the newcomers began to make their way down the path, the inmates inside the fence kept up with them, trading rumors. Someone said that their boat had been fired upon in Haifa. Someone else said they heard this group was mostly Auschwitz survivors.

"Did you see the man who was carried off the train? Was he dead?"

"No, it was a woman who fainted in the heat."

"These people are all legals with papers. They'll be out of here in a day or two."

"How do you know that?"

By now, Tedi knew better than to pay too much attention to this kind of speculation; they'd get the real story soon enough.

As soon as the new inmates reached the front gate, a different kind of chorus rose from inside the camp.

"Vienna? Is someone from Vienna? Do you know the Grossfeld family? The furriers?"

"Lodz? Here is a neighbor if you are from Lodz."

"Budapest? Avigdor Cohen family, near the High Street?"

"Slowinsky? Do you know anyone with the name of Slowinsky?"

Tedi hated this. She crossed her arms and stared at the mountains, trying to imagine what it was like up there, if it was cooler.

Her father claimed that the name Pastore was a souvenir

from the Spanish Inquisition, when Jews fled to Holland. He said his ancestors had produced so many more daughters than sons that by 1940, there were only eight Pastores in all of the Netherlands. Tedi was the only one left.

If she were to see a classmate or an Amsterdam neighbor, she would be forced to remember everything: faces, flowers, shops, markets, bridges, canals, bicycles, windows with curtains blowing out, and windows shuttered for the night. And that would poke a dangerous hole into the dike of forgetting that she was building, day by day.

So she kept her head turned away from the group gathered at the gate and tried to ignore the plaintive clamor of names until the earsplitting scream of an ambulance siren made her look. Later, other people would compare the shrill, keening screech to the sound of a cat caught under a car wheel, to an air raid alarm, to a factory whistle. Tedi put her fingers in her ears but it didn't block the volume or the pain that poured out of a frail woman who stood a few yards outside the now open gate.

She held herself oddly, with her feet turned out and her arms close to her sides. Her hands jerked like gloves blowing on a clothesline. Her head tipped back and her anguish ascended, filling the air with fear. It was hard to breathe. The sun grew hotter. A child wailed.

A nurse in a white uniform rushed forward, a syringe in her hand, but the woman wheeled around, fists raised, suddenly a crouching, punching, spitting dervish. She spun and circled so fast that Tedi thought she actually might rise into the sky, carried off by her own rage.

And then it was over. Two soldiers grabbed her so the nurse got the needle into her arm. The screaming gave way to heavy, heaving sobs, as the sum total of her misery surpassed its unnamed and unnameable parts. A shiver passed through the crowd, as though there had been a sudden drop in temperature.

A word emerged from the weeping, whimpered and repeated over and over.

"What is she saying?" people asked in a polyglot murmur.

"Is it Russian?"

"Is it a name?"

The translation was made and passed.

"Barbwire," she wept. It was Czech. "Barbwire."

In the Westerbork transit camp, Tedi had stood beside a barbwire fence and shivered for hours in the sleet, staring silently at an endless icy gray marsh. Beside her, a small, white-haired woman had wept softly. She'd worn an enormous man's overcoat, with only bedroom slippers on her feet. "They didn't let me find my shoes," she'd apologized, again and again.

Finally, she'd asked Tedi to help her sit down on the ground, where she gathered the coat around her like a tweed tent. No one saw her scrape her wrists against the razor wire. By the time she'd fallen face forward onto the fence, her body was cold.

When Tedi arrived at Atlit, she had been shocked and frightened by the sight of barbwire, too. But they had given her clean clothes, warm bread, a pillow, and amid so many reassuring smiles, she had forgotten. Now all she could see was the fence: a million razor-sharp thorns telling her that she was still something less than free, something less than human.

The nurse cradled the weeping woman in her arms, rocking her like a tired child. She signaled to one of the guards, who picked her up and carried her to the infirmary.

"Poor thing," said Hannah, tears on her cheeks. "They will take her to hospital straightaway."

"Humph," said Lillian, a plump Austrian girl with a weak

chin who was never seen without lipstick. "She is crazy like a fox. That performance will get her out of here in a hurry."

"Aren't you the heartless one," Hannah said.

"Not at all," she said. No one liked Lillian, but she was tolerated because of the hoard of cosmetics in her suitcase. "I'm only being honest. We all look out for ourselves in this world."

"That woman is never going to be right in the head," Hannah said. "And it's all the fault of those damned English for putting her into a prison camp all over again."

"I'm not so sure about that," Tedi said, placing her finger on a spiky barb. "Aren't we all hanging by the same little thread that snapped for her?"

Hannah grabbed Tedi's hand. "Enough of that," she said. "You can help me get the new ones settled in."

The main gates were closed now. All the newcomers stood, huddled together, staring at the biggest structure in Atlit, an imposing wooden barn that the inmates had dubbed "the Delousing Shed," or just "Delousing." Prison guards and translators from the Jewish Agency were trying to move them into two lines: men in front of the doorway at the right, women in a queue by a door on the left.

Tedi caught the strong, sweat-soaked smell of fear even before she saw the faces fixed in horror at the spectacle of men and women being separated and sent through dim doorways on their way to unseen showers. Beside both doors, twelve-foot-tall drums clanged and hissed, exactly like the ones near the entrances in Auschwitz, where they had also been told to surrender their clothes to be cleaned and fumigated.

Some of the women wept. Some of the men mumbled prayers. Couples called to each other with words of encouragement or farewell.

One of the translators asked Hannah to see if she could do anything with a stoop-shouldered man who refused to move or speak and was holding up the men's queue. Hannah grabbed Tedi's arm and pulled her along, too.

"Excuse me, sir," she said gently. "But this is not what you think."

He glanced at the machines and shook his head.

"I know," Hannah said. "They look like the ones in the concentration camp. But no one here will be killed. Here you will get your clothes back, I promise." He let her lead him up to the door so he could peek inside. "Look," she said, pointing to the ceiling. "You see the open windows there? None of the rooms here is enclosed. The shower is only a shower. The water may be cold and the disinfectants are unpleasant, but there are no gas chambers. And once you are cleaned up, you will have food and hot tea and delicious fruit grown by the Jews of Palestine."

Tedi could see that the man wanted to believe what this glowing Jewish girl was telling him, but he could not reconcile what she was saying with the testimony of his eyes and ears.

"Like Terezin," he muttered at last, naming the Potemkin village that the Nazis had used to fool the Red Cross, showcasing Jews playing in symphony orchestras and mounting operas for children—all of it a stage set on top of an abattoir.

"This is not Terezin, comrade," said Hannah. "Remember, you are in Eretz Yisrael. You will not be killed. You will be taken care of. If you are ill, the doctors will look after you. I promise."

He sighed. "You promise," he said with a sad shake of his head, but he followed her to a table where an English soldier, barely old enough to shave, had been watching them. The young man got to his feet, offered his hand and said, in Hebrew, "Shalom. I am Private Gordon."

"Is this man a Jew?" he asked Hannah, incredulous.

"I don't think so."

Tedi was struck by the young soldier's kindness, and then watched as his eyes wandered down toward Hannah's chest.

"Thank you, Private Gordon," Hannah said, showing off her English as she sternly ignored his attentions. "This gentleman is ready for you now. My friend and I go to help with the girls who get ready. Yes? Okay?"

"Okay." He grinned.

As she followed Hannah into Delousing, Tedi had to stop so that her eyes could adjust to the dimness. It was much cooler inside the building, but the noise was overwhelming. Hissing machines, running water, and voices rose up to the distant metal ceiling, magnified and distorted as they bounced between the bare walls. A burst of shrill laughter issued from somewhere deep in the back of the hall, a demented grace note that made her shudder.

In the changing room, they walked into a loud argument between one of the newcomers and a woman from the Jewish Agency who didn't speak enough Yiddish to make herself understood.

"What's the matter?" Hannah asked the distraught girl.

"I'm not putting my dress into that thing," she said, pointing to the revolving dumbwaiter that ferried clothes into the machine on the other side of the wall. "It's the only thing I have left of my sister."

"You will get it back," said Hannah. "Listen to me, all of you," she said, trying to make herself heard. "My friends, listen. They are only getting the bugs out of your clothes, getting them clean. There is no reason to worry. Lunch is waiting for you. Maybe you'll sit next to a handsome boy; there are many here. If you can understand me, translate for someone who does not."

The women seemed to respond to Hannah's smiling certainty and did as she asked. She is a natural leader, Tedi thought. She will run a school, a kibbutz—maybe even a government agency. And for a moment, she was sorry that she would have to forget Hannah, too.

Hannah handed her a pile of worn towels and led her to a row of open shower stalls where Tedi dropped her eyes to avoid the blur of gray flesh stretched tight over ribs and hip bones, scars and scabs. The girls faced toward the walls, hiding themselves as best they could. Some held their arms tightly against their bodies, like injured birds.

"It's the numbers," Hannah explained in a whisper. "They are ashamed of the tattoo."

In one stall, three Latvian girls, rounder and hairier than anyone else, soaped each other's backs, laughing and groaning with pleasure. "Good, good, good," they said, rolling the Hebrew word around in their mouths. They washed between their legs without embarrassment, pointing and joking with each other in a way that made Tedi blush.

She handed out the towels, confused and dizzy. Surely she had been in this same loud room with a group of girls like these, just weeks ago. Someone must have asked for her papers and put a stethoscope to her heart. She must have sneezed at the DDT powder and showered in one of these stalls. Someone had given her the dress she was wearing. Yet she remembered none of it.

What little Tedi could recall of the past two years took the form of snapshots, black-and-white and a bit out of focus, like the pictures in her family's leather-bound album. She remembered the magnificent head of hair on the Greek boy who took care of her on the boat to Palestine. She remembered the way the barbwire had sliced into the eyebrows of the woman who committed suicide at the Dutch transit camp.

Tedi had just arrived at Westerbork, betrayed to the Nazis after two years in hiding.

They had told her she was going to Bergen-Belsen the next morning. Had that happened, she might have been like the others who were terrified by the steam machines and showers of Atlit. More likely, she would have been killed there.

But they never called her name for that train, and she languished in Westerbork for a week, or maybe it had been only a few days; the cold and fear warped all of her senses. She could not recall eating anything there or lying down to sleep.

Finally, she was shoved into a boxcar with seventy-five other starved and frozen souls headed for Auschwitz. No one spoke as the train gained speed. Already as good as dead, they did not even try to comfort one another. But in the middle of the night, in the middle of nowhere, the engine stalled. A boy with a knife pried through the rotten floorboards and Tedi had been the second to squeeze through.

"Come on," Hannah said, taking Tedi's hand again and pulling her back into the noisy present. "Let's help them get dressed."

In the room beyond the shower stalls, damp piles from the steamers were heaped on a low table. A dozen dripping women rushed over to claim their clothes.

"You lied to me," wailed the girl who had not wanted to surrender her sister's dress. "Look at this," she said, holding up a shrunken, faded remnant.

"I'm sorry," Hannah said. "Sometimes the machines are too hot. But we have many clothes for you to choose from. The Jews of Palestine have given clothing from their own closets. You will have everything you need, better than what you brought."

Just then, the nurse ran in looking for Hannah, who, after a brief, urgent conversation, held up her hand and announced, "My friend, I have to go with Nurse Gilad, but my comrade, Tedi, will take care of you."

Twenty-two faces turned toward her. They were more curious than frightened now, and Tedi decided to pretend that she knew what she was doing. She led them through a door at the back of the building into a makeshift tent made out of old parachutes. Long wooden planks set on sawhorses were piled with stacks of underwear, dresses, blouses, skirts, shorts, and trousers.

The women rushed forward and began trying on clothes and offering each other advice. "Look at this," someone shouted, waving a pair of bloomers from a hundred years ago. They all laughed except for one girl who was pregnant and could find nothing to fit over the firm drum of her stomach. Tedi suspected that Hannah would have walked into the men's tent next door and grabbed a shirt and a pair of pants. She lacked that kind of nerve but felt responsible for the poor girl, who was on the verge of tears and seemed to have no friends in the group.

Tedi rummaged through the pile of clothes again with no better luck. But when a flap of yellow-gray parachute silk hanging from the side of the tent caught her eye, she grinned. "I'll be right back," she told the distraught girl and ran into Delousing, now deserted and so quiet that the sound of her sandals on the floor echoed behind her as she ran.

As she reached the front door, she stopped the young soldier who had shown such kindness earlier.

"Can you help me, sir?" she panted, first in Dutch and then in garbled Hebrew.

"I don't understand," he said.

Tedi grabbed his sleeve, made scissors with her fingers and pretended to cut. Then she pointed to the back of the building, and put her hands together as though in prayer.

"Ah." He smiled, pulled a tiny pocketknife from his pocket, and put his finger to his lips to make it a secret between them.

Tedi answered with a thumbs-up, took the knife, and dashed away.

She cut a swath of silk from the parachute and folded it so cleverly that the skirt she created looked pleated. One of the other women surrendered a blue scarf to use as a belt, to fasten it around the girl's belly. Tedi's efforts were met with praise and pats on the back.

"She looks like a bride," said one of the girls.

"A little late," someone else said, slyly, but as the comment was translated, it turned into a joke that made everyone laugh—including the "bride."

Tedi did her best imitation of Hannah and announced, "Come along, friends. Follow me." As they filed past her, one girl stopped and kissed her cheek, leaving behind a trace of fresh lavender. The smell of hope.

Zorah

Zorah tried to focus on the footsteps of the sentry making his midnight rounds, but the screams of the woman who had broken down at the gate still echoed in her head.

It was so quiet in the barrack, Zorah could hear the soldier clear his throat and the wind in the cypress trees outside. It was a sound, she supposed, that others might find beautiful and soothing but to her, it was just more proof that the workings of the world were random, that beauty, like suffering, was meaningless, that human life was as pointless as waves on sand.

Zorah hated the sea as much as she hated the wind in the trees. She hated Tedi, on the far side of the room, for the ease with which she fell asleep. But most of all, she hated the way people kept thanking God. Even now. Even here, where they were imprisoned for breaking rules made in a distant, irrelevant past, in the time before words like "boxcar" and "lamp shade" could chill you to the bone.

So many words had come unmoored from their old meanings. The English called them "illegal immigrants," but Zorah recognized the term for what it was: a polite version of "filthy Yid." What other explanation could there be for a place like Atlit?

She squeezed her eyes shut and dared God to stop her from hating everything in His creation, including this Palestine, this promised, this holy land.

In April, when Zorah had heard the news that Hitler was dead, the Hebrew blessing had nearly slipped out of her mouth, but she had fought the reflex and bit her tongue hard enough to draw blood. She would never again say, "God be praised." Her mother and father would have said it. Her grandmothers and grandfathers, aunts, uncles, and cousins would have said it, along with the professional beggars who had worked her street in the poorest of Warsaw's Jewish neighborhoods. Zorah cursed everyone in Atlit who said those words, especially the men who prayed, morning and evening, wrapped in their dirty prayer shawls. How dare they?

In the cots lined up between Tedi at the far wall and Zorah near the door, eighteen women sighed and tossed. And if none of them slept as soundly as Tedi, none burned like Zorah, who used the hours of her sleepless nights to calculate the insults of the day, all of which added up to the same thing—that no one cared to know what had happened, and not just to her, but to each of them. To all of them. What they had seen, what they had suffered, lost, and mourned. The British couldn't care less, of course. But it was no better among the Jews who took care of the day-to-day administration of the camp: the Jewish Agency bureaucrats, the kitchen workers, the doctors and nurses, the Hebrew teachers and calisthenics instructors, the bleeding-heart volunteers who were free to come and go.

Zorah knew why they avoided talk of roundups and forced marches, mass graves and death camps: if you hold a piece of rancid meat under a person's nose, he cannot help but turn away. That is an animal reflex, pure and simple, an act of self-preservation.

But the local Jews were two-faced about it, greedy for scraps of news about their own relatives, their own hometowns. They accosted dazed newcomers with questions about their parents' old neighborhoods in Riga or Frankfurt.

If you had no information, they rarely bothered to ask your name or where you came from. After that, it was all about Palestine. Where are you going? Do you have any family here? Are you a member of one of the Zionist youth movements with the fantasy names, doctrinaire politics, and summer camps that taught the fine points of ditchdigging and hora dancing? Are you ready to throw yourself, body and soul, into *Avodah Ivrit,* the work of building up the land? So *avodah,* a word for prayer, becomes the dirt under one's fingernails. But holy dirt, after all. Sacred dirt!

Zorah's scorn included her fellow survivors, too, who changed the subject after they determined that you had no knowledge of their Aunt Tzeitl or Cousin Misha. But them, she forgave.

She knew they were reluctant to tell their own stories because all of them began and ended with the same horrible question: Why was I spared? Everyone's mother had been gentle and devout, every sister a beauty, every brother a prodigy. There was no point in comparing one family's massacre to another's.

Every atrocity was as appalling as the next: Miriam's rape, Clara's murdered husband, Bette's baby, who was suffocated so the rest of the family would not be discovered.

It was unspeakable, so they spoke of nothing. Every day, the girls sat and sighed over the physique of the fellow who led them through morning exercises, or shared tidbits about the newest pair of pants in the men's barracks, or whispered about Hannah's breasts, which were growing larger every day. They clucked and preened like hens on a roost.

To Zorah, their conversations about men and food and even Palestine sounded like dance hall music at a funeral. She backed away from their offers of fruit and combs and all the other little kindnesses that threatened her at every turn. While the rest of the girls tipped their faces toward the sun and turned brown, she kept to herself inside the barrack and remained as white as paper.

She decided that all of her fellow prisoners, though wounded and bereft, were no better than wild animals. They were as heartless as the wind in the trees and as stupid as the relentlessly forward-looking Jews of the Yishuv.

"Ach," she muttered and rolled onto her back. Zorah was used to being the last one awake. Insomnia had been her companion since infancy. Her mother used to tell the other women on the street about how she would find her tiny daughter standing up in the crib, her hands on the railing, listening to the nighttime sounds rising from the street. For the entire first week in the concentration camp, Zorah had been too frightened to close her eyes at all. And even now that she was no longer afraid and the sticky Mediterranean heat made her feel dull and listless, falling asleep remained a battle.

Ultimately, the weariness of her body overcame her restless mind and Zorah did succumb, facedown on the mattress, the pillow on the floor, the sheet bunched under her sweating breasts. The other girls walked past her on the way to breakfast without bothering to lower their voices; once Zorah slept, nothing would wake her, not even the door that slammed a few feet from her head.

The barrack was deserted when she opened her eyes. "Damn it," she muttered, hurrying into her clothes, determined to get a cup of tea and a piece of bread before the daily comedy they called roll call.

The lineups in Atlit were a black joke for anyone who had survived one of the death camps, where counting off had been a form of torture. Morning and evening, the Germans had made them stand for hours, hot or cold, snow or rain, sounding the roll, barrack by barrack. If someone was slow in speaking up, they might have to repeat the whole thing twice or even three times. There were extra midnight lineups, too, called without explanation. And when a prisoner dropped to the ground, unconscious or dead, it would begin all over again.

The British counted the girls only once a day, inside their barracks in the evening. But the boys had to show up every morning as well. The sergeant in charge that day had sweated through his shirt even before the prisoners started filtering into the dusty yard in front of the mess hall. He tapped his foot and shouted for them to hurry, but they took even longer than usual as they arranged themselves in an intentionally crooked row. From the way they were glancing at each other and whispering, Zorah guessed that someone was missing: still in bed, or in the latrine, or perhaps even escaped during the night—something that had happened at least once in the three weeks since she'd been in Atlit.

The boys finally got themselves sorted, bellowing their names and saluting with exaggerated flourishes. As soon as the officer took a few steps down the line, the first prisoners took a step back and the others quickly closed ranks so the absence of one of the boys would not be noticed. By the time the sergeant had reached the end of the line, the first inmate, a cap pulled low on his forehead, gave another name and bowed from the waist. The whole crew kept a straight face and stood perfectly still until they were dismissed and strutted over to receive accolades from a group of female admirers.

Zorah watched the puffing of chests and the fluttering of eyelashes. Flirtations and romances bubbled up and burst from day to day—sometimes even from hour to hour. Zorah turned up her nose and headed for the shady side of Delousing, where the morning's Hebrew lessons were taught.

When she saw who was teaching that day, she tried to duck out. Nurit caught sight of her first and pointed at a chair in the front row, but Zorah slipped in a seat in the back as the teacher chatted up a few of the newcomers, speaking Hebrew with a liberal smattering of Yiddish to make sure she would be understood.

"It's only a matter of days, maybe a few weeks for some of you, but you'll be out of here soon," Nurit was saying. She was about forty, thick around the waist, and dyed her hair the peculiar shade of purple-red favored by the local women. Although she was liked by the others because of the chalky little squares of chocolate she handed out at the end of class, Zorah avoided Nurit's sessions. Not only did the woman love the sound of her own voice, she talked too much about luck—how lucky they were to have survived Europe, lucky to have gotten past the British blockade, lucky to be on the soil of Eretz Yisrael, where so many devoted members of the local Jewish settlement were working on their behalf.

"Today, we are going to learn the names of the flowers and plants of the land," Nurit began. "We will start with the biblical flora and continue with the trees that our people are planting, along with all the vegetables we have under cultivation. I myself spent the weekend planting bougainvillea in my garden. Do you know bougainvillea, my friends? I passed a whole day searching for just the right plant for my garden, but it was worth it. I tell you, it is the most beautiful of all flowers."

Zorah stood up abruptly and knocked over her chair. "What the hell do we care about your garden?" she said as she stamped away.

"How do you say 'pain in the ass' in Hebrew?" someone muttered.

Laughter followed Zorah as she walked off. She thought she would pass the rest of the morning trying to read the Hebrew newspaper she had "borrowed" from Nurit's bag last week. But it was too hot inside the barrack, so she wandered the grounds and kept her face turned toward the fence so no one would be tempted to talk to her.

Eventually, Zorah found herself near the front gate where a small crowd was watching the morning's departures. Arrivals were unpredictable. If the British intercepted an illegal vessel, a train or a convoy of buses would arrive and two or three barracks would fill with refugees.

But people left the camp almost every day. It seemed to Zorah that most of them spent no more than a week in Atlit. If you had the right credentials, the Jewish Agency would present you to the authorities as "legal" under the infuriating quotas the British had set for Jewish immigration to Palestine. But those numbers were a moving target, and there appeared to be different rules for children, who were released as soon as a relative came to claim them.

Zorah also noticed that whenever a private car pulled up to the camp, the "sister" or "brother" it had been sent for would be carried away without acquiring the stamp or seal or signature that kept others waiting. This was called *protectzia,* a word she learned not in any of her Hebrew classes, but from Goldberg, a gruff, gray-haired Jewish guard who worked in Atlit in order to search for clues about his mother's extended family in Germany. Goldberg was known to give away cigarettes, which made him one of the few people Zorah sought out.

She counted twenty-three people waiting to leave, bundles and suitcases piled around them. The children were the first to go, seven in all, walking stiffly beside people who were total strangers to them. Among them was Maxie, a ten-year-old who had been caught stealing shoelaces and matches. A grim-faced woman wearing an ugly black wig had her hand on the back of his neck and was pushing him along.

"Good riddance to that little shit," said Lillian, touching her fingers to the corners of her crimson lips.

"Shame on you," said a woman beside her. "Stealing probably kept him alive in Buchenwald."

"Well, I don't know what good it did him in here," Lillian replied, with a bold stare that proclaimed that she, for one, would not be intimidated by the mere mention of a death camp.

"What on earth could he trade for in this place?" Lillian demanded, as she glared down at her black Oxfords, tied with twine. "He'll be stealing wallets and purses and God knows what else as soon as he gets the chance. That poor woman has no idea what she's taking in. Then again, did you see her? Like my great-great grandmother, from the shtetl. And that wig? Horsehair! I'm sure of it. What a horror."

"Lillian," Zorah said. "You really should write a book of proverbs. I suggest you start with, 'If you don't have something spiteful to say about a person . . . why bother?'"

"And you are too clever for your own good," Lillian said.

Zorah watched as six young men crowded around the cab of a dusty flatbed truck, arguing.

"He comes with us," shouted a tall, skinny inmate, pointing at a boy with a heavy bandage on his ankle. "It's nothing—a sprain. We do not leave without him. We will make a hunger strike and shame you in front of the Jews of the world. We will report you to the Jewish Agency! To the Palmach!"

The driver pointed at the British soldiers who were watching from the guardhouses that stood on ten-foot stilts around the perimeter of the camp. "You are giving these fucking British assholes reason to laugh at us," he said. "If you don't get in right now, and without that cripple, I will leave without any of you. And I am sure as hell not driving all the way back to get you, you big-mouth son of a . . ."

Zorah grinned at the barrage of curses and realized that she had understood every foul word in the tackata-tackata version of what her father used to call "the holy tongue."

Papa had considered Zorah's gift for languages a complete waste. The old man used to chase her away from the table while he tutored her brother, even though Herschel was never going to be able to understand the Talmud. At ten years old, the boy could barely tell one letter from the next while Zorah had been able to read Hebrew and Yiddish before she was seven, and spoke better Polish than either of her parents. In Auschwitz, she'd learned Romanian and German. She picked up some Italian on her way to Palestine and was learning French just by eavesdropping on two girls in her barrack.

A young Jewish guard named Meyer walked over to the truck and took the driver aside. After a few minutes of animated conversation, the guard helped the lame boy into the front seat and told his loud champion, "Watch your manners. In a country this small, you might end up sleeping in this fellow's dormitory, or working in his brother's unit. No need to get off on the wrong foot."

The driver gunned the engine and then took off, forcing the others to chase after it. Their ringleader was the last to make it aboard, screaming and puffing until his companions pulled him on.

Zorah shook her head at the scene.

"You're not Romanian, are you?" The question made Zorah jump. Meyer, the guard who had sent them off, was smiling at her through the fence. She would have turned on her heel except for the cigarette he held out through the wire—a Chesterfield, right out of the package.

She took it without meeting his eyes, stroked the fine white paper, and put it up to her nose. The guard held out a match.

Zorah thought about putting the cigarette away, to save it for later, but what was the point? Someone would start asking questions about where she'd managed to get such a treat; then again, she realized that half the camp would know all about this little exchange within minutes anyway.

"Fuck it," she said, leaning forward to catch the flame. She inhaled deeply and glanced at him sideways.

He smiled. "Do you kiss your lover with that mouth?"

He might have been thirty years old, with wavy brown hair, a long face, strong jaw, and a pair of thick wire-rimmed glasses that had probably disqualified him from fighting in the war. Given what he'd just done for the stupid Romanians, she decided he wasn't a British stool pigeon at all, a rumor based entirely on the amount of time he spent inside the fence with the prisoners. Zorah wondered if Meyer was his first name or his last.

"Aren't you ashamed to wear such a stupid hat?" she said and walked away.

"You are most welcome," said Meyer, and doffed the Turkish three-corner pillbox.

Zorah headed for the far side of the nearest building to escape his gaze. She took three quick, delicious drags on the cigarette, so different from the cut-rate, stale, military-issue stuff they sometimes got. She could have traded a pristine butt for a chocolate bar, or a half tube of Lillian's lipstick, or the promise of getting a letter delivered to Tel Aviv or Haifa. But Zorah had no one to contact and no greater desire than tobacco.

She inhaled once more before tapping the cigarette out gently on the bottom of her shoe, then put the rest into her pocket to save until after dinner. The anticipation sweetened her whole day. Walking to and from the barrack, reading her newspaper, ignoring the fatuous conversation of the girls around her, she reached for it often, almost tasting it with her fingers. At dinner, even the bland eggplant and white cheese tasted sharper because of what was coming.

Zorah denied herself until the last minute and then slipped behind the latrine just before lights-out. She took her prize out of her pocket and massaged it gently back into shape. Before lighting it, she forced herself to pause for one final moment, watching as the last purple light of day faded to gray in the sky above the mountains.

She struck a match and inhaled deeply. The first puff, burned and sour, made her cough. But the next one was perfect and she held it in her lungs for as long as she could. She exhaled slowly, tasting the smoke as it left her. The third puff conjured a memory of her Uncle Moshe's pipe mix, which in turn recalled the flavor of Aunt Faygie's Rosh Hashanah baked apples. Zorah counted back; it had been four years since she'd eaten those apples; she had been fifteen years old.

Later, as she lay in the dark, Zorah noticed that her neck was not as tight as usual and wondered if nicotine was the cure for her insomnia. The woman on the cot beside her grunted in her sleep and rolled from her back to her side. Zorah savored the ten inches between them. On the boat from Europe to Haifa, and before that, in the DP center, in the forest, in the camp, in the boxcars, she had been piled, like a stick of wood, against other bodies that crawled with lice or burned with fever. Some had been clammy with sweat, and twice, rigid and cold. Zorah stretched out her arms, luxuriating in the space around her, the only thing in Atlit for which she was grateful.

Zorah tried to find the heavy satisfaction of the smoke in her lungs again, but the sensation was gone, like those argumentative Romanian boys who had, indirectly, been responsible for her American cigarette. Though she envied their escape, living on a kibbutz did not appeal to her. From what she had heard, it sounded a lot like Atlit: communal meals and bathrooms, order imposed by others.

Zorah wanted her own room and no one telling her when to go to bed at night or get up in the morning, or what kind of work to do. She knew these were extravagant wishes in a poor country, and she had no idea whether she would be able to make such a life for herself in a place where it seemed everyone was made to obey orders if only they were delivered by other Jews.

Not that she expected to leave anytime soon. She had no relatives in Palestine nor anyone willing to pose as family. She had never attended a Zionist youth meeting in Poland, nor had she ingratiated herself to the giddy new pioneers who were hatching all around her. But the biggest problem of all was that she had no papers. Officially, she did not exist.

She had walked out of the concentration camp so dazed and weak, she had been unable to think about what lay ahead. But when the Red Cross workers asked if she wanted a ticket back to Warsaw, she shook her head. She had been the only one in her family to make it through the first selection; there was no one and nothing to go back to.

In the DP camp, there were boys and girls who talked endlessly about Palestine as both home and hope, and since Zorah had neither she threw in her lot with them, joining with a small, well-organized group of Young Guards—the biggest of the Socialist Zionist youth movements. They boarded a train to Marseille, where they were met by a chain-smoking envoy from Palestine who led them to a flatbed truck, which jolted and bruised them for a day and a night until they reached a stretch of stony beach near a town called Savona.

A hundred other refugees were already there. The two nervous Italians in charge of the landing could offer nothing but whispered reassurances, which they repeated with less and less confidence as the night wore on. Zorah crouched and wrapped her arms around her knees, sick with worry; her rucksack had disappeared somewhere between the train and the truck, and with it her identity card.

The faint sound of an engine offshore brought everyone

to the water's edge, where they lined up like a flock of ragged birds and stared into the darkness as a rowboat splashed into view. Four muscular men wearing blue sweaters and tight-fitting caps jumped onto the sand and exchanged a few words with the Italians, who kissed their cheeks and beamed with relief.

At dawn, an involuntary gasp went up as the refugees got their first look at the ship that was supposed to carry them across the Mediterranean—a worn-out ferry of the sort used to shuttle commuters across a river or vacationers across a lake. Zorah shook her head: God had a twisted sense of humor to let her survive the efficient Germans only to drown at the hands of a bunch of bumbling Jews.

A steep gangplank was quickly assembled and the men from the boat started taking names, checking them against those on a smudged piece of paper. Zorah was surprised that this slapdash escape had actually been planned down to the detail of a ship's manifest. She hung back until she was the last one on the beach, knowing her name was not on their list.

The man holding the papers frowned at her and looked at the paper. "Levi, Jean-Claude."

When Zorah didn't move, he pointed at her and said, "You."

Did he know that Jean-Claude was a man?

"That's you," he insisted. "Levi."

The Italians ran up to them and pointed at a cloud of dust moving toward them. Zorah climbed the narrow, swaying ramp on her hands and knees.

She knew that she was not cheating Levi out of his rightful place. Nine times out of ten, a missing Jew in 1945 was a dead Jew. And yet she couldn't stop thinking about him. What would happen to her if Levi did turn out to be that one in ten?

What if he had already reached Palestine? Would the British arrest her? Throw her in jail? Send her back?

Where could they send her? She had nowhere to go, which was why she was going to Palestine.

After two weeks of worry and seasickness, Zorah was even thinner than she had been when she got out of the concentration camp. But from the day she arrived at Atlit, she realized that she had imagined a problem where none existed. She was just one more undocumented, inconvenient "illegal," like thousands of others.

On the day she arrived, a white-haired man from the Jewish Agency at the table in front of Delousing told her, "Don't worry. You might be stuck here a bit longer than most, but eventually it will all work out. You are one of the lucky ones. You are home."

Zorah had been too tired to tell him that "home" was a cramped apartment on the top floor of a dilapidated tenement where, by now, a gang of murdering thieves was cooking pork in her mother's kosher pots.

As she lay in bed, playing with the last flecks of tobacco on her tongue, Zorah wondered if Meyer could help her get out of Atlit. Perhaps he would return tomorrow and if he offered her another cigarette, she would ask if he had enough *protectzia* to send a big black car to fetch her to a little apartment of her own, or just a single room with whitewashed walls. That would be more than enough.

Zorah closed her eyes and extended the fingers of her right hand as though she were still holding a cigarette. She raised it to her lips, inhaled deeply, and waited, letting the phantom Chesterfield burn wantonly, as if she were a woman who always had a full pack of American cigarettes in her pocketbook and another in the nightstand. Zorah exhaled through pursed lips, deliberate as a film idol—though she doubted that there was, anywhere in the world, a movie star with numbers tattooed on her forearm.

She smiled at the idea. And then she slept.

Shayndel and Leonie

"I think Zorah may have a crush on the guard with the thick glasses," whispered Shayndel, as she slipped into Leonie's cot. No one else in the barrack was awake yet, which meant it was their time to talk. "In the last week, she's asked me three times if I've seen him. And last night at the party, she kept looking around as if she was waiting for someone.

"I can't imagine what your toes must feel like," Shayndel went on. "I saw you dancing with that oaf Otto. I don't think he's good enough for you, *chérie*. I don't mind hairy men so much, but given the lack of girls around here, even I could probably do better."

"Don't talk about yourself like that," said Leonie as she pushed a wisp of wiry hair behind her friend's ear. "Lots of boys wanted to dance with you."

The celebration had taken place in honor of the most

improbable and romantic coincidence imaginable: a girl from a new group of detainees had recognized her childhood sweetheart through the fence, and when they opened the gate, the two of them fell into each other's arms. Everyone was shouting and clapping, and even the English soldiers had tears in their eyes. Colonel Bryce, the camp commander, had given permission for a party. The cook had attempted a cake, and a bottle of schnapps had appeared; one of the newcomers had a violin and the dancing went on until midnight.

"They snuck the boyfriend into the girl's barrack," Shayndel said. "I'll bet nobody slept the whole night over there. Even if they hung up blankets around them, everyone must have been listening, though it would have been worse in the boy's barrack, don't you think?" she continued, dropping her voice even lower. "You know what they would have been doing, don't you?"

Leonie wrinkled her nose, which was Roman in profile and in perfect proportion to the rest of her features. Shayndel often thought the only reason that the great beauty of Atlit tolerated her attentions was the fact that she spoke French. Standing next to Leonie, Shayndel felt like a Polish peasant, with her coarse reddish mop of hair, skinny legs, and a body shaped like a potato.

"Are you a prude?" Shayndel teased, hoping she had gotten the idiom right. "I'm still set on finding us a couple of brothers when we get out of here. Brothers who want to live close by each other, you know. Nice, steady types. We'll live on a kibbutz, but on Sunday afternoon we can go to Tel Aviv, where there are shops and cafés, and we can sit over our coffee cups and watch the crowds pass by."

Leonie said nothing but squeezed Shayndel's hand, a signal for her to continue with the story she had recited every day, like morning prayers, since they'd gotten on the boat to Palestine.

"We will eat ice cream and go shopping. You will teach me how to dress and I will show you how to make the best stuffed cabbage in the world. It will be a good life for us. I'll find us the two brothers. We'll each have two children."

"Like Noah's ark," said Leonie, on cue.

"Exactly."

"Once upon a time." Leonie sighed. Nearly everything about Palestine felt like make-believe to her. The bottomless baskets of soft bread and the bland white cheese seemed like food for angels or babies. Atlit itself felt like a fairy-tale dungeon, the prisoners waiting for someone to end the evil spell and release them to live in the happy land of the kibbutz.

Hebrew was the most fantastic thing of all to her: a dead language walking in the world, a holy tongue with slang for "bullet" and "penis" and the magical power to invent or change whatever it needed, abracadabra.

"We promised to talk only in Hebrew today," said Shayndel. "Remember?"

"That's easy for you. You're the best one in class. I feel like an idiot when I don't have the words."

"You can fill in with French," said Shayndel. "I'm not strict like Arik."

"I don't like his class," Leonie said. "Nurit is much nicer."

"Did you hear Lipstick Lillian last night?" Shayndel whispered, in Hebrew. "She was talking in her sleep again. I swear I heard her say *mit schlag*. I never heard anyone talk about food so much. Such a Viennese cliché."

"'Cliché' is not Hebrew, is it?"

"Excuse me." Shayndel grinned. "Lillian is already bursting out of her dress. Can't you see her getting fat as a cow? Fat and stuck-up. Too bad."

"What did you think?" said Leonie. "People will be people in Eretz Yisrael, too. Just because we're in Palestine doesn't mean it's any different. There will be princes and criminals here, too."

"Jewish criminals, eh?" said Shayndel. "I almost like the sound of that. It makes us seem normal. But our children will not be merely normal. They will be extraordinary—tall and handsome, like in all the Zionist posters. With big muscles and white teeth."

Leonie winced.

"I'm sorry," Shayndel said.

When they had arrived in Atlit, a dentist had determined that eight of Leonie's back teeth were rotten and pulled them out. "No one notices," Shayndel insisted, pulling Leonie's hands away from her cheeks.

"Well, our four perfect children will have teeth like horses," Leonie said, to let Shayndel know that she was forgiven. "We will feed them raw milk and honey."

"And olives," said Shayndel.

"I will never like olives," said Leonie.

"You said that about the *leben,* too."

"I suppose if one gets used to drinking sour milk, one can get used to anything." Though Leonie did not know how she could bear another month of the heat, which she had heard someone say could last into October. There was only one tree big enough to give any shade in the whole camp, and the barrack often felt like an oven.

Just thinking about the word made Leonie feel sick. "Oven" used to conjure up images of cakes and roast chicken and warming bread. Now it meant only "gas chamber." Except in Hebrew, where even "oven" managed to stay in the kitchen with the sink and the icebox. Their teacher said that soon they would all be dreaming in Hebrew, which made Leonie study even harder.

"Did you dream in Hebrew last night?" Shayndel asked, knowing how much Leonie liked that idea.

"No. For that I think you need to fall in love with a native speaker. When you're in bed with a man, when you've had a little wine, that's the way to learn a language."

"Oh-la-la," Shayndel said. "Maybe you're not such a prude after all. You're getting a little . . . I don't know the word in Hebrew—amorous? Randy?"

"Not at all," said Leonie. "It's just an expression." She threw off the covers. "Let's get out of here. I'm dying for a cup of coffee—even if it's only tea."

Leonie and Shayndel were early enough to get their favorite spot in the dining hall, at a table just to the right of the door, where they could watch people come and go. The other girls from their barrack joined them there and, as always, everyone ate a little too much bread a little too quickly. A steady parade of boys stopped to flirt with Leonie and to say a few comradely words to Shayndel. After breakfast was over and the men clattered outside for the morning lineup, the girls leaned on their elbows and talked about them.

"Do you think Reuven is handsome?" asked one of the girls.

"If you like giraffes," said Lillian. "What a neck!"

"He has such beautiful eyes," said a young woman with a baby in her lap. "His children would be lucky."

"Speaking of children," Lillian said, "have you given a name to that son of yours? He's already a month old."

"Yes, I have."

"So what is it?" the girls said, all at once.

"He is Ben-Ami."

"Did you say Benjamin?" asked Shayndel.

"No. Ben-Ami," said the new mother, whose name was Rosa. "It is a new name for the new state. It means 'son of my people.' From now on, I want you to call me Vered. It means rose, too, but in the language of the Jews. We must throw off the old names with the old ways."

Lillian rolled her eyes. "That is exactly what Arik said in class. You're like a parrot. Don't you have a thought of your own?"

"You should change your name to Shoshana," Rosa-Vered said.

"Lillian was my *oma*'s name," she said. "And her *oma*'s name before that. Shoshana sounds like someone with a lisp. And if you ask me, Vered sounds like a name for a car, not a woman."

"And yet, no one asked you," said Leonie, but so sweetly that it took them a minute to realize that she'd just told Lillian to shut up. Before Lillian had a chance to protest, Tedi and Zorah flew through the door, uncombed and untucked, racing toward the nearly empty samovar.

Everyone at the table smiled. Tedi and Zorah did this nearly every morning, prompting a game in which the girls would come up with pairs of opposites: night and day, vinegar and wine, sweet and sour, hot and cold, meat and milk.

"Here come the sun and the moon," said Shayndel.

"Laurel and Hardy," said Leonie.

"Alpha and omega," offered Vered-Rosa, up on her feet, bouncing the baby to keep him from crying.

"What does that mean?" Shayndel asked.

"It appears that Rosa went to university," sniffed Lillian.

Leonie and Shayndel grinned at each other, knowing these

same girls sometimes called them "peas in a pod" and "the Siamese twins" even though they were a pair of contrasts, too. Olive-skinned Leonie had turned brown on the boat while a single day under the Mediterranean sky had broiled Shayndel's fair skin to a blister and swollen her eyes to slits. After that, she never ventured outdoors without an oversized man's hat that made her look like a child playing dress-up, even though, at twenty, she was older than Leonie by nearly three years.

They had been inseparable since first meeting on a crowded railroad platform south of Paris, on their way to Palestine. Shayndel was eager to practice her schoolgirl French on Leonie, who wanted to know if there were any big cities in the land of Israel. Their friendship deepened over the course of the journey as they nursed each other through seasickness and held each other close when the British commandeered their boat.

As they got up to leave the mess hall, Leonie said, "I'll catch up with you later. I have to go to the latrine."

Shayndel frowned. "Again? I think you should talk to one of the doctors."

"It's nothing. I've always had a delicate stomach."

"All right," Shayndel said, "I'll see you at lunch. We'll make up a little Hebrew conversation circle with some of the others."

As soon as they parted, Shayndel heard someone call her name. Hannah took her arm and said, "Walk with me."

She leaned close, as if she were about to share a girlish confidence, and said, "There's a woman coming to Atlit today. A German. She will be assigned to your bunk and I want you to keep an eye on her. Now smile and nod at me, like I just told you that Miloz, the handsome one, has been asking about you."

Shayndel grinned and nodded like a fool, less because of Hannah's instruction than her attentions. She had watched the affable and increasingly pregnant busybody, suspecting that Hannah's pushy friendliness had an ulterior motive.

"Nicely done," said Hannah, as they walked past a pair of guards. "We have been told that this person was a collaborator—a *capo*—in one of the camps. We'd like you to find out if it's true."

"We?" Shayndel asked.

"Come now," said Hannah. "You of all people must have guessed that the Palmach has eyes and ears in Atlit."

"Me of all people?"

"I know about you," Hannah said. "You were in the youth movement since childhood; the Young Guard, right? I also know that you fought bravely against the Germans in the forests outside of Vilnius. You're a hero, for goodness' sake, and anyone with eyes can see that you're not like most of the other girls, bourgeois brats or sad cases like that little French friend of yours, who seems like her insides are made of broken glass. Besides, you know all the songs and you carry yourself like a soldier."

"I think you might be making a mistake," Shayndel stammered.

"I have no time to play games," Hannah said firmly. "They aren't going to let me stay here much longer. The pregnancy is going to show any minute. Have the others noticed yet?"

Shayndel tried not to smile. "There's been some talk."

"I'll bet there has. And you can tell everyone that I am not married but I will be before the baby is born. In fact, I may be out of here by tonight, so you will be reporting to Tirzah Friedman," Hannah said.

"The kitchen director? I wondered about her."

"Of course you did! Which is why you are the right girl for the job," Hannah said. "You will act as extra eyes and ears for her. Tell her anything you discover about the German woman. After that, keep a lookout for changes among the guards, their schedules, everything about them, in fact. If you have suspicions about anyone else in camp, tell Tirzah that as well; anything that you sniff out."

"Eyes, ears, and nose, eh?"

"You're a comedienne, too? Fine. Tirzah will be asking for a helper in the kitchen in the next few days. Make sure to volunteer so she can select you." At that, Hannah squeezed her hand and walked off.

Shayndel was flattered to have been singled out by Hannah, who seemed the perfect pioneer woman: strong, blunt, cheerful, and confident. It made perfect sense that she would be working with the Jewish military forces. Hannah was exactly the kind of girl Shayndel had dreamed of becoming since she had followed her brother, Noah, to one of his secret meetings. She had probably been no more than twelve years old, but she still remembered the opening words of the speaker that night, an earnest young man who had actually been to Palestine. "To all of my brothers and sisters in HaShomer HaTza'ir, my comrades in the Young Guard, I bring greetings from the land of Israel."

The applause that followed his remarks lifted her out of her seat and changed her completely. She was no longer just a girl from a small town in west-central Poland; she was a Zionist, heart and soul, and her only desire was to go to the Young Guard summer camp so she could learn Hebrew, wear pants, and work in the fields. Shayndel got her wish the following year and became famous in that little world, not only for her command of the map of Palestine, but also for the way she forced the boys to let her march in their formations, carrying a broom on her shoulder, and for her enthusiastic, if slightly off-key, singing of folk songs. Shayndel loved every minute of camp, even when it was her turn to chop onions for her comrades' dinner.

Of course, the ultimate dream and the purpose of the movement was to settle in Eretz Yisrael, to drain the swamps and grow oranges, to reinvent everyday life in the kibbutz—the collective farm that would do away with greed, unfairness, and even jealousy. Like her brother, Shayndel adopted Zionism as her religion.

When Noah was seventeen, he had declared himself an atheist and stopped going to synagogue with their father. Shayndel found it hard to deny her mother's pleas to accompany her on major holidays, but on the Yom Kippur before her fifteenth birthday, the two of them slipped out of the house before their parents were out of bed. They spent most of the day walking with friends in the countryside, talking about the German threat and debating whether they should join the resistance or try to get to Palestine immediately, and how that might be done.

When their parents came home from the synagogue for a midafternoon nap, they found Shayndel and Noah in the kitchen, drinking tea and eating cold potatoes from the previous night's dinner. Mama hurried to the window and drew the curtains. "Everyone was asking for you at shul," she said.

"I don't care." Shayndel shrugged. "Don't try to make me feel bad about it, and for heaven's sake don't start crying. Religion isn't what we need now. Praying to God isn't going to solve anything. The only true redemption of the Jews will take place in our own homeland."

Noah smiled at her. "You sound like a pamphlet."

"Do you disagree with me?"

"Of course not," he said, reaching for an apple.

"You are no better than an animal," said Papa bitterly. "Why can't you fast like everyone else for a single day? You don't get anywhere in life without discipline. And piety."

"Piety?" said Noah. "Excuse me, Papa, but you are a hypocrite. Like everyone else, you go to shul because it is expected and then sleep through most of the service. Not that I blame you for dozing off. It's all nonsense. And you know it."

"Apologize to your father," said Mama.

"Ach," said Papa, and slammed the door.

The arguments continued, but after the Germans invaded Poland, Papa began to listen more than he talked. When Noah announced he'd decided to go to Riga, where he could book passage on a boat bound for the Mediterranean, their parents made no objection, though no amount of begging, threats, or tears would move them to let Shayndel go with him.

As the Nazis marched closer to their town and stories about what they were doing to the Jews became impossible to ignore, Shayndel brought home a few of her Young Guard friends to convince her parents to let her go to Vilna, a gathering place for Zionists from all over Eastern Europe. Her father walked out of the room before anyone said a word. Her mother served tea and listened to their arguments about the need for resistance and the relative safety of the city. But after they had left, she took Shayndel's face in her hands and said, "I understand why you're doing this. But, darling, that tall fellow is in love with the other girl, the brunette with the hazel eyes. You are making a fool of yourself."

Shayndel left home a week later, in the middle of the night, without saying good-bye. In Warsaw, she discovered that Noah had been murdered on the road by Polish thugs and wrote home to tell her parents the terrible news and ask for their forgiveness. Later, she learned that they had been murdered with all the other Jews in town—shot and buried in a field that had been her family's favorite picnic spot. She prayed that they had never received her letter.

As Shayndel walked along the back of the Delousing Shed, she noticed that one of the doors was unlocked. Seeing no one, she slipped inside, set the latch, and stood perfectly still, waiting to be sure she hadn't been followed and that she was alone. A sparrow flew through the clerestory windows and landed on a beam high above her, which she took as a good omen.

There were no towels or soap and the water was freezing, but Shayndel stood under the shower and let the grit and sweat of Atlit wash away, remembering when she would have given anything for the luxury of clean water, no matter how cold, and a little privacy. When she started to shiver, she turned off the tap and shook herself dry, like a terrier, and dressed. As she slipped back into the daylight, she ran her fingers through her hair, pleased with herself; she still knew how to disappear and get what she needed.

Shayndel followed the sound of voices to the shady side of the dining hall, where Arik was holding forth. His Hebrew classes began with the same vocabulary lists and drills as Nurit's, and like her, he ended with patriotic poems and songs. But where Nurit talked about her home and family, her garden and her neighbors, Arik always turned the conversation to politics.

"The British are not our allies," he said, speaking a little too fast for most of his students. "There was some hope that when Labor came to power we'd be able to count on them, but now they are denying the right of our people to come home. There are a hundred thousand Jews waiting in Germany with nowhere to go, and those bastards offer us a quota of two thousand? This is not the act of an ally but of an enemy."

"I heard they were going to permit another fourteen hundred a month," said a stocky young Pole named David, who had been in Atlit for less than a week but seemed to know everyone in the camp.

"Bah," said Arik, "that only happens if the Arabs agree to it, and they want the Jews out—or dead. And what the British want most of all is access to Suez and oil."

"If you're right, then the Yishuv will be at war with the British in earnest, and soon," said David, who was sitting on the edge of the bench, his elbows on his knees. "And that's too bad. My cousin fought with the Palestinian regiments, and he had nothing but praise for them."

"The limeys don't want your respect," shouted a baby-faced boy with a very deep voice. "They're in bed with the emirs and the effendis, and that makes them our enemies."

"But we are not at war with the British," someone objected.

"Not yet. But if we are to have a state and a homeland for our brothers and sisters in Europe, we must kick the empire out of here," said Arik.

At that, Miloz, the camp heartthrob, got up from his bench muttering, "I have no idea what they're talking about." Four girls followed as he walked away, and all the men in the class turned to watch them except for David, the well-spoken Pole, who caught Shayndel's eye and motioned for her to take a seat beside him. "I am David Gruen," he said. "And I believe you are Shayndel Eskenazi, yes?"

"Shhh," she said. "I want to listen to this."

Someone in the crowd said, "The minute the British are out of here, the Arabs will attack us. Isn't that right, Arik?"

He shrugged. "We will beat them. The Jews of Palestine know how to fight."

"But there are millions of them," said David, "and just a few hundred thousand of us."

At that, a man in the front row said, "Maybe you can explain this to me, Arik. In all of my years as a Zionist, in the youth groups and in all of my reading, no one ever mentioned the Arabs. Now I come here to discover that there are three times as many of them as there are Jews here in the land. Did any of you know that?"

"They are peasants," said Arik. "Worse than peasants. They are illiterate, dirty, backward. The educated ones with money use their tenants like serfs, like slaves. Besides, the Arabs did nothing with this land for hundreds of years, and I would remind you that we bought the land from them, legally. But now that we have built factories and made modern farms, now that we have jobs and schools and hospitals, the Arabs are crying that we are taking over their precious birthright."

"It sounds like the story of Esau and Ishmael," said a woman sitting in the back row. Shayndel saw that it was Zorah, her arms crossed tightly against her chest.

"Esau and Ishmael? What are you talking about?" Arik demanded. "Do you think we should let our brothers rot in Displaced Persons camps so that these people can take the land back to the dark ages? If you want to quote the Bible, what about, 'this land that God gives to you.' To you, not to Esau and Ishmael. To the Hebrews. To the Jews!"

"The rabbis taught that our misery was caused by the mistreatment of Ishmael, the brother of Isaac, and Esau, the brother of Jacob," said Zorah.

"Which rabbis?" Arik scoffed. "Diaspora rabbis? No, my dear, it is not so complicated. This was our land from the beginning, and it is our land to win back."

"You were a stranger in a strange land," said Zorah.

"So what? This is the real world," Arik said. "If we do not act, there will be none of us left to debate the fine points of the Torah."

"And that means we must become like all other nations and oppress our neighbors?"

"You know, Zorah has a point," Shayndel whispered to David, impressed at how her usually silent barrack-mate had stood up to Arik.

"Maybe," said David. "But there really is no turning back, and nowhere else to go."

"Enough philosophy for today," Arik announced. "I'll be back on Friday. Until then, speak Hebrew to each other. Now everyone stand up for '*Ha Tikvah*.'"

Shayndel thought that "The Hope" might be the saddest piece of music ever written. The song was so slow and stately it sounded more like a dirge than an anthem. Still, the melody was more powerful than any hymn's, and the words still moved her as deeply as the first time she'd heard them, a young girl with braids and a brother.

Shayndel sang quietly, under her breath.

As long as the Jewish spirit is yearning deep in the heart,
With eyes turned toward the East, looking toward Zion,

Then our hope—the two-thousand-year-old hope—will not be lost:
To be a free people in our land,
The land of Zion and Jerusalem

"You have a nice voice," David said. "You should sing louder."

"You must be tone deaf," she said, looking at his kind blue eyes, his high, thoughtful forehead.

"There's a rumor going around that you fought with the Jewish partisans near Vilnius. Maybe you knew my cousin," he said.

"You seem to have many cousins."

"Wolfe Landau?"

Shayndel stared at him. "Wolfe was your cousin?"

David nodded. "I know about Malka, too."

"Malka," she echoed. It had been a long time since she had heard or spoken either of those names, though neither of them had left her thoughts for more than an hour since she'd lost them.

"You were the third member of that troika, weren't you," he said. "I'm honored to meet you. Why don't people know who you are? What you did?"

"Why should they?" Shayndel snapped.

"Don't worry," he said. "I won't say anything if you don't want me to, though I don't understand why not. You should be proud."

"I only did what I could," she said. "They were the brave ones, the real leaders. I was just the tail at the end of the kite."

"Someday, we should fly a kite together."

Shayndel frowned.

"Or we could just go for a walk," he said, reaching for her hand. "I'm not a bad fellow. Not as dashing as Wolfe, but you could do worse."

"What are you doing?"

"I'm trying to sweep you off your feet," he said. "I think you are—I don't know the Hebrew for it—adorable."

"Ha!" Shayndel stepped back. "And I think you are exactly like all the rest of the men in Atlit, which is hungry for a woman. Any woman."

"I won't deny that." He grinned and waggled his eyebrows like Groucho Marx, then pretended to balance a cigar between his thumb and forefinger. Shayndel couldn't keep from smiling, but as she walked away from him, she was overcome with the same inexplicable sadness she had felt on the day she arrived in Palestine.

Setting foot on the soil of Israel had been a terrible disappointment—nothing at all like her dream of what the moment would be like. She might as well have arrived in Australia, for all the emotion she felt. There had been a small crowd on the beach that morning, waving and shouting, "Shalom." Others had wept for joy and kissed the ground. They had sung Zionist songs until they were hoarse, but Shayndel had been silent. She wanted to be as happy and as grateful as they appeared to be, but the only gratitude she felt at that moment was for having Leonie to care for.

And yet, this David had managed to touch her. He was funny and smart and his touch had been electric. He had called Wolfe and Malka out of the grave, suddenly alive and laughing. Not the bloody corpses she had fled from, running through the snow to save her own life. By naming them, he made her remember them, sparring and joking, always six paces ahead of her on their long legs, glancing back over their shoulders and telling her hurry, Shayndel, hurry. She would have to ask David if he had known Wolfe as a boy. She wondered what else he knew about her and what she needed to know about him.

In the dining hall that evening, Shayndel waved at Leonie but walked past their usual table to sit among the new arrivals and listen to the story of their journey and capture. They had suffered a rough crossing, caught in one storm after another. Everyone was bruised from the heaving and tossing, and one fellow had broken a wrist. There had been three sleepless days and nights before they sighted the shores of Eretz Yisrael, and then, after a British ship stopped them, they were forced to spend another day on board, stewing in the sun. When the English sailors tried to climb aboard, those who were able resisted with sticks and shovels until a canister of tear gas landed on deck, and a dozen people had to be carried off on stretchers.

"They said they were taking them to the hospital," said a young Lithuanian man with thick, sand-colored curls. "Not that I believe that for a minute."

Shayndel said, "It's likely that they did go to the hospital, unless they were suspected as spies."

"Spies?" he said bitterly. "Two pregnant women and some cripples?"

"The Jewish Agency will look after them, then," Shayndel said. "You seem to know a lot about the people on your ship."

"What if I do?"

"I'm just wondering about the girl they put in my barrack. She looked so thin and wasted. She fell asleep and we couldn't wake her to come to dinner. I hear she's German."

At that moment, David walked over and put out his hand

to the boy Shayndel was quizzing. David had big, warm eyes, Shayndel thought, and she saw that he was losing his hair even though they were probably the same age.

"I am David Gruen. And you are?"

"Hirsch Guttman, from Kovno."

"Well, Hirsch Guttman from Kovno, don't get any ideas about this girl: she's mine."

"She's the one who approached me, brother," said Hirsch.

David smiled at Shayndel. "No matter," he said. "I trust her. I'll see you later, beloved."

"What do you want to know about Hetty?" asked Hirsch.

"Hetty?"

"The German girl you were asking about. She's a good egg. Luckier than most. She spent the whole war in Berlin working as a maid for some rich family that had no idea she was Jewish. She speaks perfect German, and she had some of the best false papers you've ever seen. Even her Yiddish sounds like high German. On the boat, they gave her a real grilling to prove she was a Jew. Can you imagine? But she recited all the Sabbath blessings and she knew all the words from every Passover song anyone could come up with."

"So you think she's all right?" Shayndel asked.

His eyes grew cold. "I know what this is all about," he said. "On the boat she got sick with a fever and was ranting in her sleep, in German, of course. One of those thickheaded Poles started saying that she was a Nazi. What a schmuck. Is that why you're asking about her?"

"Goodness, no," Shayndel said. "I was just wondering because, well, she looked so tired. You'll find out that Atlit is full of gossip. Don't worry about Hetty."

"All right," he said, looking at Shayndel with new interest.

"So what's the story with you and that Gruen fellow? Do I have a chance?"

"A chance at what?" Shayndel said, adding, "You moron," in Hebrew, as she got up.

Back in her usual seat beside Leonie, she asked, "Are you feeling better?"

"I'm fine."

"Did you talk to the nurse?"

"Yes," Leonie said, relieved she did not have to lie to Shayndel about that, at least.

After breakfast, Leonie had waited to go to the latrine until she thought she might have a few minutes alone there. The pain in her abdomen was getting worse, and she was afraid that soon she wouldn't be able to keep it to herself; she had nearly doubled over at breakfast. Leonie sat with her head in her hands until she heard someone else come in and left, determined to get some medicine.

The building that housed the infirmary had once been used for storage, but the Jewish Agency had plastered the walls and put in a new wood floor, making the place seem airy and modern by comparison with everything else in Atlit. Six hospital cots made up with starched white linen stood at crisp attention along the right-hand wall; on the left were a desk, a few cabinets, and an examining room partitioned off with an old parachute hung from the rafters.

Leonie was greeted with a warm, "Good morning, sweetie," from the regular weekday nurse, Aliza Gilad. "I'm glad you're here early; the children are coming in for inoculations."

Within days of arriving in Atlit, Leonie had presented herself as a volunteer at the clinic, claiming that she had always wanted to become a nurse. Aliza made it clear that she had little confidence in someone as young—and pretty—as Leonie and assigned her only menial tasks: mopping the floor, carrying out garbage, and washing metal instruments in alcohol. But Leonie proved herself well-suited to the work of the sick bay. She didn't flinch at the sight of blood or vomit, and she was good with crying children, calm and reassuring with their distraught mothers, too. Aliza began trusting her with more responsibilities and came to treat Leonie as a protégée.

Leonie was glad to have a way to fill the long days and for Aliza's growing warmth toward her. But she had been bitterly disappointed to find that all of the drugs—even the aspirin—were kept under lock and key. There was no way she would ever "find" a dose of penicillin.

"Is Dr. Gerson coming today?" Leonie asked as she put on her apron. After meeting all of the physicians who made regular visits, she had decided to approach one of the two female doctors—a reserved and closed-mouthed Swiss.

"I don't think we'll be seeing her anymore," Aliza said. "She's got a big job in Tel Aviv."

"That's nice for her, yes?" Leonie said, trying to hide her disappointment.

"Why did you want Dr. Gerson?" Aliza asked, as she readied a vaccine. "Do you need something? Is there something I can do?"

"No," Leonie said. "I was just thinking about, well, studying pediatrics. I wanted to see what she thought of that."

Aliza lowered her voice and asked, "Are you pregnant?"

"No."

"A venereal disease, then."

Leonie flinched.

"Don't worry," said Aliza. "And don't think you're the only

one. You'd never guess who I've dosed in this place, including some of the girls you know. Even staff." She put a hand on Leonie's arm and added, "Not that I would ever tell."

The door flew open and a flock of children marched in, shepherded by three teenage volunteers from a nearby kibbutz. The girls were trying to get the little ones to sing the alphabet in Hebrew, though some were barely old enough to walk.

Aliza melted at the sight of them. "Delicious," she crooned. "Sweet as honey. I could eat you all up. Look at those cheeks. Like apples. Like plums."

Leonie thought it was a good thing that the children didn't know enough Hebrew to understand what she was saying, otherwise, they might have thought that the plump woman with the odd bun and the yellow teeth wanted to devour them, like the witch in Hansel and Gretel.

"Don't worry," whispered Aliza, as she readied the hypodermics. "We'll take care of your little problem after we finish with the babies."

Leonie was relieved and mortified. As much as she hated for Aliza to know about her problem, at least she would be cured before Shayndel grew more suspicious.

The first little girl to get a shot burst into shrill tears, which set the entire group to wailing. Their cries grew louder and more inconsolable, and nothing, not even the promise of candy, could make them stop. Each child struggled and shrieked more than the one before and Leonie began to feel like a monster, pinning arms back as Aliza came at them with the needle. Finally, the last one was inoculated and the children were led out, tears drying on their cheeks as they sucked on lollipops from America.

"I saved two red ones for us," said Aliza, putting one into her mouth as she offered the other to Leonie. They tidied the room in silence, white paper sticks between their lips. Leonie glanced at the nurse, hoping she would return to the conversation about her problem, when a half dozen sweaty boys barged in, all shouting at the same time—a shrill mishmash of Yiddish, Hebrew, Polish, and Romanian.

At the center of the racket was a pale, slender child whose face was covered in blood. "He fell making the goal," said one of the older boys. "I told them he was too small to play with us, but he whined and begged until we let him. And then he fell and he hit his head."

"Where is he?" came a woman's voice from outside. "Danny? Are you all right?"

Leonie didn't recognize her at first. Tirzah must have been washing her hair, which was still damp and hung halfway down her back, brown with golden streaks. In the kitchen, it was all bundled into a thick black net, which made her look older and more severe than the beautiful, distraught woman reaching for her son.

"I will not have this madness in my clinic," said Aliza, at the top of her lungs. "Leonie, get rid of these wild animals right now."

Leonie grabbed the box of lollipops and waved it over the boys' heads. "Outside for a treat," she announced, and they followed, as eager and as docile as the toddlers.

When she returned, Danny was lying on a cot with Tirzah beside him, her hand on a large white compress covering most of his forehead.

"It was just a little cut," Aliza said to Leonie. "It only looked bad because it was on the scalp, which always bleeds like crazy."

Tirzah frowned, dubious about the nurse's breezy diagnosis. Then again, she frowned about almost everything.

The inmates were glad when Tirzah's son visited from a

kibbutz somewhere in the south. Danny's monthly trips meant there would be a cake at least once during his stay. His presence also spiced up conversations at meals, as newcomers engaged in ever-more-outlandish speculations about the chilly woman who ran the kitchen for the Jewish Agency. She wore no wedding ring; did that mean Danny was a bastard? Perhaps she was a widow. Or maybe her husband divorced her for the way she oversalted her soup—or for fooling around with another man.

Danny was a sweet kid, a skinny seven-year-old who had his run of the camp and spent his days playing with whatever children happened to be there. When they were very young, he organized games of jacks or tag, but when there was a group of boys his age or older, he pushed himself into their races and matches.

Tirzah stroked her son's cheek. "Doesn't he need stitches? When is the doctor coming?"

"There is nothing for the doctor to do," Aliza said crisply. "The bleeding stopped and the cut is right at the hairline so you won't even see the scar, if there is one.

"Here, Danny," Aliza said, taking a piece of chocolate from her desk drawer. "Have some candy. You were a brave boy. Do you think we should give one to your mother? She was not nearly as brave as you."

There was a knock at the open doorway followed by a question in English. "Everything all right in here?"

"Yes, Captain," said Aliza.

"Colonel," Tirzah corrected her.

"The boy?"

"He is fine."

Colonel John Bryce, the British commander of Atlit, removed his hat and stepped inside. A short man in polished boots, he made a little bow to Aliza.

"Does he need the doctor?" he asked in Hebrew.

"No. He is fine," Aliza said.

The officer looked at Danny. "Are you fine?"

Danny smiled and replied in English, "I am very good, indeed."

The inmates hated John Bryce solely on principle. He was not a vindictive or petty man and he permitted the Jewish Agency free rein within the camp. Even so, he was considered a prig and a fool for his insistence on following rules to the letter, often causing delays and complications a more lenient commander might have avoided.

Not much was known about him; he was a career officer in his late forties, his skin deeply lined from years of service in India. He had fought in North Africa during the war against Germany and was ending his career in Palestine.

His feeling for Tirzah was so obvious that Leonie had to turn away, embarrassed and a bit envious. She thought it extraordinarily romantic that he had risked exposing himself by rushing to her side this way. Tirzah kept her eyes on Danny, so it was not easy to read her face.

"Well, then," said Colonel Bryce, finding there was nothing for him to do. "Carry on."

Aliza took another look at Danny's wound and secured a much smaller bandage over it. "It looks very dramatic," she said, pinching his cheek. "The girls will swoon over you.

"Keep him still for the rest of the day and send him to me in the morning for a quick check," she said to Tirzah. "And don't make too much of this. Boys will be boys. They smash themselves up and they heal. Don't smother him."

After everyone left and Leonie began to sweep up, Aliza asked, "So, tell me. Is the pain sharp? In the lower abdomen? Do you have a sore throat?"

"How do you know all of that?"

"It's my job to know," she said, and motioned for Leonie to go behind the curtain. A moment later she appeared with a hypodermic. "Turn around," she said and lifted Leonie's skirt. "I'll give you another shot in a few days."

"Thank you," Leonie whispered.

"No need," Aliza said. "Come outside. I need a smoke."

They sat on the bench on the shady side of the shed and shared a cigarette in silence. After a short while, Aliza said, "I could never do what Tirzah is doing."

"What do you mean?"

"What do you think I mean? Fucking for her country!" Aliza smirked. "I shock you, do I? How old are you, anyway? Seventeen?"

"Almost eighteen."

"I suppose I look like an old lady to you, but if she is thirty-five, I am only ten years older, which isn't too old, if you know what I mean. Besides, I know what goes on in the world." She took a long drag on the cigarette and shook her head. "I suppose women have always been asked to do this kind of thing. You can get a man to tell you almost anything in bed. But by now, Tirzah must be an expert about the British prison authority and maybe something about the police department, too. Still, for a Jewish woman to have to stoop so low? It makes me sick.

"Of course, when you really stop to think about it, she deserves a medal and a pension, just like any other soldier. What a sacrifice. What a shame."

Leonie said nothing but she wondered whether Aliza might have misjudged the situation. Bryce was obviously in love with her. Danny was fond of him. As for Tirzah? Leonie guessed and thought, Poor woman.

II

September

Rosh Hashanah, September 7

Tirzah had let it be known that the evening meal that started the Jewish New Year would be special, so speculation about the menu had become a topic of discussion and debate.

"There is a big argument about the proper ingredients for carrot tzimmes," said Shayndel as she reached for another potato from the mountain before her.

Tirzah, who was chopping a bowl of onions, made no reply.

"I think there's even a wager about whether there will be sweet or savory noodle kugel."

Shayndel thought she heard Tirzah laugh. "What?" she asked. But the cook only continued chopping.

Usually, Shayndel didn't mind Tirzah's reserve. In the three weeks since she'd begun working in the kitchen, she had found it a relief to spend time with someone who did not treat her with kid gloves. After David told the men in his barrack that she had been a partisan fighter, everyone except Leonie had stopped acting normal around her—no more joking or gossiping now that she was considered a champion of the resistance, a heroine of the Jewish people.

The tales of her exploits got grander with every retelling: she was said to have single-handedly killed a dozen Nazi soldiers in a machine-gun bunker; she had walked into a Polish police station in broad daylight to steal identity papers; she had rescued scores of families moments before the Germans had come to arrest them.

There was some truth to all of the stories—especially the one about the police station theft—but there were holes in them, too. She had been too stubborn to admit that she couldn't throw as far as the boys, and tossed the hand grenade so badly that Wolfe had put himself in the line of fire to retrieve it and pitch it into the gunner's nest. Still mortified by that fiasco, which had nearly cost all of them their lives, she refused to talk about any of her wartime experiences. But her reticence was taken as a proof of modesty, which made her stock rise even higher.

Shayndel began to spend more time in the kitchen, where she could count on Tirzah to be as curt and bracing as horseradish. The room was narrow and cramped. There was a large army cookstove and piles of battered, burned pots and pans—enough to accommodate the Jewish laws that separate meat and dairy. The sink was far too small for all of the washing-up. Tirzah kept the space as clear and uncluttered as possible, without so much as a stool that might tempt a person to sit down and linger over a mug of tea.

Shayndel worked hard in the kitchen, chopping and

washing, but wished she could do more as Tirzah's agent in Atlit. Occasionally the cook inquired about a new arrival, but mostly Tirzah wanted details about the guards: which men slept on duty and which were easily bribed, who had a wife and children at home, who was smitten by which of the Atlit girls.

Shayndel was to report any changes in any of their schedules. She learned all the guards' names and was surprised to find out that not all of the Arabs were Muslims; several were Christians. But it had been two weeks since she learned anything new. Her "spying" became as routine as clearing tables and sweeping the floors, and she wished Tirzah would confide in her about what other kind of information the Palmach was looking for; maybe then she could be more useful.

Shayndel sighed as she picked up another potato, wishing she had some shocking morsel of news that would jolt Tirzah into conversation. But even the gossip from the barrack was stale. Traffic into Atlit had slowed to a trickle, which had prompted Arik to spend a good part of his last Hebrew class complaining that the Mossad Le'aliyah Bet—the committee for secret immigration—was doing a bad job of procuring seaworthy vessels. The few ships that did manage to limp to shore near Tel Aviv and Haifa were old, slow, and easily captured. The passengers resisted, singing Zionist songs as they raised sticks and fists at British troops armed with bayonets. The Mossad encouraged these doomed displays, supplying banners that read, "The Nazis killed us. The British won't let us live." The pictures ran in the London and New York newspapers as well as in Jerusalem.

Shayndel dug the eyes out of another potato and glanced over at Tirzah, now stirring the onions in a huge frying pan. She was a handsome woman, whose age showed only in the lines around her eyes. Trim and strong, she took big strides as she walked around the compound. No one knew anything about her except that she had a son and that she slept with Bryce, the camp commander.

Potato after potato after potato, Shayndel grew so bored that she decided to provoke Tirzah into talking. "I heard someone lost an eye when the *Montrose* landed," said Shayndel. "Do you think it's worth the suffering to those poor people on the boats?"

Tirzah made no reply.

"I know the headlines do us some good, but the refugees on those boats are exhausted and sick. It's sort of cruel."

Tirzah shrugged without looking up, so Shayndel tried another tactic. "I think that boys get out of Atlit faster than the girls. I know we need soldiers and farmers, but I thought that women were meant to work side by side with the men in the fields. And aren't they training girls to fight?"

"I can't imagine that little French friend of yours shooting a rifle," Tirzah said.

"Well, I can," Shayndel said quickly, even though Leonie's hands probably couldn't manage anything bigger than a pistol.

"I suppose you know her better than I do. To me she looks like a mental case, but the nurses say that she handles herself well with the sick."

"It sounds like you gossip as much as we do."

"For us, it isn't gossip," Tirzah snapped, making it clear that the conversation was over.

Shayndel held her tongue for a minute and then changed the subject. "Aren't we going to make something sweet for the holiday?"

"Don't worry about that," said Tirzah, a hint of amusement in her voice.

"What? Oh, tell me! I'd kill for a piece of apple cake. Will there be kuchen? You don't trust me even with that much information?"

"Don't be silly," she said. "But at the rate you're going, there won't be enough potato kugel for even half of the crowd. Go get me a couple of girls who know how to peel vegetables without wasting half of them."

Shayndel took off her apron and walked out into the bright sun. It seemed strange to be cooking for Rosh Hashanah in such withering heat. She associated the holiday with cool nights and changing leaves and the smell of her mother's kuchen.

Tedi was the first person she saw, sitting on a bench in front of the mess hall, paring her nails. "Can you peel a potato?" Shayndel asked.

Tedi grinned. "Is that a joke or an insult?"

"Tirzah sent me out to get some extra hands."

"I'm happy to help," she said. "Actually, I'm happy to do anything at all."

The next person Shayndel spotted was Zorah, walking toward the barrack with her head down and her hands in her pockets. Not the best of company, thought Shayndel, but she was in a hurry. "Zorah, we can use some help in the kitchen."

"Is that an order?"

"Don't be an ass."

"So it is an order," Zorah said, and followed her back to the kitchen.

When they arrived, they found Tirzah standing beside Tedi.

"Look at how this girl uses a knife," she said, picking up a potato skin that had been peeled in a single strip. "At last I have someone who knows what she's doing."

"A compliment from our chef?" Shayndel let the insult pass amid the good feeling and aroma of the holiday kitchen. She wished Leonie were there, too.

"I was always good with my hands," Tedi said, as she finished another potato. "I used to make doll clothes at home. My teacher said I should be an artist."

"Maybe you'll become an artist here," Shayndel said. "A sculptor, perhaps! There must be great art in Eretz Yisrael, don't you think, Tirzah?"

Tirzah wiped up the potato skins and threw them into the garbage bin. "There are many more important things to do to insure that Jews will never again be treated like cattle. So there will be a place in the world for people like you."

"What do you mean by that?" said Zorah. "'People like you'?"

"Nothing," Tirzah said and turned back to the stove. She found it difficult to face these women. She knew they had suffered unimaginable horrors and wanted to feel more compassion for them. She wished she could embrace them, like the volunteers who came to Atlit purely out of kindness, to cut hair and polish nails, or play with the undersized, nervous children.

Zorah glared. "People like us," she repeated. "You think that if you had been there, you would have fought the Germans and saved yourself, and your elderly parents, too. You know nothing about what happened.

"I want to know where you were when the Germans came for us, year after year. Where were the Allies? Where was your English soldier boyfriend?"

The only sound came from the big pot of soup on the stove, rattling in a boil against the lid. Tirzah silently cursed herself for having said anything. She tried to limit her exchanges with survivors to the task at hand. She knew only the bare outline of Shayndel's story, though Tirzah approved of the way she held herself and her willingness to work hard. But Tirzah could not abide the victims—the ones who stared blankly or the ones who spit fire. She was disgusted by their nightmares, their tears, and their horrible tattoos. It was wrong of her, of course. She was ashamed and confused by the anger they brought out in her, and sometimes she thought her assignment in Atlit was a kind of punishment for the hardness of her heart. She had never been easy with people, guarded and aloof even as a child. She married Aaron Friedman only because she was pregnant, and when he walked out two weeks after Danny was born, Tirzah's family blamed her. She moved to a kibbutz where no one knew her, and refused to speak to her parents or her brother for years.

"You have no answer to that question, do you?" Zorah smirked. She grabbed another potato as if she were going to strangle it and promptly cut a deep gash into her thumb.

"No blood on the food," said Tirzah, handing her a towel. "Go have the nurse see to that."

Zorah banged out of the room and the three women worked in silence. Tirzah retreated to the back of the kitchen.

"Zorah is a hard case," said Tedi after a few minutes.

"She was in the camps," Shayndel said. "Sometimes, early in the morning, I hear her crying in her sleep."

"And yet, that girl with the baby—remember her? She was in Buchenwald," Tedi said, wiping her hands on a towel. "I don't recall her name, but she was sweet as honey. How do you explain that?"

"Enough talking," Tirzah said. "There's too much to do."

Zorah kicked at the dust and was halfway to the infirmary before she realized that she was virtually alone. There were no boys playing soccer, no men loafing in the shade, shirtless in the afternoon heat. The benches behind Delousing were empty of women fanning themselves, chatting, or dozing.

The infirmary was shuttered, but Zorah's cut had stopped bleeding. She was not about to go back to the kitchen, which meant there was nothing to do but return to her barrack. As she opened the door, a skirt caught her full in the face.

"Sorry." A girl wearing only a slip rushed over to retrieve it. "I was trying to catch that."

The place was a madhouse. It seemed like every piece of clothing had been tossed up into the air and left where it had fallen, with dresses, skirts, blouses, and underwear scattered everywhere. Women rushed from one end of the room to the other, eyes shining, hands outstretched. Everyone was talking at once.

"This might fit you."

"Let me try that!"

"Would you tie this for me?"

There was a queue beside Leonie's cot, as girls waited for her to adjust a belt, smooth a wrinkle, or turn up a sleeve, and then pronounce them, "*Tres jolie*. Very pretty."

Zorah lay down on her cot and faced the wall, but even with a pillow over her head, there was no blocking out the giddy banter of dressing, primping, and praising.

"Mascara! Where did you get that?"

"My turn."

"My turn."

"Is this too short?"

Rosh Hashanah had always been her favorite holiday. As the sun set and a new year began, the world seemed filled with promise. Her father would return home from the brief evening service smiling. He would compliment her mother's soup and the meal passed pleasantly and ended in song. Her father had a beautiful voice.

But as the month wore on and one holiday followed another, his mood would sour. He complained about the stifling heat or the cold drafts in the prayer hall. He grumbled about her brother's inability to keep up and the hypocrisy of the rich men, who had the best seats in the synagogue but talked business throughout the service. By the end of Sukkot, he was back to slapping Mama for overcooking the chicken.

Even so, when the sun began to set at the start of Rosh Hashanah the following year, Zorah would hope again.

She felt a light touch on her shoulder and turned to see Leonie standing beside her, holding out a white blouse with yellow buttons. "This should fit you," she said softly as she placed it on the foot of the bed and hurried away before Zorah could say no.

She waited for a moment, sat up, and placed her hand on the soft, dotted swiss cotton. The buttons were made of heavy plastic in the shape of flowers, with five petals each.

She touched one of the buttons and wondered if Meyer would notice them. The idea shocked her and she drew her hand back as though she'd been bitten. She glanced over her shoulder to see if anyone had seen her nearly succumb to the nonsense around her, which she knew was nothing but sex madness. All she really wanted from Meyer, she told herself, was another cigarette.

The door banged open as Shayndel and Tedi rushed in. Shayndel stripped off her shirt as she strode through the room. "Wait until you see the boys," she said. "It's amazing what a shave and a comb can do."

Tedi stopped at Zorah's bunk.

"How is your hand?" she asked.

"It was nothing," said Zorah.

"Come here," Leonie said, waving to Tedi and Shayndel. "I have dresses for you. The dark red is for Shayndel and the blue is for Tedi."

"You seem to be enjoying yourself," Shayndel said, slipping on a cherry-colored shirtwaist.

Leonie picked up a brush and set to work on the tangles in Shayndel's hair. "It's nice to feel useful," she said.

A strange, mournful sound filtered into the room. The conversation quieted and then stopped altogether as the half-musical, half-animal wail hovered for six, seven, eight seconds and then changed suddenly into a high-pitched staccato shriek.

"What on earth was that?" Leonie shuddered.

"A shofar," Shayndel said. "It's a sort of trumpet blown at Rosh Hashanah and Yom Kippur. It's made of a ram's horn. You never heard a shofar?"

Leonie shook her head. "My uncle had no use for religion."

"What about your parents?"

"I was a baby when I went to live with my uncle's family. It's a terrible noise, no? So primitive."

"I always liked it," Shayndel said. "In my summer camp, they would blow a shofar to wake us up in the morning. They must be using it to tell us that it's time for Ma'ariv. They're keeping the gates between the men's and women's sides open for evening prayers."

"Will you go?" Leonie asked.

"I don't think so." She shrugged. "It's a short service and given the state of my hair, they will be done by the time you're finished with me."

Shayndel thought about her last Rosh Hashanah at home, when she had refused to sit with her mother and stood in the back of the women's section, whispering and laughing with the other Zionist girls.

Leonie slipped a pair of tortoise-shell combs into Shayndel's hair and held out a mirror. "Look how pretty you are," she said. "Let me find you some lipstick."

"Don't bother," Shayndel said, staring at Zorah, who was fastening the last of her flower buttons. Eyebrows arched all over the barrack as Zorah twisted her hair into a loose knot at the nape of her neck. She stood up, faced her audience, and made a stiff curtsy before she walked outside and headed for the men's side of the camp.

She approached the group that had gathered in a semicircle around Anschel, a wiry man of twenty-five or so, whose spectacles and wild black beard lent him an air of religious authority. Everyone agreed that Anschel was more than a little crazy. On his first night in Atlit, he had made a scene in the dining hall when they brought out a platter of chicken, pounding the table and screaming when no one could give him the name and credentials of the butcher who killed and salted the birds. He had also tried to break up one of Arik's classes, shouting that Hebrew should be reserved for holy purposes only.

Anschel certainly prayed like a madman, his eyes squeezed tight, swaying back and forth so violently that he hit his head against the wall behind him. He had begun the evening prayers for Rosh Hashanah the moment he counted nine men around him and mumbled through the service so fast that no one could keep up.

"Who made him the rabbi?" someone demanded as Anschel began folding his prayer shawl. "We aren't going to let him do that tomorrow, are we?"

"I thought that the Jewish Agency was sending a real rabbi."

"I heard they weren't doing anything. No prayer books. No rabbi. Nothing."

"Who told you that?"

Zorah had kept her distance, watching the proceedings and discussion from behind a small group of women who had come to pray. But one of the men caught sight of her. "Who is this lovely lady?" he crowed, grabbing her arm.

"Zorah, is that you?" said one of the regulars from Arik's Hebrew class. He licked his lips. "Don't you look nice? See how the old shoe is turned into a glass slipper."

"Too bad no one can turn a donkey into a handsome prince," Zorah replied, and walked away as slowly as she could, pretending not to hear the hoots and whistles at her back. As soon as she was out of their sight, she ran back to the now deserted barrack, where she loosened her hair, put on her own shirt, and left the white blouse, neatly folded, on the foot of Leonie's cot.

"I hope Tirzah won't be angry that we took so long," Shayndel said, as she and Tedi hurried toward the kitchen.

"I guess not," Tedi said as they opened the door on a scene of cheerful pandemonium. The kitchen was crowded with far too many kibbutzniks, elbowing past each other and chattering as they piled platters with salads and casseroles, fruit and bread, and enough cookies and cakes to fill a pastry shop. In the dining room, the tables had been draped with white cloths and set with wineglasses, bowls of apples, and centerpieces of pine boughs and wildflowers.

Shayndel tried to pick up a plate, but it was grabbed out of her hands. "I work in the kitchen," she explained.

"Not tonight," said a girl with a mass of curly black hair barely restrained by a green-print kerchief. "Tonight, you will be served by your comrades from Kibbutz Yagur and Kibbutz Beit Oren.

"Do you know which kibbutz you'll be going to?" she asked. "I'm at Yagur, just over the hills. Maybe you'll come to us?"

"No, no," said a thin boy with buckteeth. "It's too hot there. Today up in Beit Oren, we were wearing long sleeves all day. Little Switzerland, we call it."

The doors to the dining hall thundered with the sound of pounding fists as the residents of Atlit, dressed up and hungry, whistled and shouted for their dinner.

Someone improvised new lyrics to an old love song: "Tirzah, my darling, I perish for the sight of your chopped salad. I cannot bear being separated from your noodle soup for even another moment."

The kibbutzniks laughed and looked toward Tirzah. She shrugged and waved her wooden spoon like a scepter, and the doors were unlocked.

After a stampede into the dining hall, there were ooh's and aah's about the tablecloths and flowers.

"Who is getting married?" someone shouted.

"All I need is a groom!"

"Here I am."

The noise rose to a crescendo as people took seats and expressed opinions about the decorations and the kibbutzniks who lined the walls of the room. "Where is our dinner?" shouted one of the young men who was juggling the apples at his table. Anschel, the religious fanatic, leapt up and cried, "Quiet. Be quiet, all of you. It's time to bless. What's the matter with you?"

Voices fell as a soft "shhhh" made its way from table to table.

"Who is blessing lights?" Anschel demanded. "Where are our candles?" He glared at the kibbutzniks. "What are you people, gentiles?"

One of the girls ran into the kitchen and returned with matches and a pair of candles. "I'm sorry," she whispered.

A woman wearing a headscarf stood up and lit the candles. She cupped her hands and floated them above the flames in slow circles—once, twice, three times—before covering her eyes with her fingers and murmuring the prayer.

Anschel lifted a cup above his head and glared around the room, waiting for others to do the same. Around each table, the men eyed each other and silently determined which one would stand for the blessing. As they raised their cups, he began, "Blessed are You, Lord our God, King of the Universe." The piercing nasal drone of his voice held everyone in thrall at first, but then others joined, creating a baritone jumble of melodies and accents that conjured a congregation of absent fathers and grandfathers. Tears flowed as the goblets were emptied, but Tirzah gave them no time to mourn, banging the door open wide with a tray piled with golden loaves of challah. She was greeted with applause and chatter, which continued through the brief blessing for bread, which was passed and devoured.

The apples were sliced, dipped into honey, and fed by girls to boys and by boys to girls amid an orgy of unambiguous finger licking. Leonie nudged Shayndel and pointed at Ilya, a notorious Revisionist who was making eyes at Masha, the rabid Communist, now batting her lashes back at him.

"A miracle," said Shayndel.

A roar greeted the appearance of chicken and potatoes and Tirzah was dragged out of the kitchen for another ovation. Even though the portions of meat were small, there were no complaints in the dining hall. Shayndel called that a miracle, too, though Leonie thought it had more to do with the wine and homemade schnapps, smuggled in by the kibbutzniks.

"Please" and "thank you" were used as never before. And while the conversation was lively and loud, there was barely any political argument or gossip. "More miracles," Leonie shouted to Shayndel, who was sitting right beside her until David squeezed between them and held out his hand.

"We have not been formally introduced," he boomed, obviously tipsy.

Shayndel blushed. "I . . . I told you about David," she stammered, although she had done no such thing. For two weeks she'd been trying to think of a way to weave David into the story she and Leonie told one another early each morning. She had no idea if he had a brother, or if he would like Leonie. Finally, she had decided it was better not to trouble her friend about David since she wasn't sure how she felt about him.

"We're out of water," Shayndel said and hurried away with the pitcher.

As he watched her walk away, David sighed, "I am going to marry her."

"You hardly know one another," Leonie said.

"Love has nothing to do with time, not in this world anyway."

"So you are in love with Shayndel?"

"Yes, but I'm not sure she feels the same."

"She is a very good person," Leonie said, gripping his arm and speaking directly into his ear. "You must be very good to her. You must take care of her. She takes care of everyone else. She never thinks of herself."

"Of course I will take care of her," said David. "You can keep an eye on me. If I'm not up to the job, you'll let me know."

"Me?" Leonie said. "I would be like an extra wheel. Like putting milk into a cup of wine."

"But what about you?" he asked. "Every man in this room is in love with you—well, everyone but me. Why do you chase them all away?"

"You are drunk, monsieur," Leonie said, wrinkling her nose at the alcohol on his breath.

"Yes, but that does not mean I am wrong. Why are you so chilly?" David tried to put his arm around her, but she moved her chair and watched as eight kibbutz girls delivered platters of cookies, cake, and strudel, and bowls of fruit compote. Shayndel followed, a big grin on her face and a plate in each hand.

She placed one heaped high with sweets in the middle of their table. "This is for everyone to share," she said. "But the kuchen is mine. See, this one is made with apricot, this has plums, and the third is apple with raisins—which is what I grew up with."

Shayndel picked up her fork with a flourish, like a maestro with a baton. She took a small bite of the first two cakes and nodded her approval after each. But the third kuchen required a second taste as she discovered almonds and bits of dried apple that had been moistened with liqueur, and a sweet blend of spices she couldn't name. This was so far superior to her mother's baking that Shayndel put her fork down out of loyalty.

"Is it good?" Leonie asked.

"Unbelievable," Shayndel whispered, so serious that everyone at the table burst into laughter.

David stole a bite from her plate and pretended to swoon, while under the table he pressed his thigh against hers. She frowned and tilted her head toward Leonie, letting him know she was not going anywhere without her friend. David saluted and stumbled off, returning a moment later with Miloz.

"You sit here," David said, pushing him into the chair beside Leonie. He pointed at Shayndel and said, "There is an accordion outside, and I simply have to dance with you. Please, mademoiselle?"

Shayndel started to say no, but Leonie waved her away. "Go on. He will not be denied."

Nearly everyone in the hall stared at the vision of Leonie and Miloz side by side. Leonie's soft brown waves framed her heart-shaped face; a pair of perfect brows arched above eyes the color of gray clouds on a sunny day. She was the living proof that Parisian girls—including Jewish ones—were congenitally stylish.

Miloz seemed even more striking sitting beside her. With a long neck and jet-black hair that set off the milky whiteness of his skin, he looked like a Roman statue. It was impossible not to imagine them married and the parents of the most attractive Jewish children in history.

The attention made them self-conscious and acutely aware of the fact that they had nothing to say to each other. Miloz mashed a piece of cake into a pile of crumbs; Leonie sipped her water. They sighed in union, which made them laugh and turned their discomfort into an alliance.

"Let's go watch the dancing," said Leonie.

He pulled her chair out for her and offered his arm, which set the men from his barrack to shouting, "Hurrah!"

Zorah watched them, in spite of herself, and looked around the hall one last time to make sure that Meyer hadn't arrived without her noticing. That means he is at home with his wife and children, Zorah thought, as she hurried outside, passing through the gauntlet of Arab guards who slouched on either side of the door, watching the festivities.

As the room emptied, Tedi noticed that the guards were eyeing the dessert table, and brought them a plate of cookies.

"Thank you very much," said a small man with a heavy mustache.

"You speak Hebrew?" Tedi asked.

"Hebrew and Arabic. I have English, and a little Farsi, too."

Another man, who bore a striking resemblance to Arik, the Hebrew teacher, reached for a three-cornered cookie. "My mother makes something like this." After tasting it, he grimaced.

Tedi laughed. "Your mother's are better, yes?"

"Hers are sweeter." He reached out to touch her hair and said, "You are sweet, too."

Tedi stepped back. "I will get you something better."

She sent one of the kibbutz boys over with strudel. The guards waved at her, mouths full, and the Arik look-alike held up a sticky thumb.

Tedi waved back and then walked through the kitchen to the back door. She passed Tirzah and a group of kibbutzniks who were smoking and talking far too fast for her to understand.

"Good night," Tedi said. "Many thanks."

The clearing in front of the dining hall, noisy with laughter and music, was full of dancers, but Tedi was too tired to join in. Her face ached from smiling back at the stares and comments from the kibbutzniks. She wondered if she would always be treated as a curiosity: the tall blonde Jewess.

She walked toward the eastern fence, which faced onto a half-plowed field, pungent with the smell of broken sod and crushed weeds. The mountains were a dark shadow in the moonless night.

After the closeness inside the dining hall, the air was sweet and cool. She took a deep breath and turned her face to the sky. It seemed impossible that these could be the same stars she had looked up at six months ago, impossible that she was seeing them through the same eyes.

On the night of her escape, the icy air had hit her like a slap in the face, harsh but welcome after the fetid heat and terror inside the boxcar. There had been a full moon that night, which seemed as outsized and unreal as a paper cutout in a theater set.

After ten of them had squeezed through the floor of the cattle car, they found themselves facing an enormous field, flooded with moonlight. Tedi saw the others start to run but then drop to the ground, disappearing in the weeds. She followed suit, lying on her back and staring up at the moon as the sound of boots grew closer. One of the soldiers had a bad cough. One of the others swore as he stumbled over a rail tie. They seemed in no hurry and Tedi realized that they were unaware there had been an escape.

Her fingers burned in the cold; she wished she had thought to bury her hands in her armpits, but she didn't dare move. She became terrified that she might sneeze. Go away, she prayed. Go away.

Finally, the engine coughed back to life and the train pulled out, but Tedi waited until she heard someone else move before she dared lift her head. They scrambled for a line of trees, where they huddled close and rubbed each other's hands back to life.

Tedi sank down and sat in the dust of Atlit. After the Germans marched into Amsterdam, Tedi's best friend had told her, "You're so lucky. You look like a poster girl for the Hitler Youth." Gertrude had said it without malice, but Tedi was ashamed. A few weeks later, her parents announced that they were sending her into hiding at a farm outside Utrecht.

"I don't want to go," she wept. "I want to stay with you. Why don't you send Rachel instead?" But the decision had been made; her sister was too young to go to strangers. They would find somewhere else for her as soon as they could.

On the night before she was to leave, Tedi's mother sat on the bed beside her and brushed her hair. "You will be all right, sweetheart," she said, "but our Rachel has no chance of passing."

The memory of her mother's words sent a chill up Tedi's back. She tried to think about something else, but tonight she was too tired to fight the past. Rachel had been as dark as Tedi was fair, intellectual where Tedi was artistic, moody where she was sunny. Tedi was the favorite daughter, and both of them had always known it.

"I'm sorry," Tedi whispered.

Two days after her little group escaped from the death train, a group of British soldiers found them, gave them tea, and wrapped them in blankets before putting them on a truck headed for the Displaced Persons center in Landsberg. There she found more barbwire, more barracks, and endless lines in which she waited to talk to officers and Red Cross workers and black-market "fixers," who flourished in the chaos. She was sure that someone could help her get home, which was all she could think about. So many of the others talked about getting to America or Palestine, Argentina or Canada; she wondered if she was the only Jew in Europe who wanted to stay.

Her mother had said they were all to return to the apartment on Bloemgracht as soon as they could; that was the plan for "after."

Tedi got as far as the train depot in Stuttgart, which is where she ran into Arne Loederman, her father's business partner for seventeen years, since she was a baby. It took her a moment to recognize the frail old man calling her name. He wept at the sight of her, skin and bones.

He told her that he had been in Bergen-Belsen. He had seen her father, mother, and Rachel there; her Uncle Hermann, Auntie Lu, and their sons, her cousins, Jakob and Hans, too. He raked his fingers down his cheeks and looked at the ground. He didn't have to say it.

Tedi shivered, as cold as she'd been in the moonlit field. Even her fingers were numb. It was not a surprise. She had known they were dead, felt it even as she insisted on getting back to Amsterdam.

Mr. Loederman held his arms out to her and held her close, weeping bitterly on her shoulder. She did not return his embrace or cry and finally, he pulled away. He took both her hands in his. "You must travel back to Amsterdam with me, Tedi," he said, without meeting her eyes. "Half the business belongs to you. You remember Pim Verbeck, the old foreman? He promised to take care of things for us. Whatever is left will be your inheritance. I will take care of you."

But Tedi said, "I am going to Palestine."

Mr. Loederman's eyes filled with fresh tears. "I suppose I would do the same if I were younger. You must write to me when you get there. I will send you what I can. Here." He tried to press a few coins into her hands.

Tedi would not take them. "I have to go," she said.

"Wait. Let me buy you something. Food, a pair of shoes, something."

Tedi was already running away from him, hoping to catch up to the people she had been traveling with, the ones who were headed for Palestine. They had tried to talk her into coming with them and leaving behind the whole poisoned graveyard that was Europe. But she had kept her mind fixed on Amsterdam, the markets and the cinemas, the light on the water, the bakery down the block from her house, her favorite bridges. Once she got home, she promised herself, she would never complain about the dampness, or the long winter nights, or even the smell of the canals at low tide.

But Mr. Loederman had erased her longing and turned her homesickness and nostalgia into anger and loathing. Why had he survived? Why not her father, who had been a better man—kinder, smarter, and younger, too? Why was Tedi alive and not Rachel? Where was her mother? Her cousins? Her friends? Suddenly she imagined Amsterdam full of ghosts, reproaching her from every window, every storefront, every doorway.

In Palestine, at least, no one would burst into tears at the sight of her.

Sitting cross-legged on the ground, Tedi traced her name into the dirt and remembered Mr. Loederman's wife, Lena, an old-fashioned woman who wore crocheted collars. They had had a grown son, a daughter-in-law, and a grandson. All dead, she realized. She should have hugged him back.

The accordion raced up a scale. Young voices rose into the night. Tedi put her fingers into her ears and listened to the sound of her own breathing, one breath at a time, as her father had taught her when she was seven years old and miserable with the mumps. Papa had sat beside her on the quilted white counterpane. "Shah, darling, shah," he said, putting a cool hand on her burning forehead. "Take a deep breath. Good. Now, take the next breath. Then another breath, and another, and another, and *voilà*! You will be somewhere else, all better, no more headaches. The sun will shine and we will eat too much chocolate and we won't tell Mamma."

Tedi was rocking and weeping, her fingers in her ears, wanting her father, wishing that she could be that seven-year-old girl again, wondering how a lifetime could be burned and buried when it was so close that she could still feel the comfort of her father's hand on her face.

But the hand landed on her shoulder instead, grasping her firmly from behind. Tedi screamed and threw her elbow back as hard as she could and jumped to her feet, fists clenched.

Zorah was on the ground, clutching her thigh. "Bloody hell," she sputtered. "You idiot. Why did you do that?"

"I'm sorry," said Tedi, dropping to her knees. "I'm so sorry. Are you hurt?"

"I'll be all right," Zorah said, sitting up and rubbing her leg. "I didn't mean to startle you."

Tedi was rocking back and forth, her eyes squeezed shut, her arms wrapped around her sides.

"Really," Zorah insisted. "It's not that bad."

"They would grab from behind like that," Tedi whispered. "One of them would hold me down. They both laughed. They covered my face. It was as if I wasn't even there, just my . . ."

Zorah put her arm around Tedi's shoulders. It took a long time until she stopped rocking and trembling. The accordion played a tango from start to finish. Then there was a big-band ballad and a local folk tune. Finally, Zorah ventured a few words. "It was hell for women in the camps. I know."

"I wasn't in a concentration camp," Tedi said. "I was in hiding. I was at a farm in the countryside. All day long, locked inside the barn, and at night the farmer's son would come. Sometimes he brought someone else, an older man, and the two of them, sometimes every night.

"When I couldn't stand it anymore, I said something to the mother. She slapped me. The Germans came the next day."

Tedi started rocking again. "Don't," said Zorah, pushing the heavy hair away from Tedi's damp forehead. "Those bastards will rot in hell forever. But you got away, didn't you? You are far, far away from all of that. You're safe now, right?"

Zorah put her arm around Tedi's shoulders and held her still. "You're in the land of milk and honey, right?"

The sound of the party rose and fell, as though it were coming from a boat circling the shore.

"It's late," Zorah said finally. "Time for bed." She stood up, brushed the dust from her skirt, and offered Tedi her hand.

When Tedi got to her feet, she wrapped her arms around Zorah. "Thank you," she whispered, surprised at the delicacy of the fierce little woman who banged through Atlit like a clenched fist.

"No need for thanks," said Zorah, trying to break free.

But Tedi held on until Zorah stopped struggling. And for a moment, or perhaps no more than a fraction of a moment, Tedi was almost certain that Zorah hugged her back.

It was very late when Shayndel crept into Leonie's cot and woke her up.

"What's the matter?"

"David and me . . . I ended it."

"What happened?" Leonie asked. "I thought you liked him."

"I do, I mean I did, at first anyway. But I can't take it anymore. He is only in love with the idea of me. I make him feel important."

"I think he has great respect for you."

"It has nothing to do with me," Shayndel said, "and certainly nothing to do with what I want. He goes on and on about war like it is something beautiful and noble, which only means he's never seen it himself. War is hideous and it leaves you covered in shit. I cannot kill anyone else. I will not. Not even for the Jewish state. Someone else has to do it this time. I will work on a chicken farm and shovel manure. I will add up long columns of numbers in an office without windows. Anything but that."

"What does David say when you tell him this?" asked Leonie.

"He doesn't listen. He lectures me about the duty we all owe the Jewish people and the dream of a state. He puts his hand under my dress like it's his right and he says I must make sacrifices."

"What do you mean? Did he try to take advantage of you?"

Shayndel smiled. "Hardly. We've been going at it behind the last barrack almost since we met."

"I had no idea," said Leonie. "Good for you."

"Not particularly," Shayndel said. "Let's just say he doesn't know what to do to make a girl happy."

"There are ways to teach them about that. Or at least, that's what I've heard. And when there is real feeling . . ."

"You don't have to tell me about sex," Shayndel said. "In the forest, there wasn't much to do at night, and we all learned how to make each other happy. But this is not about fooling around. It's about him, David.

"Tonight he was completely impossible. I told him it was finished between us, and then he laughed at me and said I had cold feet. Like I was a little girl. Like I didn't know my own mind! Now all I want is for him to disappear so I don't have to argue anymore. Tomorrow wouldn't be soon enough. Do you think I'm right?"

"*Chérie,* if you do not love him, you are right. And it seems clear that you do not love him."

"I guess I wanted to be in love with someone. But not him. I'm just sorry that I didn't tell you about him from the beginning. I felt badly that you didn't have a boyfriend, too. That I betrayed our little plan with the two brothers."

"Our plan? That was more like a game, a nice little story we told each other," Leonie said. "Making plans is a game. Life chooses for you."

"Do you really believe that? That we are like leaves floating on the river, wherever it takes us?"

"This is not a bad thing," said Leonie. "It is not a good thing, either. That's just how it goes."

"So nothing makes sense?"

"How could you make sense of our lives?"

Shayndel lay still for so long, Leonie said, "I'm sorry if I offended you."

"I took no offense. I was just thinking what it would be like to keep that philosophy in mind on Yom Kippur."

"It is the day of judgments, no?"

"Yes. God is the judge who writes in the heavenly book who will live and who will die in the coming year," Shayndel said. "I wonder why I never objected to that idea. How can I permit anyone to speak of God sitting on His golden throne and deciding that Malka and Wolfe should be murdered, and millions of others, too? It is horrible."

"Were they believers?" Leonie said. "Your friends?"

"They believed in Palestine and the dream for a homeland."

"May it be so," said Leonie, using the ancient Hebrew formula.

"I thought you didn't know anything about the prayer book."

"I don't, but my grandfather used to say that. They took me to see him only a few times when I was a girl, but when I left and I said, 'See you again, *au revoir,*' he would answer, 'May it be so.' I used to think he was joking, but maybe he was a little serious, too. He died in his sleep, my grandfather, in his own bed, long before the Germans marched into Paris. He was not even sixty, but now I think he was a lucky man."

"On Yom Kippur, everyone weeps for the dead," said Shayndel, who had not cried when her friends had died, nor since.

"Weeping is terrible for the complexion," said Leonie, holding Shayndel close, "but it is very good for the heart."

Yom Kippur, September 17

Yom Kippur dawned overcast and muggy; it was going to be a hot day. Some of the men got up for early prayers, but without a regular breakfast hour or roll call, nearly everyone slept late. Tedi crept out of the barrack and walked through the quiet camp without seeing a soul.

There were a dozen people in the mess hall, and all of them looked up as she entered. Some raised their water glasses defiantly, showing off their disdain for the day-long fast, but others quickly dropped their gaze. There was no tea that morning or fresh salad, nor would there be any regular meals, but because children and the sick are exempt from the rules of self-denial, platters of fruit and cheese and baskets of bread had been set out, covered with dish towels to keep off the flies.

Tedi was surprised to find Zorah there. She was sitting alone, staring at an apple on the table in front of her.

"Can I join you?" she asked, waiting for permission to sit down. They had barely spoken since Rosh Hashanah, when Zorah had shown her such kindness.

"Suit yourself," Zorah said. "Where is your breakfast?"

"I'm not hungry, not yet anyway. I never really fasted on Yom Kippur. In my family, we—"

A boy stuck his head through the door and announced, "The Poles are starting Musaf."

"What is that?" Tedi asked.

"It's an extra service after morning prayers," Zorah said.

"Aren't you going?"

Zorah felt the call to prayer in her body. Her feet twitched and her heart raced, but she had no intention of giving in to the urge. "Why should I go?" she said, as if she'd been insulted.

"You seem to know so much about such things, the prayers, the Bible, the commentaries, even. Some of the girls call you 'the little rabbi.'" Tedi thought the name suited her, given that Zorah had begun to smell like a book—an oddly comforting combination of paste and ink and dust.

"That's no compliment if you consider the maniacs and lost souls who care about such things around here. Later, I'm going to have a big lunch with the Communists. Just watch me."

"I meant no harm," Tedi said softly.

"Ach," Zorah relented. "Don't listen to me. I need a smoke, that's all."

Tedi and Zorah sat at the table for an hour, watching as people wandered in and out. Only mothers with children walked through the doors without embarrassment or apology, urging their little ones to eat and taking sips of water when they thought no one was looking.

Zorah said, "I'm going to get some air." She left the apple untouched and wandered the perimeter of the camp, trying to avoid the chanting and muttering and bursts of song. But as the day wore on, boredom and curiosity got the better of her, so as the afternoon services began, Zorah went for a tour of the four separate observances.

The largest was held by the Poles in the promenade between the men's and women's barracks. Anschel, the religious zealot, was gone, and a rabbi had been imported for the service—a robust old man with a short gray beard; he wore a long white robe, the ceremonial garb of grooms, corpses, and Yom Kippur supplicants.

The Hungarians met behind one of the men's barracks, and the handful of Romanians who chose to pray fit beneath the overhang in front of Delousing.

The Communists and Socialist Zionists got together in the shade behind the mess hall, where they argued about whether to say any prayers at all. They agreed that formal worship was a waste of time and a distraction; still, a few of their number wanted to do "something." Finally, a short Russian with the loudest voice declared, "Enough. We can recite some words strictly out of solidarity, to honor the dead and the traditions of the dead. We say the words, we remember, and then we get drunk and have a good cry."

His friends brought that phrase into the dining room, repeating it to each other as they filled their plates and debated about how long it would take before religion withered entirely in the new Jewish state.

Zorah walked through and sat down beside Tedi, who had not moved all day.

Lillian was there, too, nibbling at apple slices. "My people were never religious fanatics," she said, in a voice meant for everyone in the hall. "My grandmother used to bake special butter cookies that she served only at tea on Yom Kippur. Her friends from the neighborhood would come to the house. 'Enough already,' she used to say to them. 'We are civilized people, after all.'"

"I wish she would shut up," Tedi whispered to Zorah.

"That will not happen until they wrap her in a shroud," Zorah said. She pointed at a boy sitting across the room. "What's going on with him, the one they brought in yesterday?"

The skinny ten-year-old had a full mouth, a piece of bread in one hand and a half-eaten pear in the other. He was sweating and swaying in his seat.

"He's been eating like that all day," said Tedi.

"Someone should stop him," Zorah said, but it was too late. He fell to his knees and started vomiting on the floor.

Zorah shook her head. "I saw someone die from eating like that. It was the day the British liberated the camp."

The smell hit Tedi hard. But as much as she wanted to run outside, she felt obliged to stay and listen to Zorah.

"They set up a feeding station with a sort of tube, filled with lukewarm gruel," she said. "I didn't know the man, or who knows, maybe he was my cousin. There was nothing left to him but eyes and bones. They carried him to this pipe and he opened his mouth, like a bird being fed by its mother. He closed his eyes and swallowed and swallowed until . . .

"No one thought to stop him. Someone said he ruptured his stomach. There were no doctors. So many died the day after liberation. Too weak. Too sick."

"I was never that hungry," Tedi whispered. "I was lucky."

Zorah turned on her. "Don't ever say that. Don't let anyone say that to you."

Tedi looked like she'd been slapped.

"Ach, maybe they're right," Zorah relented. "Maybe it's better not to talk of this at all. What's the point?"

"Exactly," said Tedi. "What is the point?"

"I'll tell you the point," said Zorah. "It is unbelievable what I saw, what I lived, what happened to you, to everyone here! The point is that nobody knows what happened, and if we pretend it didn't happen, then it didn't happen and it will never stop. People died from starvation even after they were given food because no one paid attention. A fifteen-year-old girl jumped off the deck of the ship that carried me to Palestine, and do you know why? Because everyone kept telling her, 'You are so lucky. You are young. You have cousins and uncles. Lucky girl.' She was bleeding inside from everything she'd been through. 'Don't cry,' they told her. 'Lucky girl,' they told her. She jumped into the sea."

"Shah, be quiet." Tedi put her hand on top of Zorah's. "They are staring at us."

"I don't care."

"Well, I care," said Tedi. "I don't want people looking at me like that. I don't want anyone to ask what happened to me. My memory is private. My grief is private. My . . ." She searched for a way to put it. "My shame. I mean, you won't tell anyone, will you?"

"Of course not," Zorah said. "What do you take me for?"

"You see? There are times when silence is better. When we must put the past behind us, in order to live."

Zorah crossed her arms against her chest. "So in order to

live, we must annihilate the past? Then what about your parents? Aren't you responsible for their memories? If you don't speak of them, it's like you kill them all over again."

Tedi was on her feet.

"I'm sorry if this causes you pain," said Zorah. "But I am not wrong."

"Leave me alone," said Tedi and ran out of the room.

Zorah stayed where she was, watching as groups of people passed by the open doors as each of the services ended. Some of them came to the door, looked inside, and then hurried away. She picked up an apple and brushed the cool, smooth skin back and forth against her lips. The smell made her mouth water. Her stomach rumbled. Eat it, she told herself.

When Tedi walked back into the barrack, Shayndel called her over to Leonie's cot, where the two of them had passed the day, talking and napping.

"Do you want to come to the last service of the day with us?" Shayndel asked.

"Did you go this morning?" Tedi asked.

"That's too much sitting for me," said Shayndel. "Neilah is short, and I want to say Kaddish for my family."

"I thought only men can do that," Tedi said.

"This is the twentieth century," Shayndel said. "I'm not asking some stranger who never met my mother and father to pray for them. Besides, if we go to the Socialists, no one will care what I do."

"Will you say it for me, too?" Tedi asked. "I don't know the words."

"Of course. I am saying it for Leonie, too. You can add the amens with everyone else."

It was not clear how it happened. The Russians claimed that the idea was theirs, but it might have been the work of the local rabbi, who had been seen talking to the Romanians and Hungarians earlier. However it came to pass, as the sun moved toward the horizon, the entire population of Atlit—nearly three hundred that day—gathered as a single congregation. They streamed toward the promenade, dragging benches, chairs, and wooden boxes through the dirt.

Although the crowd was quiet, there was something festive in the air as people arranged seats into uneven rows. The injured and the pregnant were urged to sit first. Others, dizzy from fasting and heat, sat down without prompting. The dust of the long day settled around them in the golden light.

"Where are their shoes?" Leonie asked, pointing to a group of men who were standing in bare feet.

"It's an old custom of mourning," Shayndel explained as she, Tedi, and Leonie sat among the women who had, without direction or discussion, taken seats to the left of an untidy aisle.

As the rabbi moved to the front of the crowd, everyone grew still. The mood dimmed so quickly, Leonie looked up, expecting to see a thick cloud covering the sun. But the sky was clear except for a single thin band of purple stretched over the mountains.

The rabbi covered his head with a large white prayer shawl and stood silently for a long moment before he picked up a book and began to chant in a clear, reedy tenor voice.

With the first note, Shayndel began to weep, silent and almost motionless. The tears came not so much from her as through her, as every note and phrase called up random shards of memory.

"Blessed, blessed," said the rabbi, and she saw her father's signet ring.

"Hallelujah," he chanted, and she thought of her mother's favorite blue apron.

"Open my lips," the rabbi recited, and she remembered the little scar on her brother's forehead.

She was overcome by the weight of what she had lost: mother, father, brother, friends, neighbors, comrades, lovers, landscapes. Odd details surfaced, like flotsam rising from a sunken ship: her father would only eat the dark meat of a chicken; her mother loved Laurel and Hardy films and the Beethoven piano sonatas.

She remembered the last formal photograph of her family, taken a week before Noah left them, headed for Palestine. She had just turned sixteen. When her father brought the picture home, he couldn't get over how much his children resembled each other. Her mother agreed. "Your noses, your chins!" she exclaimed, tracing her finger over the glass. "Just like my father."

All gone.

Leonie and Tedi sat on either side of Shayndel, but she could not bear to look at them. She could do nothing but weep. The tears reached her lips, orphan tears; she found them strangely cold.

Leonie put her arm around Shayndel's waist. Tedi rested her hand on Shayndel's shoulder. They pressed their bodies against hers, holding her up, reminding her that she was not alone, that she was still loved.

Leonie and Tedi wept softly, too, less for their own losses than out of sympathy for Shayndel, whom they had never seen cry. She worked so hard, smiled so freely, and seemed to forgive the everyday pettiness of Atlit so easily. She had made them think she was different—undamaged and immune to grief. But of course she was as lost as everyone else, as lonely and haunted by ghosts that only she could see and hear. Her pain as bottomless. Together, the congregation of Atlit wept. As the sun dropped and the sky blazed and blushed and dimmed, for nearly an hour, they rose for some prayers and sat for others, reciting the sibilant Ashkenazic Hebrew liturgy of a thousand gutted sanctuaries.

Tedi, Shayndel, and Leonie kept their seats, silent, holding on to one another. Zorah watched them from a distance. She stood at the back of the crowd, a few paces removed from the Orthodox girls—the ones who kept their arms and legs covered even on the hottest days, the ones who never danced in the same circle as the boys.

Zorah kept her mouth closed throughout the prayers, pursing her lips and frowning during the communal confession of sins and the plea to the great Father, the formal outcry as the gates of judgment were closed, the somber wailing of God's oneness, the triple repetition of His kingship. Then, "Adonai is God," repeated seven times, each one louder than the last, sounding more and more like a demand for justice, until finally the words stopped and only the bleat of the ram's horn answered.

Zorah used to hear the last shofar blast as a call to wake up and begin again, a clarion trumpet. But this was noise, a feral howl, signifying nothing. The final note drifted and hung in the air. The sun had set and the twilight was soft on their heads. No one spoke or moved until the sound faded and silence reigned.

But it was only a few moments before a loud sneeze broke the spell. Someone said, "Gesundheit," and laughter followed. People stood and stretched. Men began to fold their prayer shawls and conversation began to percolate until the rabbi called out.

"My friends," he announced. "A moment more. Let us end this Day of Atonement, this Sabbath of Sabbaths, together." The crowd turned back, reluctant but obedient, on their feet as he lit a foot-long, blue-and-white braided candle and recited the blessings that separate time into sacred and profane.

The evening prayer service followed—a rushed affair, murmured by only a few men, until the rabbi announced the mourners' prayer.

It was the slowest Kaddish Zorah had ever heard, every syllable weighted by groans and sighs. Pious women on either side of her covered their eyes with their fingers, soundlessly mouthing the words.

Glorified and celebrated, they recited. *Acclaimed and honored, extolled and exalted beyond all tributes that man can utter.*

Zorah knew that most of the people around her did not understand what they were saying. For them, the ancient prayer was a kind of lullaby, a balm for the afflicted. She wondered if they would be standing if they realized that they were praising the God who had decreed the murder of their families; that they were expressing gratitude and affection for the One who had annihilated everyone and everything they had loved.

We need a new Kaddish for 1945, she thought. An honest Kaddish that would begin, "Accused and convicted, heartless and cruel beyond anything the human mind can understand."

They chanted, *God who brings peace to His universe.*

Silently, Zorah translated, "God who brings Nazis to His universe."

Amen and amen, they assented.

"No more and no more," said Zorah.

"Amen, already," came a shout from the crowd, ready to be finished, ready to forget, ready to eat.

The last lines of the prayer took up the case for peace: *God who brings peace to His universe, make peace for us all and all of Israel.*

Zorah wondered where peace might be located in a world burned beyond recognition.

Some of the boys started singing the last words, *oseh shalom,* picking up the tempo and transforming it into a folk song. They kicked away the chairs, grabbed one another and started dancing in a tight circle, arms around each other's shoulders and moving so fast that the smallest boys were lifted off their feet and carried along, shrieking.

After a while, they started singing a new song, a modern Hebrew hymn extolling the bricklayers who build a new state. Zorah joined in, willing to praise miracles made with human hands.

"I never heard you sing before," said a familiar voice at her ear.

Zorah did not turn around. Meyer moved closer and asked, "Did you miss me?"

"Only when I was dying for a smoke," she said.

"I thought about you all the time," said Meyer.

"I assumed you were with your family—your wife and children."

"I am not married, Zorah. I had to go home to make arrangements for my sister. My mother died last year and my father can't take care of Nili, or he won't be bothered. She is Mongoloid. Do you know what that means? She is twenty but with the mind of a little child. I cannot care for her so I took her to a place for women like her in Jerusalem. It was clean and pleasant, but I know that my poor mother is turning in her grave. What else could I do?

"I'm here only to see you," he said, close enough for Zorah to feel the heat of his body and smell the sour breath of his Yom Kippur fast. "I won't be coming to Atlit anymore, but I am going to write to you. I don't expect you to answer, and even if you want to, I'm not sure I'll be able to receive letters. This way, you don't have to pretend you're indifferent to me, and I can pretend that you are not."

The singing had stopped and the crowd was moving quickly toward the dining hall.

"I wish I could send you cigarettes," Meyer said, slipping a packet into her hand. "But they would only get stolen. Still, whenever you get a letter, you should know that I was thinking about sending a whole carton of Chesterfields. I am a romantic, right?"

Zorah fought the urge to face him, to wish him well, to say good-bye.

"Pray a little for my safety, will you, Zorah?" said Meyer. "I will kiss you good night wherever I am."

Zorah heard him walk away and counted to thirty before she turned. He had reached the gate. Without turning or looking back, he raised his hand to wave. As though he knew she would be watching.

The Clinic

It was late in the afternoon, and the infirmary was so quiet that Leonie and Aliza had dragged their chairs outside. "Soon the days will be much cooler," said Aliza, handing a cigarette to Leonie. "It isn't even two weeks until October."

"October," Leonie echoed. The cloudless skies and wilting heat had erased her sense of time. In Atlit, new faces appeared almost every day, like leaves in spring, and then scattered, sometimes within a matter of hours. The days dragged, yet somehow the weeks flew. Two months had passed since her arrival, and soon she would witness a change of season.

Leonie could no longer remember all of the women who had passed through her barrack. Some of the recent arrivals had included the weakest and sickest she had seen; they landed within days of a convoy of strapping girls who had spent the war in England. Healthy or ill, it seemed that everyone was in transit—nearly everyone.

Whenever she saw another truckload of refugees leaving Atlit, waving and singing, Leonie felt like a leper in quarantine. Sometimes, she wondered if she was under suspicion. Had someone discovered how she spent those last two years in Paris? Would they send a policeman to shave her head and drag her back to France?

But that fear did not keep Leonie awake at night. She assumed that her situation was simply a matter of fate. Life was unplanned, purely random. That was the only logical explanation for why Shayndel was stranded in Atlit. In a rational universe, Shayndel, the partisan heroine, would have been released immediately and given a medal for her courage during the war. Tedi, the tall, well-liked blonde, should have been settled on a blooming kibbutz weeks ago. As for Zorah, she was no worse than dozens of bitter survivors who had come and gone. Leonie knew that there was nothing sinister or sacred about their predicament—it was just bad luck.

She looked up from the yellow dust on her shoes to the brittle thorns in the fields outside the fence. Atlit was dull and dimly frightening, but unlike everyone else, she was not desperate to leave. As long as she was here, she did not have to make decisions and was free from disasters of her own creation. Besides, she knew it was only a momentary respite and that soon, without warning, she would lose Shayndel and Aliza, the only people in the world who cared what happened to her.

Leonie handed the cigarette back to Aliza and asked, "Did you bring the newspaper?" The nurse nodded and unfolded the broadsheet she had in her pocket. She had to smuggle the papers into camp; the British preferred to keep the immigrants ignorant of the conflicts swirling around them, though of course, the news seeped in daily in spite of regulations.

Aliza ran her eyes up and down the front page, searching for a story to read aloud. She stuck to pieces about milk production, or reviews of plays and concerts, or heartwarming accounts of holiday festivities; nothing she thought might cause Leonie to frown or, God forbid, weep.

Leonie no longer had to ask Aliza to slow down as she read. As long as people didn't mumble or speak too fast, she understood what they said. The written word was another story; on the page, she could barely puzzle out "pioneer," which had been one of the first Hebrew words she learned in the DP camp. Two eager young men from Palestine had pursued her and spoken with breathless passion about how she could take part in building a homeland. She was enchanted by the promise of a fresh start and by the idea that she was needed.

But from the moment Leonie had gotten on the boat, she knew that she had added a new fraud to her portfolio. She was surrounded by people who knew the lyrics to countless Zionist songs and seemed to have the map of Palestine committed to memory. After two months, Leonie was still confused about the geography of the country. Was Jerusalem on the other side of the mountains in the east? Was it cold in the north of the country? Could it possibly be any hotter in the south? She was too ashamed to ask anyone.

Her clearest ideas about the landscape and life of Palestine came from Aliza's descriptions of Haifa. Leonie glanced over at her unlikely friend, who was reading an article about a proposal for growing pineapples in the Jezreel Valley.

Aliza was older than Leonie by nearly thirty years. She wore thick-soled black shoes and olive green socks with her white uniform. A disaster of freckles covered her broad cheeks and wide nose, which had no acquaintance with powder. She was a bighearted woman who loved to talk about herself.

Leonie could picture the steep streets that wound up the hill to where Aliza lived with her husband, Sig, a bus driver, in an apartment with views of the sparkling sea. Leonie knew the names of the Arab markets that had the best cheese, and which bakeries sold the best bread, because the high point of Aliza's week was the elaborate Saturday luncheon she made for an ever-changing cast of cousins and nephews, uncles, aunts, and nieces, served at a wrought iron table on a tiny balcony, filled with flowers.

"Who came to lunch last week?" Leonie asked. "Did Uncle Ofer pick another fight with your brother-in-law?"

Aliza laughed. "They fight about everything."

"Even pineapples?"

"Mostly they argue about politics," Aliza said. "This time, Ofer was yelling about the British and how it's time to throw them out, once and for all. He calls them occupiers now, and started banging on the table about how the Palmach has to stand up to them for what's going on up north. He's furious at the English for shooting at the refugees crossing the border over the mountains."

"But isn't Ofer the one who loves everything English? The one with the pipe and the teapot?"

Aliza laughed. "I must talk about them too much."

"I like hearing about your family," Leonie said. "But tell me, the Palmach . . . is that separate from Haganah?"

"Not separate. Palmach is part of the Haganah. In fact, the British trained the Palmach unit to defend Palestine against the Germans," said Aliza. "But now they fight for the Yishuv—

the Jews of Palestine, all of whom are united in support of you. Oh, not just you, Leonie. No need to blush.

"I mean all of you immigrants. You are real miracle-workers, believe me. In Eretz Yisrael, where we disagree about everything—including pineapples—everyone agrees that the Jews of Europe must be able to come here. There is no solution but to burn that damned White Paper and make good on the promises of the Balfour Declaration."

Aliza had never spoken with such passion about politics before. Leonie shrugged apologetically. "I understand the words," she said. "But what is the White Paper? Balfour? I'm sorry to be so stupid, but I don't know—"

Aliza interrupted. "Don't apologize. You were just a baby when this was decided. Look at you." She shook her head. "You're still a child. All you need to know is that in 1917, the English foreign secretary, Balfour, wrote a letter that promised the Jews a homeland in Palestine. It was a promise that they went back on in 1939, when they put handcuffs on Jewish immigration with a document called the White Paper."

Aliza folded the newspaper and slipped it back into her pocket. "If they had kept their word, we could have saved so many lives. It makes me sick just thinking about it. There are a million survivors still in Germany. And I heard that the Allies are starting to lock them up inside the death camps. This is beyond imagining.

"My uncle is right," Aliza said. "Quotas and blockades will not stop us. And the truth is, the English have always preferred the Arabs to the Jews. In fact, they are anti-Semites, though there are exceptions, of course," she said. "Like our little commandant here in Atlit.

"But enough politics for today," she said, getting to her feet.

"I'm going over to the kitchen and see if I can get a lemon or an orange so I can show you how to give an injection." She put her hand under Leonie's chin and smiled. "I suppose you'll get married right away. But it's always good to have a trade, just in case."

Leonie watched her go, overwhelmed by affection. Aliza seemed happiest when she was taking care of others, or telling them what to do. She never complained and seemed content with her life. Leonie wondered about the heavy gold earrings that she wore every day—her only adornment. Maybe they were a gift from her husband, or perhaps they had belonged to her mother. Aliza never mentioned children; Leonie wondered if she couldn't have any, or if she'd lost sons during the war.

Despite all the time they spent together, the two women knew almost nothing about each other. Leonie was too shy to inquire, and there was an unspoken rule against asking survivors about their experiences.

Leonie stood up and went back inside the infirmary. It might be an hour before Aliza returned; as much as the nurse disapproved of Tirzah's affair with Colonel Bryce, they seemed to have plenty to talk about. Leonie wandered between the cots, looking for something to do. She had already cleaned up after the morning's roster of ills: a bad splinter, coughs, rashes, constipation, diarrhea, and chest pain that turned out to be indigestion. Starvation and malnutrition followed by abundant fruits and vegetables made for a lot of stomach trouble.

The little clinic was busiest when a group of new immigrants arrived. Doctors and extra nurses would appear for a day of physical examinations, inoculations, and paperwork. The seriously ill were taken to hospital immediately, leaving only cases of simple dehydration, sunburn, cuts, and sprained ankles for the regular nurses. Many days, Aliza and her colleagues did little more than bandage scrapes, give enemas, and dose the children with vile-tasting fish oil.

Leonie was sweeping under the cots when Aliza rushed through the door, her arm around a red-faced girl, clutching her belly. Three more women ran in behind them, all of them talking at once.

"Leonie, lay out the rubber sheet behind the curtain there and bring some towels. And the surgical kit," Aliza ordered. "You girls, come and help me get her up on the table.

"All right now, Elka," she said, sternly, "how far along are you?"

"I was due last week," she panted. "The women in my family carry small."

"You should have told me as soon as you got here," Aliza grumbled, as she draped a sheet over Elka's legs.

"I didn't tell anyone. They wouldn't have let me on the boat if they knew I was so far along. But I didn't care. I wanted my baby born in Palestine. No one was going to stop me. No one." She gasped as the next contraction grabbed her and her face turned scarlet again.

"Don't hold your breath," said Aliza. "You can make all the noise you want to." Elka obeyed immediately with a bellow that sent her friends into peals of laughter.

Tirzah arrived with a steaming kettle of water, and Aliza sent Leonie back to the kitchen with her to fetch more. A crowd had already gathered outside, waiting for news and pacing like an extended family—even though no one knew the mother's name.

"How much longer, do you think?" someone asked Leonie as she rushed by.

"Who wants to bet it's a boy?"

Tirzah lit the burner under a big pot of water, and chased Leonie out into the mess hall to pace until it boiled. Fifteen impossibly long minutes later, she carried the pot back through the waiting crowd, where no one was smiling.

"What's going on?" someone asked her. "It got awfully quiet all of a sudden."

Leonie rushed inside and felt as though she'd walked into a tomb. The stillness was so profound, for a moment, she thought she was alone. But as her eyes adjusted from the bright sunlight, Aliza materialized, leaning over a blood-streaked doll laid out on a towel, massaging the tiny chest, then stooping to place her lips over the baby's nose and mouth. Elka's eyes were squeezed shut, and though her friends held her, her legs shook so violently that the table below her rattled. The room stank of blood and shit.

The pot of hot water slipped out of Leonie's hands and crashed to the floor. The women around Elka jumped, but Aliza seemed not to have heard the noise as she whispered into the baby's ear between breaths. Elka started to whimper. The wall clock tapped out a dry dirge, more terrible every second.

Until a faint, husky mew rose from beneath Aliza's hands. "Good girl!" she said gently. "Let me hear you." She picked up the baby and laughed as the cries grew louder and more human. "Ten fingers, ten toes. You have a beautiful daughter," Aliza crowed, as she swabbed the baby clean, wrapped her in a towel, and placed her in Elka's arms.

"Mazel tov, little mother. Look what a pretty mouth she has. Have you picked a name?"

"Aliyah Zion."

"Beautiful!" Aliza approved.

Leonie asked, "What does it mean exactly?"

"It means 'coming up into the land of Israel,'" Elka said.

"And the family name?" asked Aliza, who had laid a fresh sheet over Elka's legs and was cleaning her up beneath it.

"The family name is Zion."

"That is your husband's surname?"

"Don't speak of him," Elka spat.

Aliza dropped her head, assuming he was dead. "I'm so sorry," she said.

"Don't be sorry. He's alive, though if I ever see him again, I may remedy that situation."

"You don't mean that," said one of Elka's friends.

"Don't I?" she said. "He should have been here. He could have gotten on the boat with me, but his mother wanted to wait for a bigger ship. A better ship. And he decided to stay with her instead of coming with me? He can go to hell. Surely there is someone in Palestine who has a backbone. Someone who doesn't have a goddamned mother!"

Her words hung in the air like a dark cloud, as the clock scolded, *tsk, tsk*.

Elka's friends turned their faces away from her, and she began to wail, clutching the baby's face to her chest so tightly that Aliza rushed forward and pried the bundle out of her arms.

"Gently, little mother," she said. "Leonie, take the baby outside for a moment. Show everyone that she is well, but don't let anyone touch her. And for God's sake, put a smile on your face."

The crowd pushed forward, surrounding her and praising the bow-shaped lips, the tiny fingers, the thatch of golden brown hair. But Elka's sobs were growing louder and more desperate. "Mama!" she screamed suddenly. "Where is my mama? Why doesn't she come?"

Leonie brought the baby inside but Elka did not stop crying, and refused to hold her child. Aliza tried to calm her with tea and then with brandy. She offered gentle reassurances and then scolded her about her duty to the child. Nothing worked—not even her own baby's inconsolable howls. Finally, Aliza gave Elka a sedative and fed the baby a bottle.

The following morning, Elka was unchanged. No matter what anyone said or did, no matter how loud the baby cried, she would not even look in her direction.

On the second day, Leonie recognized the dull, unfocused gaze in Elka's eyes as the one she had seen on a girl who had pulled out her own hair by the handful, and on the man who would not get out of bed. A few of the so-called crazy ones raged and ranted, but most were listless and empty, like Elka.

Aliza lost patience with those cases quickly, certain that they were the victims of their own weakness and not any real disease. She gave Elka the benefit of the doubt for an extra day, but after seventy-two hours with a screaming baby and a completely indifferent mother, she asked for "Dr. Nonsense," which is what she called the psychiatrist.

Dr. Nonsense was Simone Hammermesch, an elegant Belgian woman with white hair, manicured hands, and a half-dozen languages at her disposal. She pulled up a chair beside Elka's bed and took her hand, waiting quietly for an hour before saying a word. Then she leaned close and murmured in soft, reassuring, motherly tones, until Elka seemed to relax a little. Still she said nothing.

Leonie watched the doctor work but hoped that Elka would not succumb to her kind, hypnotic voice; that she would get out of bed without letting slip the secret that had laid her low.

Dr. Nonsense was persistent and patient, but after two long

sessions at the bedside, all she managed to get out of Elka was, "Leave me alone."

She sighed, patted her snowy chignon, and got to her feet and called for Aliza. "Please get the patient dressed and bring her to my car. I'll call the maternity ward about the baby."

After they left, Aliza helped Leonie make up the cot with fresh sheets. "Don't worry," she said. "After a little rest, Elka will be tip-top. Someday, you'll run into her on a street corner and you'll go for a cup of coffee and laugh about this whole thing. She might not even remember it happened. I've seen this before, many times.

"Now go get me a syringe, won't you, dear?" she said, taking a small orange out of her string bag. "I haven't forgotten about showing you how to give a shot."

The next day, Leonie stayed away from the infirmary, lying in bed with a pillow pulled to her belly so that the others would think she was suffering from cramps.

"I don't know how you stand going there day after day," Shayndel said, sitting beside Leonie after the others had gone to breakfast. "The sight of blood alone does me in. Don't you find it depressing being with sick people? The pain, the wounds, the scars, the smells. Ugh."

Leonie shrugged. In fact, she envied the ones with wounds and scars and even, God help her, the ones with the numbers on their arms. No one asked those people why they were furious or miserable, why they refused to dance the hora, why they did not grab for the candy bars sent from America. Everything was permitted and forgiven them, at least as long as they dressed and took their meals and kept their stories to themselves.

Leonie's skin was unblemished. She had not hidden in a Polish sewer or shivered in a Russian barn. She had not seen her parents shot. Atlit was her first experience of barracks and barbwire. She had survived the war without suffering hunger or thirst. There had been wine and hashish and a pink satin coverlet to muffle her terrors.

Near the end of December in 1942, at five in the evening it was already dark on the Paris streets. Leonie rounded the corner, holding the lapels on her coat so that no one could see the yellow star. She was on her way home, to the apartment she shared with her uncle and cousin in a run-down corner of a district where Jews were rare. Her uncle had bribed someone so they didn't have to wear the badge at first, but after a change in the police department, they had been forced to register. Leonie hated the way people stared at her now, and when she felt an arm slip through the crook of her elbow, she nearly screamed, certain she was about to be arrested.

"Don't worry," whispered Madame Clos, the tobacconist's wife. "The Germans have been to your apartment. They took your cousin and your uncle. I've been watching out for you. Come with me."

Madame Clos was a tall woman and Leonie had to run to keep up with her. They hurried toward her building on the far end of the block. Leonie knew that she would never see her uncle or cousin again; after the brutal roundup of thirteen thousand at the Velodrome the previous summer, no one believed they were being "evacuated." There was no "resettlement." No "work camps."

Leonie followed Madame up steep flights to the top floor, trying to muster a little pity for the only family she had. Even as a young boy, her cousin had been horrible to her. "You're a little bastard," he would smirk, echoing his father. "And your mother wasn't even smart enough to get knocked up by a rich man."

When she was seven years old, Auntie Renata—her mother's sister—had walked out on Uncle Mannis, a petty criminal and a gambler. When Leonie started to grow breasts, her uncle leered and pinched. "It helps them grow," he said with a smile that made her stomach drop. He opened the door to her room when she dressed in the morning, and laughed when she told him she kept a knife under her pillow. The week Leonie turned fifteen, she got a job in a candy factory and stayed at work as long and late as she could.

Breathless after the sixth set of steps, she waited as Madame Clos rummaged for her keys and unlocked an enormous wooden door. She dropped her bag in the foyer and led Leonie into a room crowded with furniture: large, dark sideboards, bookcases, and far too many chairs. Heavy red drapes covered the floor-to-ceiling windows, making the place feel like a theater. The silk flower arrangements added a funereal note. On the couch, three pale girls sat in a row, wearing crocheted shawls over short silk slips.

Madame Clos put her arm around Leonie. "Let me present my nieces, who have come to live with me in these dark days: Christine, Marie-France, and Simone."

Simone, Leonie remembered, was a redhead.

Tirzah

The tap on the door was barely audible, but Tirzah had been keeping an eye on the time. At five minutes past midnight, the guards were settling in for the start of the second watch, but the Jewish holidays had disrupted schedules everywhere in Atlit, and it had been nearly a month since Bryce had slipped into her room.

He arrived, as always, trailing the scent of talc and Bay Rum. He had told her that it was the commonest cologne in the world, but it was new to her, which delighted him. Just as it pleased her to have given him a nickname, something he never had before. These were the gifts they gave each other, the only kind they could give.

The room was dark, except for a candle, but even in the shadows they were shy about looking directly at each other. Bryce took Tirzah's hand and kissed a small crescent-shaped scar at the base of her right thumb, grateful for the knowledge of its provenance—a burn from a loaf of bread she had baked as a child in her grandmother's kitchen.

Tirzah put both her hands on his freshly shaved face and imagined him at his mirror, preparing for her. He moved closer so she could feel the heat under his pressed shirt. Then it was up to her—it was always up to her—to lean toward him, to give him her mouth, to blow out the candle, to take off her robe and let him surprise her, as he always did, with his tongue and his fingers everywhere. They lost themselves on the narrow cot so quietly and so slowly, it was as if they were dreaming themselves inside one another's skin. They did not so much kiss as inhale each other's panted breath until they broke apart, spent and breathless.

Usually she was the one to doze for a few moments after they made love, but this time Bryce fell asleep. Tirzah tucked her arm under him and pulled closer, feeling the bones of his spine against her belly and chest. She ran her tongue over her teeth and tasted his toothpaste. She brushed her cheek against his thinning hair and savored his Bay Rum.

Everyone in Atlit knew about their affair. The other officers winked at her, managing to be both lewd and respectful at the same time. The nurses and teachers had made it abundantly clear how distasteful they found her "sacrifice." Tirzah despised her countrymen's hypocrisy about sex. Virginity was not quite the all-important prize it had once been—especially not among the young Socialists of the Yishuv. In Palestine, it was considered patriotic to open your legs for young men of fighting age; yet, if an unmarried girl had the bad luck to get pregnant, she could be demoted or even fired from a job. And if a woman was unofficially "encouraged" to seduce an enemy officer who could provide important information in the struggle for the homeland, well, the sooner that sort of thing was over and hushed up the better.

The real secret about Tirzah's affair with the colonel was wrapped in the cotton wool of expediency. Sleeping with the enemy was an odious but justifiable means to a Zionist end, but falling in love with such a man verged on the treasonous.

Tirzah had been completely unprepared for that possibility and was still a little shocked whenever she caught sight of Bryce during the day. He was far too short and fair for her, an entirely different species from the men she'd been attracted to in the past. Watching him walk across the compound, she had to stop herself from laughing at the idea that the great love of her life had turned out to be a middle-aged, ginger-haired bantam from a place with a name that sounded like a sneeze or a brand of whiskey. Cardiff.

No one would suspect the passion hidden behind his formality, or his talents as a lover, or his belief in the justice of the Jewish claim in Palestine. Tirzah's superiors pretended that every last Brit was a closet Nazi, which made it easier to do anything and everything to chase them out of the country and claim it as their own. But that story had nothing to do with her Johnny.

Eight months earlier, when the Palmach sent her to spy in Atlit, she had thought him the image of a narrow-minded, buttoned-down Englishman. But then he opened his mouth and addressed her in complete and grammatical Hebrew sentences. When he pronounced her name properly, she had blushed. That caused him to stare and stammer. And so it began.

Mostly, they spoke Hebrew, but he told her in English that he loved her. She had no reason to doubt him. Everything else he had ever said to her had been true. Bryce would let her know when a new group of refugees was due to arrive, whether by train or by bus. When trains pulled in at night, he neglected to assign enough men to guard the inmates as they made their way from the end of the tracks, around the fence, and to the gate. Helpers and spies embedded in the transports managed to spirit away dozens of "black" immigrants—ones without papers—hiding them in the fields before they could be counted. She had kept count, and Bryce had been responsible for the escape of at least seventy-five refugees.

He had once tried to translate an American turn of phrase about the British strategy on Jewish immigration; "closing the barn door after the horses have escaped." Tirzah had laughed at the expression, which sounded absurd in Hebrew. The image stayed with her, though. She imagined herself as a lone horse trotting off into the distance, wondering where to go.

She wondered if Bryce knew about her disastrous marriage. He knew a lot about her, mostly because he asked. Where did she grow up? Did she play with dolls as a little girl or did she climb trees? Did she like to read? Which of her schoolteachers did she remember? When she answered—whispering as though relating state secrets—he kept perfectly still, memorizing every word. He probably knew a good deal more about her from her dossier, too. It wouldn't be hard to connect her to the Palmach; indeed, most of what she knew about Bryce came from their files: A career officer, he was well liked by his men but lacked the sort of ambition that would have avoided a dead-end posting like Atlit. The woman in the photograph on his desk was his wife, though Tirzah had yet to discover her name. Their sons, however, she knew were George and Peter, both of whom had enlisted in the RAF. George had been killed early in the war, flying a mission over Germany.

At unpredictable moments in her day—writing lists, peeling vegetables, washing a countertop—Tirzah would recall the insistent gentleness of his hands on her sex, the firmness of his mouth on her breast, the fondness in his voice when he spoke about her son, Danny. These furtive attacks of joy took her breath away, and for the first time in her life she uttered the prayer that thanks God for small blessings. And in the next breath, she cursed the God who would let happiness bloom on such a doomed stalk.

Bryce woke up and turned over. "Sorry," he said, and put his finger to her lips. "What is the Hebrew word for 'bittersweet'?"

"Ha," Tirzah said. "Our first cliché."

He flinched. Had the bed been any larger he would have pulled away from her, but there was nowhere to go, so he kept still. It would be another hour before the next change of the guards, when he could leave without being seen. After a long pause he asked, "Danny is coming tomorrow, isn't he?"

Tirzah heard the forgiveness in his voice and wondered if his feelings for Danny had anything to do with the loss of his son.

"Yes," she said.

"I've gotten some of that toffee he likes. I'll bring it to the kitchen."

Bryce would stay away from her room until the boy left, but he didn't mind these brief separations. When Danny was in camp, Tirzah's eyes seemed to absorb the light, and the lines around her mouth grew softer. He wished he could do more than bring candy to her son, something more for her, too. He daydreamed about getting her an apartment in Tel Aviv like some of the other officers had done for their girls. They could be together for more than three hours at a time; they could share a meal and watch the sun set.

But even as he imagined the scene, he knew it would never happen. Tirzah was not that kind of woman, and he wasn't sure what would happen between them if he asked for anything more than what they shared in her airless little room. Perhaps the facade of her affection would crack. As much as he wanted to believe that she cared for him, as much as he thought he could feel it in her mouth and see it on her face, he would never be completely certain of her feelings.

They were long past pretending about their part in the drama that was unfolding in Palestine. She asked bald-faced questions about camp operations, down to the assignment of sentries and patrols. He answered her in detail, a willing coconspirator.

Bryce hated his assignment in Atlit. He thought it was outrageous to keep these people locked up like criminals, especially having read some of the classified reports about the liberation of the death camps. He had seen photographs considered too ghastly for public release, but even more troubling to him were rumors that the Allies had known about the concentration camps and the railroad lines that served them for months or even years. The idea that the RAF might have stopped the killing was even more horrible to him than the images of dried-up bodies stacked like cordwood. He felt implicated in a secret crime and ashamed of his uniform.

He fantasized about marrying Tirzah and training Jewish regiments to fight the Arabs, who were gearing up for war against the Jewish settlement. But he knew those were pipe dreams. He had watched men "go native" in India. It was an occupational hazard and in the end, it was always the woman who paid the price. He would never put Tirzah in that position.

He also knew that eventually his superiors would take note of his laxness or uncover his complicity. They would demobilize him and send him home, where he would take up fishing, like his father. He would drink too much, also like his father. He would read all the newspaper accounts about Palestine and wonder what happened to Tirzah and her little boy. He would imagine writing to her—long, honest letters—but never put pen to paper.

The sound of footsteps hurried them out of bed. Tirzah wrapped herself in the sheet and watched him dress. She hoped that things between them would come to an end before Danny learned that he was supposed to hate the colonel who took such an interest in his mother.

"Tirzah," Bryce said. "Things are heating up in the north."

"I know," she said. The newspapers were full of stories about tensions at the borders with Lebanon and Syria, where refugees from all over the region were making their way over the mountains on foot. Anti-Jewish sentiment in the Arab world had grown during the war years, making life increasingly perilous for Jews there; restrictions, harassment, and riots had become common even in places like Baghdad, where the Jewish community had flourished for so long. The "Zionist threat" was now a rallying cry, uniting the Arab world against Jewish plans for a homeland, and against British interests and their handling of the mandate in Palestine.

Hoping to pacify the Arabs, the British commanders were ordering the surrender of Jewish immigrants on the northern frontiers—a directive that was flagrantly defied by the kibbutzniks at the border. It was rumored that the Palmach had sent reinforcements to help the refugees—nearly all men of fighting age—to negotiate the rough terrain.

"There's talk of our chaps moving another division up there, to make the point," Bryce said. "They want to seal that border, and things are coming to a boil. You should know."

"All right then. Yes," said Tirzah, feeling as though she had been paid for her services.

"I wish I could spend a whole night with you," he said, ignoring the tension in her voice and succumbing to his own longings. "Just once, you know?"

Tirzah pictured them in a room overlooking the sea. She would make them coffee in the morning.

As he moved toward the door, she got out of bed and hugged him from behind. "Johnny," she whispered.

At first, she had called him Johnny as a strategy, to make him seem less powerful and to keep herself from feeling like a whore. Then it became a way to make her feelings for him seem casual. Now, no matter how much she tried to make it sound cool or ironic, it was an endearment.

"*Laila tov,* Johnny," she said. "Sleep well."

Esther

Zorah had made it so clear that she preferred her own company, a whole day could go by without anyone saying a word to her. For the most part, this suited her fine, but it meant she was among the last to learn about the books. A large donation had been delivered in the morning, but by the time she found out about the boxes, there wasn't much left.

All of the novels and histories were gone, as was everything printed in Yiddish, German, Polish, and French. She made do with a Hebrew grammar with the covers torn off and a pristine collection of biblical fables written in English, and spent the next three days in the barrack, stripped to her underwear in the heat, absorbed by the challenges on the page.

Language was Zorah's favorite game and her greatest talent. She gave herself over to the puzzle of ancient cases and unused tenses inside the crumbling Hebrew volume that had once belonged to Saul Glieberman. He had left his spidery signature on the inside cover and placed check marks beside what Zorah agreed were the most difficult declensions.

The book of fables was a greater challenge since her English vocabulary was limited to words gleaned from movie posters in Warsaw and picked up from the British soldiers in Atlit. She would read a sentence over and over until a cognate would emerge—"night" revealed itself thanks to *nacht* in German and Yiddish; the similarities to *noc* in Polish and *nuit* in French were like an added bonus.

A single word could make a whole phrase come clear, which then created context for the next. After wrestling an entire paragraph into focus, Zorah would look up from a page red-eyed and physically hungry to tell someone—anyone—what she'd understood. After a frustrating afternoon stuck on the meaning of "blanch," she sought out Arik, who had served with the British army's Palestine brigade in Italy. But "blanch" was not a word he knew, so Zorah dragged him over to ask one of the English guards, who laughed when he read the sentence about an enormous mythical bird that could cause eagles and vultures to turn white.

The books devoured Zorah's days and left her so tired that she fell asleep without much trouble and woke up early, eager to get back to work in the solitude of the barrack. But after breakfast on the sixth day of her studies, she returned to find two new arrivals asleep on the cots beside hers—a mother and her young son.

For that day and the next, they did nothing but sleep. From breakfast to lunch, from lunch to dinner, they were so quiet and motionless that Zorah could forget they were there.

By the third day, the two of them had recovered enough to

sit up between meals. They kept very still, huddled together, but Zorah heard them whispering in a Polish dialect she recognized from her Warsaw neighbors who had been brought up in the country—people her father had called peasants, spitting out the word like a curse.

The mother's name was Esther Zalinksy. The little boy, Jacob, clung to her like an infant, even though he was as big as a five- or six-year-old. He might have been older; it was hard to tell with children stunted by hunger and fear.

Zorah watched them during meals. Jacob never looked in the direction of the other children. Esther ran her hand through his brittle black hair. "You are my good boy," she murmured, "my own good boy."

He gazed up at her with such naked adoration, Zorah began to suspect that he was slow, the way her brother had been slow. But then she overheard him translate the Hebrew for "bread" and "light" and "nurse," but only into Polish, never Yiddish.

There were other refugees in Atlit who did not speak the Jewish mother tongue, but they were from places like Holland and Italy, where Jewish communities were small and more assimilated; or else they were French or Hungarian and from wealthy families who had worked hard to distance themselves from their uncultured, Eastern European past. But in Poland, Yiddish was the first language of every Jew, no matter how educated or rich.

When Esther and Jacob finally ventured out of the barrack, Zorah muttered, "Good riddance," and opened her book. But she was too restless to concentrate, and started wondering where they had gone.

She walked to the latrine and then circled Delousing, until she spotted Esther and Jacob sitting on a bench in the sun. Zorah took a place at the other end and turned her back toward them, pretending to be lost in her book as she eavesdropped.

Esther worried and fussed over Jacob: Did the cheese agree with his stomach? Had he moved his bowels that day? Was he too hot? Could she get him water? Where were his shoes?

Esther returned again and again to the subject of Jacob's bare feet. Even though many of the other children in Atlit went shoeless, she fretted that he would hurt himself, or that the other women would think her remiss for letting him run wild.

"I cannot wear them," he said, as she tied his shoes again. "They are too small. Please, Mama. They hurt me."

"I must find a way to get you some proper shoes," said Esther. "If only I wasn't so stupid with languages. You must ask for us."

Zorah thought them an odd pair. Though Esther's looks were faded, she had once been a pretty girl, blue-eyed and fair, with a button of a nose and round cheeks. The boy was dark-haired and sallow, with a narrow face and a long nose. His fingers were thin and long while hers were like sausages.

He must favor his father in everything, thought Zorah. And then it occurred to her that Esther might not be a Jew at all. She could have been the maid in a prosperous Jewish home; liaisons like that were common enough. Sometimes they ended with a dismissal and an envelope of cash. Sometimes, when there was real feeling, there was a rushed trip to the *mikveh,* a secret wedding, and a blue-eyed baby.

Once this suspicion took root, Zorah kept a greater distance between herself and Esther. She stayed inside with her books again, and when either Jacob or Esther took a chair beside her in the dining hall, she moved to the other end of the table.

After witnessing this at lunch one day, Tedi followed her outside and asked, "Why are you avoiding Esther?"

"I have no idea what you mean."

"She keeps looking at you. She must want something, perhaps only to talk. But you run away from her and the boy like they have measles or something."

"I didn't know that you could read minds," Zorah said. "But I have no reason to avoid her or to talk to her. I could care less."

"Is it because she is not Jewish?" Tedi said.

"Did she tell you that?"

"All you have to do is look at her."

"That is funny coming from you, who look like a—"

"I look like my grandmother," said Tedi. "She was a good Dutch Lutheran. Even so, I am a Jew."

"And she is not?" Zorah asked.

Tedi shook her head. "I don't think so."

"So why is she here?"

"For the boy, I imagine. But there is no reason to be unkind to her. Just because she is not Jewish doesn't mean she is stupid. And the child sees everything. They need a friend in this place and you speak the language."

"There are plenty of other people here who speak Polish," said Zorah, putting an end to the conversation. "Go ask one of them."

That night, Zorah lay awake for hours listening to the high, thin whistle of Jacob's breath. He was lying on Esther's bed, where he often slept, curled around her legs like a puppy.

She did not understand why these two bothered her so much. Why should she be offended by the irony of a Polish gentile trying to pass as a Jew? Maybe Esther had promised the father that she would take the boy to Palestine, which Zorah supposed would make her a Zionist hero.

Or maybe she disliked Esther just because she was a Pole.

The Poles had been just as monstrous as the Germans. The Nazis did not require her neighbors to spit on her family the day they were taken away. They had spit again when she returned, after the war, to see if anyone else had survived.

Her father had been right on this point: the Polish people were blockheaded boors who hated Jews from the soles of their feet. I do not have to be nice to Poles, Zorah decided. Not even a Pole with a half-Jewish child in Palestine.

A low groan rose from the bed beside her. Esther was sitting straight up on her bed, panting and clutching at her stomach. Grabbing her dress, she rushed to the door.

Zorah realized she would not get much sleep that night, which meant she would be too tired to finish the story she was working through: an ancient fable woven around the first chapters of Genesis, recounting an argument between the sun and the moon about which was to be more powerful.

She glanced over at Jacob and saw that he was lying facedown on Esther's pillow, clutching the sides of the bed as though it were a life raft. Zorah watched his shoulders heave as he sobbed without making a sound.

He is afraid his mother has left him, she thought, and counted to sixty, waiting for someone to do something for the boy. He might even think she has been killed.

Zorah counted to sixty twice more before she got up and sat beside him.

"Your mother will return soon," she whispered.

His body went rigid.

"She went to the toilet. She will come back."

He turned his head. Tears glittered in his lashes.

Zorah ran her hand back and forth across his back, slowly

and evenly, not stopping until he turned his face to the other cheek and she felt her hand rise and fall over a sigh that released him into sleep.

She let her hand rest where it lay, his heart keeping time beneath her fingers.

Anger burned at the back of Zorah's throat. She wanted nothing to do with this. Nothing at all.

She had kept herself alive through wretched days and worse nights by holding fast to a single thought: *If I forget thee, my slaughtered companions and my murdered kin, may my hands wither and my tongue lose the power of speech.*

She had seen evidence, cruel and sad, that the world was an instrument of destruction. Bearing witness to that simple truth had kept her from madness. Nothing else was required.

But Jacob's beating heart had something else to say. Through the tips of her fingers it insisted, *Come, let us go up to the mountain and sing the song of the child who sleeps and trusts.*

The pulse under her hand was the irrefutable proof that destruction had an opposite number whose name was . . . Zorah could not think what to call it, but her mouth flooded with the memory of a white peach she had eaten as a little girl, sliced by her mother, shared with her brother. The sky was clear and blue after a summer rain. They were sitting at the window looking out at the sturdy brick building across the street where her friend Anya lived. The building had been bombed to dust with many of the souls inside, but the memory of the peach and the light on the bricks and Anya's gap-toothed grin remained with her, still beautiful.

Zorah looked at the number on her forearm, which rose and fell, slowly and gently, with Jacob's sleeping breath, and the word came to her.

The opposite of destruction is creation.

A gray, foggy light had begun to filter into the barrack by the time Esther returned. When she saw Zorah sitting on her bed, staring at Jacob as though he might disappear at any moment, she gasped.

"He is fine," Zorah whispered in Polish. "He woke up and I told him that you would be back."

"Thank you," said Esther. "You are very kind."

Zorah shook her head. "I am not kind."

Later in the morning, Esther took Jacob to the children's Hebrew class, which was taught by an earnest young woman with a toothy smile and a withered arm. The students, fascinated by the strange combination of cheerfulness and deformity, were quiet and obedient in her presence and soaked up her lessons effortlessly. But instead of staying to watch as she usually did, Esther left him there.

She found Zorah sitting on her cot with a book and said, "I wished to tell you that I am sorry for last night. The food here does not sit well with me."

"None of us is used to this food," said Zorah, without looking up. "Especially in the beginning."

"It is not only the food that bothers me, miss. I am worried about a subject, that is to say . . ." Esther stammered. "There is something I need to know, which keeps me from being able to . . . I'm sorry to bother you, but if I could have just a moment of your time. There is a question. I mean to say, I have a question of great concern."

"I can't tell you anything about getting out of this place," Zorah said. "I've been stuck here longer than anyone."

"It is not that," said Esther. "I heard them say that you are learned in the religion."

"You wish to speak to a rabbi," said Zorah.

"No," Esther said quickly. "I would not dare. Besides, there is the language . . . so please, miss . . ."

"Why do you address me formally?"

"What am I to call you?"

"No need to call me anything. Just tell me what you want," Zorah said, exasperated but curious.

Esther smiled. "You see? You are kind. But I'm afraid that in order to ask you this question, I must impose a little on your patience so that you understand. You will permit me?"

Zorah shrugged.

Esther squared her shoulders and took a deep breath, as though she were about to recite a lesson.

"My real name is Kristina Piertowski, or it was until we got on the boat and I took the name of Jacob's mother.

"God has blessed me with this little boy, but I did not give birth to him. His mother was the kindest, most cultured woman I ever met. She spoke Polish, German, and French, as well as the Yiddish. As a girl, she had dreamed of becoming a physician, but it was very difficult for women, and then, of course, she was a Jew. She married Mendel Zalinsky, a good man who adored her. A furrier. She was already thirty-five when they married. Jacob was born the next year.

"I was his baby nurse. I held him from his first day in the world and I loved him. The other nurses in the park used to say that you could lose your job if the children grew too attached to you, but Madame Zalinsky was not like that. She said, 'The more he is loved, the better he will be able to love.' You see what I mean? A generous woman. A wise woman.

"We were in Krakow and Mr. Zalinsky saw what was happening. He sent us to a cottage on the outskirts of a little town in the country, not too far that he couldn't visit sometimes, but far enough that he thought we would be safer." Esther stopped for a moment. "I heard that he was shot trying to bring food to an old woman who lived down the street from us. At least Madame never knew, God be praised.

"We were all right in that village for a little while, but there was a next door neighbor who wanted the house for himself. So that son of a bitch, pardon me, said something to the police, may he burn in hell.

"Madame told me that if anything were to happen, I was to take Jacob and go. She gave me a fur coat with golden coins sewn into the lining. She told me to use the money for us both, and not to neglect myself. Can you imagine? That she should think of me at such a time?

"The day it happened, she kissed us both and sat down in a chair facing the door. I can see her still, sitting so straight, with a little valise on the floor beside her.

"I took Jacob to my grandparents' farm close to the North Sea. We were many kilometers from the nearest town and far from the main roads; it was a good place to hide. My grandparents thought Jacob was my son. Grandfather called him 'the little Jewish bastard' when he thought I couldn't hear. But we were all right until the Germans marched through and took everything—the livestock, the half-grown potatoes, the grain we had stored for the animals. After that, it was bad. I traded furniture for fish. We burned the floorboards for heat. There were weeks we ate soup made with nothing but wild mushrooms and onions. This is bad for a growing child, you know? I fear that Jacob will never be even as tall as his father, who was not a big man. But he is smart, my Jacob. You see it, don't you? He is his mother's son."

"Does he know about her?" Zorah asked.

Esther seemed startled by the question. "Yes. No. I mean, in the beginning I would tell him bedtime stories about his mama and his papa, what they looked like, how much they loved their little boy. We would say prayers for them, and I would make him promise always to remember their good names.

"But then I worried what would happen if a soldier stopped us and asked about his father. So I stopped talking about them, and when he called me Mama, I said, 'Here I am.' And it is true that I love him as much as his own mother. And it is true that I had her permission to love and be loved by her son, but . . ."

Esther stopped and pressed her hands together. "Someday I will tell him. I only pray that he will forgive me and still call me Mama."

"But what made you come to Palestine?" Zorah asked. "Did the parents speak of it? Did the mother tell you to bring him here if she did not return?"

"They were not Zionists like some of them here," said Esther. "They were not religious, either, though they never ate pork. Madame said it was just their custom. They were good people, kind people, hardworking."

"But why didn't you just stay in your grandparents' house and raise Jacob there? This was not your journey to make. The boy might have died on the way. Didn't you know how dangerous it would be?"

"Do you know how dangerous it is for a Jew in Poland today?" Esther said, bitterly. "Jacob is circumcised. Someday, he would be found out, and what would become of him? He would discover the truth of his birth, and what could he do? He would hate me, and why not? Poland is filled with such hatred, you cannot imagine.

"Not far from where my grandparents lived, there was a Jewish family, a dairyman and his sons. One of the boys returned to the father's house; the only one who survived, I think. The neighbors saw him and clubbed him to death on the road. In broad daylight they did this. They dragged his body to a ditch and pissed on it, and then boasted about what they had done. The men went around telling the story like it was something to be proud of. In Poland they say, 'Too bad they didn't kill all of the Yids.'

"Everything there is evil, poisoned. How could I let Jacob stay there? I could not stay there, myself. So I took the coat with the coins in the lining, which I never touched, not even when we were eating grass soup, and the coat took us to Italy, where we fell in with some people looking for a way to get to Palestine. I gave them some money and they got us onto a boat and now, miss, I come to my question."

Esther looked directly at Zorah for the first time and said, "Before we got on the boat to come here, I walked into the sea and made myself a Jew. Like a baptism. That is how it is done, yes?"

"Yes," said Zorah. "That is how it is done."

"So now I am Jewish? Like Jacob?"

"Yes," Zorah nodded, knowing full well that her ruling would not sit well with the rabbis; perhaps not even with most Jews. So she said, "There is no need to ask anyone else about this matter, ever again. If someone asks you about your family background, you look him in the eye and say, 'I am a Jew.'"

"I am a Jew," Esther repeated.

"Jacob is lucky to have you as his mother." The word slipped out of Zorah's mouth, but she did not wish it back. Sometimes "luck" was just another word for "creation," which was as relentless as destruction.

Esther would love Jacob no matter what happened. Jacob would sing "*Ha Tikvah*" whether Zorah joined him or not.

"I understand why you have been so quiet," Zorah said. "But now you must learn the language."

"I'm afraid it is far too difficult for someone like me."

"Someone like you?" Zorah said. Changing from Polish to Hebrew she asked, "Are you not the mother of Jacob Zalinsky?"

"Yes," Esther replied slowly, in Hebrew. "Yes, I am the mother of Jacob Zalinsky."

III

October

October 6, Saturday

Shayndel was washing the tables in the mess hall after breakfast when Tirzah called her into the kitchen. She pointed at a brick of what looked like beige cheese on the counter. "You said you'd never tasted halvah. This comes from a place where they make the real thing, the best. Try it."

Shayndel was startled by the gesture. It might have been a reward for her recent assignment, updating the schedule for every guard in Atlit, but it also felt like a friendship offering from this unfailingly distant woman.

"Thank you," she said, and took a big bite. The texture, somehow oily and grainy at the same time, made her feel like she had a lump of sand in her mouth. She couldn't decide if it was sweet or salty, and tried not to grimace. "It's made from sesame seeds, right?" Shayndel asked as she poured herself a glass of water.

"It looks wonderful." The voice came from the doorway, where Colonel Bryce stood as if waiting for an invitation to enter.

Shayndel had never been so close to the camp commander. At this range she could see how slender he was and the gray hair at his temples. His uniform was faded, though pressed and well fitted. He removed his hat and tucked it under his arm.

"You may have some, if you wish," Tirzah said. "She doesn't seem to like it."

He pinched off a corner between his thumb and fingers. "Lovely. Very fresh," he said, in Hebrew.

"Languages are a hobby of mine," he explained in response to the shock on Shayndel's face. "Is that the correct word, Mrs. Friedman?" he asked Tirzah. "Hobby?"

"Yes, sir."

Bryce took a few more crumbs of the halvah and smiled at Shayndel. "I remember the first time I tried this stuff; I thought it tasted like dirt."

"Never mind," Tirzah said coldly.

"Thank you anyway, I mean, thank you so much," said Shayndel. She realized that she had never addressed Tirzah by name. "It was nice of you to think of me."

Tirzah shrugged and crossed her arms while Bryce put his hat on the counter and began tapping his finger as though he were working a telegraph. After a moment, Shayndel realized that they were waiting for her to leave. She pulled the apron over her head. "If you don't mind, I think I will go see what the new physical education instructor is up to. Good morning, Colonel."

"Good morning," he said.

Tirzah was rattled by Bryce's visit to the kitchen—something he had never done before. The whole camp was doubtless buzzing about it already. "To what do I owe this honor?"

"I have gotten word from Kibbutz Kfar Giladi," he said. "On the Lebanese border. I believe you have cousins there."

They both knew she had no family that far north. "Yes?" Tirzah said.

"There was a rather large incursion of Jewish immigrants late last night; maybe sixty or seventy Jews from Iraq and Syria. The British were there in some numbers, as I understand it. The Palmach was also in force and things got messy. Shots were fired."

"Casualties?" she asked.

"Two dead and two in hospital."

"I'm sorry to hear that."

"It was very unfortunate," he said. "Our patrols managed to capture most of the group that got through, and I just received word that those detainees will be brought here, to Atlit. At least fifty of them. They will be arriving within the next twenty-four hours. I have orders to hold them in a separate barrack, under special guard. I thought you might wish to inform your superiors at the Jewish Agency about this, if only to increase the delivery of bread and such."

Tirzah nodded, knowing as he knew that she would have found out about the incoming refugees within the hour anyway; there would be a phone call for her or a message delivered by a milkman or a volunteer "teacher" with a pass freshly stamped by the Jewish Agency. "It is quite possible that my people are already well aware of this," she said, acknowledging their customary minuet of indirection and euphemism.

"In any case," he said, "I wanted you to have every chance to prepare the kitchen. And one more thing: I seem to recall that your son is due to come for a visit."

"Tomorrow."

"It might be better to postpone the trip this time."

A shiver ran up Tirzah's back.

"There is talk of repatriating this particular group of refugees—and as quickly as possible."

"You can't be serious," she sputtered. "It hasn't been safe for Jews in Iraq since 1940. The Baghdad pogrom—two hundred innocent men murdered. The whole Jewish community blackmailed, terrorized. If you send back fifty avowed Zionists, they will be murdered, and it will put every Jew in the Arab world at risk, too."

"I doubt it would come to that," Bryce said. "Our chaps are well in command of things there at the moment."

"At the moment," Tirzah mocked.

"I understand your position," said Bryce.

"Do you?"

"Yes, I do, in fact," he said. "I believe that at some point, quite soon, the Yishuv will stage a military attack against the mandatory forces on behalf of the immigrants from Europe, in particular."

"You think there is going to be an attack here?"

"I am not the person in this room with access to that intelligence," Bryce said, breaking the rules of their game for good. "But given the risk, I would keep Danny away from here right now."

Tirzah nodded.

"Very well," Bryce announced crisply, and put on his hat. For a moment Tirzah thought he might actually lift his hand to his forehead and salute, but instead he lowered his voice and gently said, "Shalom, Mrs. Friedman."

Tirzah watched him from the door, his shoulders back and his head high, as though he were marching in formation. The more she thought about it, the more she agreed with his suspicions. The story of the Iraqis' capture was sure to be in tomorrow's newspapers. The Palmach would not permit this deportation and they would have to act fast. Everything was about to change.

Tirzah folded thick brown paper around the halvah. She wondered if Danny would remember Bryce at all: the candy he brought for him, his kind green eyes. She wondered if they would ever touch one another again.

Shayndel left the kitchen confused. She had assumed that the relationship between the officer and the cook was one-sided: the besotted old colonel wrapped around the finger of a younger woman who was making a terrible sacrifice on behalf of her country. But it seemed obvious that the feeling between them was mutual. Did that make Tirzah a collaborator? Had she been passing information to the enemy?

The suspicion ran counter to Shayndel's instincts. It was possible that Bryce could be a double agent, but not Tirzah. Poor thing, thought Shayndel, not that she would want any part of my sympathy.

As she rounded the corner of Delousing, Shayndel had the strange feeling she had walked out of a prison camp and into a theater. Virtually every inmate in Atlit seemed to be gathered, either watching or taking part in a parody of a calisthenics class.

The strongest men and boys—forty in all—were lined up in the clearing near the fence, while a dark, stocky man she'd never seen before was delivering a nonstop monologue while running in place.

He was wearing the sort of gray undershirt associated with American GI's, and shouted, "Knees up, children," as he lifted his combat boots high with every step. "It's only been five minutes and we're going to run for another ten. After that, we start the jumping jacks and it really gets hard.

"Don't look at the man next to you," he wheedled, switching from Hebrew to Yiddish and back. "Look at me. Watch me. I'm running and yelling at you at the same time and I could do this all day. By the time I'm done with you, you'll be able to walk from Haifa to Tel Aviv without stopping. Hup, hup, hup.

"You are hot? Then take off the shirts, fellows. You, too, ladies." He grinned at the dozen girls who were taking part, lined up in a back row. Leonie and Tedi were among them and called for Shayndel to join them, but she waved and headed for the shade of the corrugated awning.

"Knees up, feet up, my little Jews. No more Diaspora arms and legs," he shouted, flexing his biceps like a circus strongman, then grinning and mocking his pose. "Eretz Yisrael needs you to have muscles like Nathan." The young boys mimicked him, clenching fists at the end of arms that looked like chicken legs.

"Bravo," Nathan approved.

Even as he joked, Shayndel could see he was taking the measure of his class, frowning at the men who quit, smiling at those who kept up. He looked at Shayndel and quickly saluted.

Tedi joined her, panting. "I thought I was fit."

"He's just showing off," Shayndel said. "He was certainly giving you the eye."

"He's flirting with everyone," Tedi said.

But Nathan was, in fact, running his eyes up and down Tedi's impressive legs. She stuck out her tongue, which only made him lick his lips with such slow, erotic effect that everyone turned to see whom he was teasing.

"Back to work, children," he ordered, and led them through another twenty minutes of jokes and exercise. When he dismissed his sweating students Nathan made a beeline not for Tedi but for Shayndel.

Short and powerful, he was clearly a fighter, with a broken nose, tobacco-stained teeth, and big, meaty hands. "You're the one who works with Tirzah in the kitchen?"

"Yes. I'm going back there now."

"I'll come with you then. I see that you're friends with the tall blonde and I hear you're also close to that pretty little French girl. Oh-la-la. Can you put in a good word for me there? Which isn't to say that I don't find you totally adorable, as indeed I do. You're not married, are you?"

Nathan was older and much rougher than most of the volunteers who appeared and disappeared in Atlit. As they walked, she saw him sizing up buildings and distances like a commando, even as he talked nonstop nonsense until they reached the kitchen. Once inside, he dropped his cheery manner like a jacket and turned his back on her. "It is good to meet you," he said to Tirzah, and led her to the far corner of the room.

Shayndel tried to eavesdrop on their conversation as she ran back and forth between the dining hall and the kitchen preparing for lunch. She was sure they were plotting something. At one point, she heard them mention her name.

"What about me?" Shayndel demanded. "What is going on?"

"You'll know when you need to know," Tirzah snapped.

"Ach," said Shayndel, and banged the door hard as she went to join her friends.

"What's going on?" Leonie asked.

"Don't ask me." Shayndel sulked as she tore a piece of bread into little pieces.

Just then Francek, a dour Hungarian, sat down across from them. He put his hands down flat on the table and announced, "They're moving everyone out of G barrack. They put some of the men in D, the rest in F."

He looked at Shayndel and demanded, "What does this mean?

"They must be bringing in a new group," she said.

"Hello, children," Nathan interrupted noisily, as he forced his way between Leonie and Shayndel.

"You, pretty girl of all," he said to Leonie in mangled French, as he reached his arm around her.

"You are a stupid monkey," Leonie replied. "You have fur all the way down to your knuckles, and I think that monkeys smell worse than even pigs." She picked up her plate and walked away.

"What did she say?" he asked Shayndel eagerly. "Does she like me?"

Francek interjected, "What can you tell us about the new group of prisoners?"

"Don't get too excited," said Nathan. "Better to think about pretty girls and let the Yishuv take care of things. Your job is to get ready for life in Palestine, to grow strong and to learn Hebrew. And lucky for you, I am not only the best physical education teacher in all of Palestine, but also the best Hebrew teacher. I'll bet you haven't learned the most important words in your official classes, have you? Do you know how to say 'cock'? 'Titties'? One lesson with me, and you won't need any review."

A crowd of men and boys gathered around Nathan as Shayndel picked up the dishes and headed back to the kitchen, where she found Leonie at the sink.

"They are all monkeys," she said, as Shayndel reached for her apron.

"If only he knew what you said to him."

"He would have found it charming," Leonie scoffed. "Believe me, that sort of man hears nothing but the sound of his own voice. I think the men here are all as arrogant as baboons, and proud of it."

Shayndel nodded. "I think it has something to do with proving that they are different from—"

"From Jews?" said Leonie, ferociously scrubbing ancient dirt from the bottom of a pot. The French considered Jewish men effeminate and impotent, but also sexually insatiable. The Germans thought they were financial wizards with hidden stores of gold, yet too stingy to buy themselves decent clothes. Effete and barbaric; brilliant and small-minded. And dirty. Always dirty.

Francek burst into the kitchen. "They're putting up bars over the barrack windows."

Shayndel and Leonie followed him outside, where Nathan took each girl by the arm. "Let's take a little walk together and see what's happening, shall we? But you, my good man," he said to Francek, "relax a little. Sometimes, what looks like a problem is actually a gift."

"I don't like riddles," said Francek.

"You must be Hungarian," said Nathan. "My grandfather is Hungarian. He doesn't know how to take it easy, either."

By the time they got to G barrack, near the northern perimeter of the camp, workers were hammering the last nails into a double layer of chicken wire over the windows. A padlock had been screwed into the door. The British soldiers stood a little apart from the scene as inmates shouted curses at them, including a dozen especially filthy Hebrew epithets newly acquired from Nathan.

"This isn't going to end well," Shayndel warned.

Nathan shrugged. "Let them blow off a little steam."

The younger boys started screaming, "Nazi, Nazi, Nazi," aiming pebbles at the Englishmen. When one of them was hit in the eye, they all wheeled around quickly and pointed their rifles at the crowd.

Nathan stopped smiling and rushed forward, standing between the guns and the prisoners.

"That's enough," he shouted to the inmates. "Listen to me now. It's time for my afternoon class. I'm going to hold some races and the winners get a new package of American chewing gum."

The men and boys were not so easily bought off, and it took Nathan a lot of shouting and swearing to get them to back down. Eventually, they did follow, but his class turned into an angry debate about politics and ended in a fistfight.

In the kitchen that evening, Tirzah kept her back to Shayndel. The silence between them seemed to grow thicker and more tangled with every minute, and by the time Shayndel hung up her apron for the night, she was worn out by anger and resentment. Had she done something wrong? Did Tirzah distrust her after that odd scene with Bryce? Did Nathan say something about her?

Just as she was about to walk out the door, Tirzah stopped her. "A moment, please."

Shayndel could not recall ever hearing her use the word "please." Tirzah gestured for her to sit down beside her on the step. She lit a cigarette and offered it to Shayndel, who shook her head.

"Suit yourself," she said and smoked in silence. Shayndel waited, annoyed but aching with curiosity. She looked out through the fence at a harvested field, dull gold in the slanting light of sunset. The sky was purple streaked with low orange clouds, like a tinted photograph with a caption like, "The beauty of autumn in Palestine."

At last, Tirzah got to her feet, stepped on the cigarette butt, and said, "Follow me."

She walked briskly, leading Shayndel toward a storage building that had been turned into bedrooms for some of the staff. Unlocking the door, she pulled the chain on an overhead bulb, revealing what amounted to a large closet furnished with a cot, a stool, and a small table. The walls and floor in the narrow room had been painted battleship gray.

"Lovely, isn't it?" Tirzah said.

"That's a pretty coverlet," Shayndel said, pointing at the red comforter, the only bright spot in the room. The walls were bare, except for a framed studio portrait of a towheaded toddler wearing short pants and holding a stuffed lamb.

"He was a lovely baby," Shayndel said, waiting to be told what she was doing there.

Tirzah closed the door and perched on the stool. "When you go back to your bunk tonight, you'll find that we moved in that new German girl from A barrack."

"Not the one who doesn't bathe," Shayndel groaned. "Not Lotte?"

Tirzah shrugged.

"But she's crazy as a cuckoo. Anyone can see that. Why you haven't already shipped her off to a mental hospital I don't know."

"We have reason to suspect her."

"I know she's German. We all know that. That other German girl you had me spy on turned out to be a regular Jew like everyone else."

"We've had collaborators and kapos from concentration camps here," Tirzah said. "Men who beat their fellow Jews to death to save their own skins, informers, sadists, spies, common criminals. Even some gentiles who thought they could get away with murder by coming here."

"Don't tell me what people are capable of," Shayndel said. "Everyone in this place has seen worse than you can ever imagine."

Tirzah opened her mouth to answer, but thought better of it and bit her lip.

As much as Shayndel hated when survivors used their suffering to make a point or get their way, she was glad to see Tirzah flustered for once.

"We have disturbing information about this woman," she continued, with a measure of deference. "She was identified as Elizabeth Boese, one of the female overseers at Ravensbrück."

"If you already know who she is, what do you need from me?"

"Our informant saw her only from a distance on the docks in Haifa. We wish to confirm it."

"But why on earth would she come to Palestine?"

"People take the chances they find," Tirzah said. "And people do stupid things. Besides, this one is insane, you said it yourself."

"All right," Shayndel said. "All right."

"Also that Polish woman," said Tirzah. "The one who calls herself Esther."

"The one with the little boy? What about her?"

"Don't play dumb. All you have to do is look at her. Not Jewish."

"And the boy?"

"I am only asking you to find out what the story is there. And quickly. I need answers about these people immediately."

"Why the hurry?" Shayndel demanded. "And why won't you tell me what's going on? The empty barrack with the padlock on the door? That Nathan character, whispering in your ear? And this morning, in the kitchen with . . ." She stopped before mentioning Bryce's name.

"It's not up to me." Tirzah looked Shayndel in the eye for the first time all day and said calmly, "As soon as I can tell you, I will."

"All right," Shayndel said. "I will find out what I can about those two women." As she opened the door, she added, "And again, thank you."

"For what?"

"For the delicious halvah."

Tirzah smiled.

As she walked through the fading light, Shayndel thought about what she had been asked to do. She kicked at the dust and wondered if someday, someone would arrive in Palestine and accuse her of sabotage. She had been a terrible shot, and such a slow runner that she had often been a liability to her comrades-in-arms. It would not be incorrect to say that I caused the deaths of my dearest friends, she thought. I would never deny it.

An anxious drone of conversation stilled as Shayndel made

her way through the barrack and past the blanketed shape on the bed beside Tedi. She could feel the eyes on her, and when she got to her cot she looked around and announced, "I don't know anything. I swear."

Even Leonie looked doubtful.

Tedi hurried over, wringing her hands. "Please, Shayndel, I beg you, let me change places with you. I simply can't breathe with that woman next to me. You have to get her moved out of here."

After nearly ten weeks in Atlit, Tedi had become familiar with the smells of death and decay, despair and self-loathing, arrogance and shame. Some of those odors sickened or choked her, but she recognized them and noticed how they faded after a few days of healthy food and uninterrupted sleep. But the stench rising from Lotte was entirely unlike anything else, and it made her heart pound.

"I will never be able to sleep," she said.

Shayndel smiled. "You could sleep through an earthquake."

"No, really, I cannot breathe. I am afraid of this . . . smell," Tedi said, knowing she was sounding a little crazy. "Please," she begged, "change beds with me."

"I'm sorry. But I need you to stay where you are," Shayndel said. "You know a little German, don't you?"

"Hardly. I had a year in school."

"That's more than me. I want you to find out where she comes from and how she got here."

"I don't know enough of the language for that," Tedi pleaded.

"I'm sorry, but this is important," Shayndel said firmly. "They think she might have been in one of the camps—Ravensbrück. It is also possible that Lotte isn't her real name."

When Tedi started to object, Shayndel touched her hand

and turned the order into a request that no one in Atlit could deny. "But there is also a family here, in Jerusalem, who thinks she may be a . . . cousin."

Leonie, on the cot beside them, had been listening and knew Shayndel was lying. No one was looking for Lotte except possibly Tirzah, which meant that the German girl was suspected of spying or collaborating, even if she was as crazy as everyone seemed to think.

Leonie was not convinced that what other people called insanity was a disease, like tuberculosis. But unlike Aliza, who thought "crazy" was a moral failure if not a dodge, Leonie believed that "madness" was a symptom of an overwhelming, untamed secret.

Everyone in Atlit had secrets. Sometimes, Leonie caught glimpses of darkness in the faces of the otherwise cheerful Zionists, revealed by a strange pause or a stuttered answer. There were hints of untold details in terse stories of escape, heroics, and of course, in the whispered confessions of concentration camp suffering; but then a groaned sigh would ward off questions of how or why. Most people managed to keep their secrets under control, concealed behind a mask of optimism or piety or anger.

But there were an unfortunate few without a strategy or system for managing the past: somnambulists and mutes, overwhelmed by disgrace over the random accidents that chose them for life; hysterics and screamers, unable to forgive or forget a moment of cowardice or betrayal—no matter how small—that had kept them from dying.

Leonie was certain that the people everyone else called insane really needed nothing but time, rest, and patience so that their private poisons could settle and dilute. The result might not be happiness or contentment, she knew. But after a while, rage might mellow to surliness, and catatonia settle into mere stiffness, no more threatening than a limp. Eventually, eccentricity would be forgiven as a sad souvenir from a terrible time, perfectly understandable, even normal, given the circumstances.

Leonie had discovered the trick to managing her own secret when she got off the boat in Palestine. In front of her, a young boy with a concentration camp tattoo on his arm walked down the gangplank carrying a bulky suitcase on top of his head. That had reminded her of a photograph she'd seen in a book, of African women bearing enormous bundles of firewood. The caption had explained that what made it possible for them to transport such heavy loads was "exquisite balance."

Leonie decided that is what she would do with the twenty-three months she had spent on her back and on her knees, learning German. She held her secret aloft and apart from herself. She imagined walking across a vast, empty plain among those silent, dignified black women. Exquisite balance.

The next morning, Leonie wolfed down her breakfast and ran back to the barrack to talk to the German girl.

"Fraulein?" Leonie said. "Excuse me? I work in the . . ." She stopped, trying to remember the German word. "Sick house. Yah?"

Two suspicious, close-set brown eyes appeared from beneath the blanket and stared. Her hair was so greasy that Leonie couldn't tell if she was blonde or brunette. The woman lowered the blanket a bit more, revealing a mouselike face with sharp features and thin lips.

"Claudette Colbert?" she whispered.

Leonie smiled. "People used to tell me I looked like her, before I got so thin."

"You are German, Claudette Colbert?"

"No. I am French. I am called Leonie."

Lotte pulled the blanket back over her head.

"I wish to help you," said Leonie. "I know what you are suffering. I know that you have a secret, but here everyone has secrets. No one is without guilt. But if you do not bathe and mingle a little with the others, they will take you away and put you in the insane asylum, where they will force you to reveal what it is you wish to keep to yourself."

Leonie waited for an answer until she heard voices at the door. "I believe that it is better to let our mistakes rest in peace. How can we live if the past is hung around our necks?

"Think about what I said," she whispered. "We will talk again later."

October 7, Sunday

Zorah had spent a sleepless night listening to the women around her toss and moan. Even the ones who usually slept like babies had twisted their sheets into knots. As dawn began to seep into the barrack, Zorah turned onto her back and for a moment felt as though she were drifting on still water, surprised and pleased by the buoyancy of her cot. Then someone brushed past, and she was back on dry land, with Shayndel crouched in the narrow space beside her, whispering into Esther's ear.

Zorah waited until everyone was awake, pulling on clothes and shoes, before she got up and sat beside Esther. "What did she want?"

"She says she has to ask me some questions," said Esther, fighting back frightened tears. "She says I must talk to her honestly and tell her the truth, but I know, I just know that they are going to take Jacob away from me. They will send me back to Poland and put him in an orphanage. Why don't they just kill me here?"

"Leave it to me."

Zorah had not meant to say that. She did not want to be involved in Esther's life. She did not want to be counted on. She wanted to fall asleep in silence and wake up in silence. But Esther had no one else, and there was no taking it back.

"Leave it to me," were Bracha's words. Bracha had slept beside Zorah in Auschwitz, on the wooden bench closest to the floor. They held each other as girls around them disappeared. No matter how hopeless the situation, Bracha would say, "Leave it to me," as though she were telling a three-year-old not to fret about a misplaced doll, as though she had the power to change anything on the night when lice, cold, and hunger had driven Zorah to whisper, "I've had enough."

Only a few years older than Zorah, Bracha had been her protector, her big sister, her mother. She picked her up when she fainted, and taught her the awful skills of survival, like using her own urine to treat the cuts and cracks on her hands. "Do it," Bracha ordered. "If you don't they can get infected. Do it."

For six months, Bracha had helped her fall asleep by running her fingers across Zorah's itching scalp. One night, Zorah had dreamed that she was a dog, napping on her owner's lap in a sunny parlor, and she had burst into tears upon waking.

Bracha got sick with dysentery four months before liberation. First she grew feverish, then she couldn't leave the latrine, then they took her to the infirmary. And then the last person on earth who cared about Zorah Weitz was dead.

Zorah was convinced that Bracha might have lived had she concentrated on her own survival. Her death had sealed Zorah's belief in the futility of kindness; but her sacrifice also made Zorah feel obliged to stay alive—if only out of spite. She turned her grief and anger into the service of getting out of the concentration camp on her own feet.

For the sixteen weeks (112 days, 2,688 hours) between Bracha's death and the liberation of the camp, Zorah did not lift a finger or say a word if it did not serve the needs of her body. She expended as little energy as possible, hoarding her strength and sharpening her senses so that she could be the first to pounce on any stray crumb of food or scrap of paper or cloth to stuff into the lining of her coat. When the Russians arrived, the other girls cringed in shame as the strong young men stared at their starved, sexless nakedness, but Zorah thrust out her hand and pointed to her mouth, and she ate first.

After Bracha died, Zorah believed that her purpose on earth was to spit in God's eye. And that was how she managed, until she met Jacob and Esther.

"Leave it to me," Zorah said.

"You will talk to Shayndel?"

She nodded.

"You are an angel."

Zorah pulled away as Esther tried to kiss her hands. "Don't be foolish."

"You must permit me to make your bed for you."

"If you do that, I will never speak to you again."

Shayndel had walked with her head down and her hands in her pockets as she headed for the kitchen, rehearsing the tirade she wanted to deliver to Tirzah. She felt awful about scaring Esther before the poor woman was even awake. As Shayndel rounded the corner, she nearly collided with a driver unloading boxes from the back of an unfamiliar bakery truck.

"What did the guards say about all of the extra stuff?" said Tirzah, as she held the door open for them both.

"I told them it was a Jewish holiday." The driver grinned. "That always does the trick."

Tirzah turned the lock and started taking sweets out of the boxes. A large, round coffee cake filled the room with the smell of cinnamon. "They didn't have to send so much," she grumbled.

"I'll have some before I go," said the driver.

"Shayndel will get you a cup of tea," Tirzah said. She reached deep into one of the cartons and pulled out a pair of wire cutters. The other boxes held cookies, strudel, and tightly wound coils of rope, flashlights, and daggers.

"Careful with that," said the driver as Tirzah unwrapped a dish towel from a glass bottle full of a clear liquid. "Where do you want me to put all this?"

Tirzah moved the slop pail and pulled up a trapdoor in the floor. As they began loading the contraband into the hiding place, she looked at Shayndel and said, "Take the sweets out to the dining room and make sure no one comes in here for a while. Understand?"

Shayndel felt like singing. There was going to be an escape. Escape! Her mind raced. Who would be in command? Would they ask her to help with the other girls who had no experience in such an action? Or would they leave the women behind? What if the rescue was meant for the men only? Or perhaps only for the men who were going into the barrack they'd just turned into a prison?

She could not tolerate being left behind. She would insist that they take her. She knew about the plan, after all. She would—

"Shayndel," Tirzah barked, "why are you standing there? Bring the food out already."

She carried the coffee cake into the hall, and instantly created a noisy diversion. By the time Shayndel returned to the kitchen, the driver was gone and everything was back in place. Before she could open her mouth, Tirzah warned, "Don't ask. You'll be told what you need to know when it's time."

Shayndel could keep quiet but she could not keep still. Her mind hummed: escape, escape, escape. She worked feverishly, cleaning the kitchen in no time, and decided she would try to sneak into Delousing again, hoping that a cold shower would help her calm down. But when she walked out of the kitchen, she found Zorah waiting for her.

"I have to talk to you," she said. "Now."

"What's the emergency?"

"I want you to leave Esther alone."

"Don't get so excited."

"You're after her," Zorah said. "I saw you this morning. Whatever it is you suspect, leave her alone."

"I was asked to find out something about her background, her origins," said Shayndel.

"Why? Are they going to enforce race laws in Eretz Yisrael?"

"I am only doing what I was asked to do."

Zorah sneered. "And if they told you to take the little boy away from her, would you do that, too?"

Shayndel did not know how to answer that.

"Ha!" Zorah pounced. "I didn't think so. And I am going to be watching out for her, for both of them—Esther and Jacob—to make sure nothing happens to them. And that means I will be keeping an eye on you."

"A real guardian angel. What happened to our angry cynic?"

Zorah opened her mouth but before she could argue, Shayndel said, "Don't worry. I won't tell anyone about your secret heart of gold."

At lunch, Tedi was the last to join the rest of the girls from her barrack. "You look terrible," Leonie said, as Tedi sat down. "Are you ill?"

"I couldn't sleep," she said, glaring at Shayndel.

"Come to the infirmary later and have a nap," Leonie offered. "The beds are much softer and I can set up a curtain."

"Sounds like a delightful invitation," said Nathan, putting his hands on Leonie's shoulders as he walked up behind her. "Don't fight it," he cooed as she slapped him away, then gestured at two new men who had followed him. "Allow me to present my friends, Bob and Uri."

Shayndel shook hands with them first, sizing up what she recognized as the Palmach's reconnaissance team for the escape. The first man was a very tall, muscular blond who made his way around the table, ending with Esther and Jacob, who stared up at him open-mouthed. "I know you are wondering what kind of Jewish name is Bob. My family moved here from Australia." He grinned. "And I like to be different."

"Bob and Uri are here to help me teach physical education," said Nathan.

"Of course," muttered Zorah. "And I am here for the rest cure."

"Rest cure, eh?" said Uri, who was compact and swarthy like Nathan. "You have quite a vocabulary for a new immigrant."

"Zorah is tall smart," Jacob piped up.

"You mean *very* smart," corrected Nathan, patting his head. "And yes, these fellows are here to help me get everyone strong and fit for life in Eretz Yisrael, even you, Mistress Weitz of the sharp tongue."

"How do you know my last name?"

"Darling," Nathan drawled, "I know everything."

"Weitz? Is this the great beauty that Meyer told us about?" Uri asked, and winked at her.

Zorah took a sip from her mug, hiding her reaction to Meyer's name. It had been three weeks since she had last seen him, on Yom Kippur. It had been eight days since his second letter arrived. Both of them had come to her in official-looking envelopes, handed over discreetly by Goldberg, the Jewish guard.

Meyer's first letter had been utterly formal and so bland, it might have been written by a dutiful nephew to a maiden aunt, inquiring about her health and the weather. But in the second, he had described a sunset over the Mediterranean, sprinkled tobacco crumbs into the folds of the paper, and signed it *M.*— which had seemed wildly romantic to her.

"Miss Weitz is blushing," boomed Nathan.

"Leave her alone," shouted Jacob, who jumped up and punched at Nathan's arm.

"Meyer has a competitor." He laughed, picking the boy up and holding him over his head.

"Put him down," said Esther.

Zorah glared at Shayndel, who chimed in, "Enough, Nathan. Put the boy down."

"Aren't you the lucky one," he said, sitting Jacob on the table, "to have so many lovely women in your corner."

Jacob frowned at him, his hands still clenched into fists.

Francek appeared at the front door and shouted, "They're here."

Everyone ran outside and toward the front gate, where two dun-colored buses were parked, their blacked-out windows shut tight, as a dozen British soldiers were climbing down from a flatbed truck behind them.

Nathan cupped his hands around his mouth and yelled, "Let them out of there, you pigs."

As the troops surrounded the buses, Francek cried, "English Nazis."

The other men took up the phrase, chanting, "English Nazis, English Nazis."

Bryce surveyed the scene from the doorway of his office: the shouting inmates, the nervous soldiers, and his own men standing at attention. He walked across the road and stood with his back toward the gate, watching as a British staff car sped toward them.

The two officers seemed surprised by the jeers and catcalls that greeted them as they got out of the car. They returned Bryce's salute without enthusiasm and followed him to his office.

The crowd quieted, waiting to see what would happen next. The Jewish guards—Goldberg and Applebaum—were summoned into Bryce's office, fueling another round of angry speculation about their role in a place like Atlit. But as time passed and the sun grew hotter, the insults and chanting resumed.

A stone sailed over the fence with enough force to hit one of the soldiers, who slapped at the back of his neck and cried, "Shit."

"Shit, shit, shit," echoed a delighted chorus of little boys, who were hushed only when Applebaum and Goldberg reappeared and hurried across the road and through the gate.

"Comrades," Applebaum called as he waved for people to gather. "The colonel has ordered that all male internees must return to their barracks before the men can be unloaded."

"Screw them," Francek exploded. "Why should we agree to that? We've never been locked in during the day."

"My friends," said Goldberg, "think of the poor men inside those buses. They are exhausted and hungry and I don't have to tell you how hot it must be with the windows closed."

Francek put his finger on Goldberg's chest. "Shame on you," he said, poking hard. "You are a collaborator, a lackey, a stooge. The both of you."

"Stop it," said Shayndel, worried that Francek's antics would somehow jeopardize the escape plans. "Our brothers are suffering and we have to do whatever we can for them. Even you, Frankie," she said, pinching his cheek as if he were a child.

"Let's go," she said, and started walking back toward the barracks.

Leonie took her arm. Tedi and Zorah followed, and the rest of the women fell in. Finally the men started to move, too, until only Francek was left, yelling and poking at Goldberg. Nathan and Uri grabbed him under the arms and carried him off, kicking and sputtering.

It took nearly thirty minutes before the last of the Atlit men disappeared. Meanwhile, the women stood in small, quiet groups within sight of the buses, watching until a soldier walked out of Bryce's office and gave the order.

The men staggered out, their faces dripping with sweat, their shirts soaked through. They blinked into the bright light, trying to get their bearings as British soldiers surrounded them and waved their rifles toward the front gate, where Goldberg and Applebaum offered greetings and encouragement in Hebrew and Arabic.

Shayndel counted thirty-nine prisoners. They were all young men, black-haired and olive-skinned. None of them had seen a razor for days and their faces bristled.

The soldiers herded the new inmates back toward the barracks. "Doesn't everyone have to go through Delousing?" asked Leonie. "Why aren't they taking them for a shower?"

"I don't know," Shayndel said, "but I don't like it."

It was a strangely quiet parade. No one shouted family names or hometowns; it was clear that none of these dark-skinned men was from Poland or Lithuania or any place these girls once called home. The men seemed to wilt before their eyes; their shoulders sank, their heads dropped.

"This is terrible," Shayndel said and called, "Be strong."

"I don't think they speak Yiddish," said Zorah.

Shayndel changed to Hebrew, shouting, "Welcome, friends. Shalom! Shalom!"

A dozen heads turned toward her. White teeth flashed against brown skin. Fingers were raised in a V for victory.

Tedi smelled cumin and onions. "*Shalom aleichem,*" she cried.

"*Aleichem Hashalom,*" several voices replied.

The girls clapped and waved, and started to follow along on their side of the fences that separated the women's and men's quarters.

Tedi started the singing.

As long as the Jewish spirit is yearning deep in the heart,
With eyes turned toward the East, looking toward Zion,

The dark-eyed men threw back their shoulders and joined in.

Then our hope—the two-thousand-year-old hope—will not be lost.

Voices rose from inside the men's barracks, where faces were crowded close to the windows.

To be a free people in our land,
The land of Zion and Jerusalem.

As soon as they reached the end of the song, they started over, but louder and much faster. By the third repetition of "*Ha Tikvah,*" the melancholy anthem had become a marching song, a hoarse demand for action. The last man to enter the barrack turned and raised his fist before a guard shoved him inside.

The singing stopped when the door slammed and the men inside the other barracks began calling out, "What is happening?"

"Nothing yet," shouted Tedi. "But we are watching."

After a short time, six soldiers marched in formation to Barrack G and took six of the new inmates to Delousing.

"Why are you so tense?" Leonie asked Shayndel as they waited for the men to emerge.

"I'm not tense."

"*Chérie,* you are chewing your lip, tapping your foot, and drumming your fingers on your own arm."

Shayndel could not think of a lie to cover up her nerves. She felt as though her senses were stretched to their limits, as keen as they had been in combat. But she was also unfocused and anxious to find out more about the escape plan. Luckily, the doors to Delousing opened before Leonie could press her any further.

All attention shifted to the clean-shaven men, their wet hair glittering like onyx in the sun.

"How handsome they are," said Tedi.

"I wouldn't have thought you'd find that sort attractive," Leonie said.

"You think I'd go for that Australian fellow?"

"He's tall and blond like you. And good-looking, you have to admit."

"Not my type," said Tedi.

"Don't you two have anything better to talk about?" Shayndel grumbled.

"Not at the moment," said Leonie.

"What should we be talking about?" Tedi asked, wondering why Shayndel suddenly smelled like burning leaves.

"Well, I'm going to go chop some onions before my mind turns into glue."

The men waved and saluted as they were rushed back to the barrack. "Come tell me if anything interesting happens," Shayndel said.

"What could happen?" Tedi asked.

"Maybe you should ask one of them to marry you," Leonie said, poking Tedi in the ribs.

"I'm done with you two," said Shayndel, and she tried not to run on her way to the kitchen. She was determined to force Tirzah to tell her something before she lost what remained of her self-control, but she found the cook in a rage of her own.

"Those monsters aren't going to let them come to the dining hall," she fumed, filling a basket with hard-boiled eggs, olives, and bread. "They are going too far," she said, thrusting a water pitcher at Shayndel just as Applebaum arrived.

"Can't we manage something besides water for them to drink?" he asked. "Tea at least?"

"This is a question for your commander," said Tirzah, without meeting his eyes. "I would need permission."

He answered with undisguised contempt: "Perhaps the request would be met with success if you asked him yourself."

Tirzah met his gaze. "No need," she said icily. "I'll get it ready."

Applebaum shrugged. "I'll come back for it."

"Son of a bitch," she muttered under her breath.

After helping Tirzah prepare the baskets, Shayndel slipped outside to look for Nathan, who, she was certain, knew how the arrival of the prisoners fit into the plans for the breakout. She found him standing near the eastern fence, deep in conversation with Bob and Uri.

"They asked each of them how they got over the border," said Nathan. "They wanted to know who helped them, if they had contacts in Baghdad."

"It's good that none of them knows anything."

"About what?" Shayndel demanded. "Why are these men being treated so differently? Why are they locked in?"

"You're a smart one. Can't you figure it out?" said Nathan.

"Are they being sent somewhere else?" Shayndel guessed.

"Not if we have anything to do with it," Bob muttered.

"So this escape plan is all about rescuing them?"

"You see," Nathan said. "I told you she was a smart girl."

"What about the rest of us?"

"Listen, comrade," said Nathan, draping his arm around her shoulder, "we are going to start a new calisthenics class this afternoon so it will appear that my friends here have an official purpose in Atlit. Bob will be making a special class for the girls, so see to it that we have a good showing."

"Does that mean we're all going?" Shayndel insisted.

But Nathan only chucked her under the chin and walked away.

Tirzah had put off her visit to Bryce's office as long as she could. She dreaded the place, and not only because of the photograph of his wife and sons. She hated the old British map of Palestine on the wall, the locks on the filing cabinets, and the width of his desk, which seemed to measure the gulf between them. She forced herself to stand tall and pretend not to see the knowing glances—real or imagined—cast at her by the soldiers at the prison gate and then by the sentries at the administration building.

She relaxed a little at the sight of Bryce's unfailingly polite clerk, who seemed young enough to be her own son. Private Gordon got to his feet and said, in halting Hebrew, "Good afternoon, Mrs. Friedman. He is telephone. He will be with you in moments five or six."

Tirzah smiled. "Your Hebrew is improving."

"Thank you. It is difficult with me. I study and talk in Haifa shopping. Here, no one will talk."

Bryce's voice grew loud enough to be heard through the wall. Tirzah and Gordon glanced at each other uneasily. A few minutes later, he opened the door, his neck and ears flushed.

"Mrs. Friedman," he said, surprised to see her. "Is there some problem? Do you have everything you need by way of supplies?"

"I have run out of salt," she said. "I would like to use the telephone to order more."

Private Gordon got to his feet. "If you don't mind, Colonel, I need to round up some more envelopes. Shall I send someone in my absence?"

"No need," said Bryce.

She followed him inside the office and sat down. "It is not only the salt," she said. "My son needs to see the dentist tomorrow. I wish to make a telephone call to make sure the appointment can take place as scheduled."

"Of course," he said, turning the phone around and pushing it toward her. "Tomorrow, you say?"

"Yes. The only time he can be seen is at night," said Tirzah. "He is to arrive rather late, in fact. During the half hour after the second watch."

"I see."

"I believe tomorrow is a night that Goldberg is usually posted at the front gate."

Bryce nodded. "Yes, that is correct."

Tirzah took the receiver and asked the operator to place the call. They waited in silence for several minutes, their eyes fixed on each other's hands.

"No one answers," she said.

"Would you like to wait and try again?"

"It is not necessary. Is it?"

"Would you like me to ask Gordon to bring you a cup of tea?"

"No, thank you," said Tirzah.

Tirzah and Bryce stood up. She smoothed her skirt. He moved the telephone back to its customary place.

They both realized that these might be their last few moments alone. The breakout would change things in Atlit. Bryce was risking his career. Tirzah might be assigned elsewhere. There was no way of knowing.

Bryce broke the silence. "I will miss seeing Danny."

"Colonel," she said, switching to English. "I wish to thank you for your concern for my boy."

"A pleasure, Mrs. Friedman."

"Good-bye," she said, in English.

"Let us say instead, Shalom," said Bryce.

"As you wish," Tirzah said. "Shalom."

When Leonie saw the knot of women gathered outside her barrack door, she ran toward them and pushed her way inside. Aliza was shouting at the top of her lungs, "Enough, enough," while Lotte, crouched on top of her cot, shrieked, "*Hexe, hexe, hexe*."

Her skirt was stained with dirt and menstrual blood, her feet were filthy, her ankles covered with angry red welts.

"Wait," said Leonie, stepping in front of the nurse. "Let me."

Lotte stopped screaming. "Get the witch away from me,

Claudette Colbert," she said. "She is an evil witch and I know what she wants."

She dropped her voice and whispered, "She wants to cut open my legs and put glass needles inside to watch me die. She wants to kill me. Everyone here wants to kill me. The one dressed like a nurse will break my bones. She is not a nurse at all. That's a disguise. She is a witch."

"Calm yourself," Leonie said. "You can trust me, can't you? I won't let anyone hurt you."

"Thank goodness you speak German," said Aliza. "The doctor told me to bring her to the clinic, but I told him I will not permit such dirt in my infirmary." She pointed at Lotte and shouted, "You need to be washed and fumigated."

"She wants to kill me," Lotte shrieked.

"Stop screaming," Aliza hollered.

Leonie took a step closer to Lotte. "She is not a witch, really. She wants only for you to bathe, and I think that is a good idea. You will feel so much better when you are nice and clean. And to be honest, fräulein, you have no choice in this. You must do as we say, or they will take you to the hospital."

"No hospital."

"That's it. I'm going to send a couple of the guards to get her," Aliza said.

"It won't be necessary," Leonie said. "I think she is afraid of your uniform. Perhaps it would be better if you let me take her to Delousing."

"I'm not sure you can manage this."

"You can see that she listens to me," said Leonie.

"I will send someone to help you."

"No need," Leonie said.

"Oh, yes, there is. Nurses in the mental wards are always

getting bitten and punched. Bring her to the infirmary as soon as you're done."

After Aliza left, Leonie said, "You see? I sent the nurse away. But if you don't do as I say, she will return with soldiers, and the doctor."

"No doctors."

"So you will come with me?"

"We are going to Hollywood, Claudette Colbert?" Lotte asked, with a knowing wink that sent a shiver up Leonie's back.

"We are going to get you clean. You'll have a shower, fresh clothes, and you'll feel like a new woman." Leonie held out her hand, walking backward, as Lotte climbed off the bed with the blanket wrapped around her.

Outside, Tedi was waiting with a towel and a change of clothes. "The nurse sent me," she said, and turned her head away from Lotte's smell. "Ugh. Let's get this over with."

Lotte followed them, dragging the blanket in the dust. When they reached the back door of Delousing, Leonie told Tedi, "Wait for us here."

"The nurse said I should stay with you."

"Just stand by the door. I'll call if I need anything."

Tedi needed no further convincing.

Lotte seemed to relax a little as they entered the dim, cavernous room, but the sight of the showers made her sprint toward the door. Tedi caught her and dragged her all the way into the stall, where she crouched on the floor with her hands on top of her head.

"If you do not wash right now," said Leonie, "I will get the doctor."

"No doctors," Lotte hissed. She hurried to her feet and

pushed her chest out defiantly, as though she were facing a firing squad. "I am ready."

Tedi turned the faucet full on, and although the water was cold, Lotte did not flinch.

"Very good," said Leonie gently. "You see the soap over there? Start with your hair and your face."

"Get *her* out of here," said Lotte, pointing at Tedi, who was glad to retreat to her post near the door.

Leonie watched as the water transformed Lotte from a troll into a normal-looking woman. She was a little older than the rest of them—twenty-eight or even thirty. Her hair was light brown and fine. Someone had hacked it off at odd angles, Leonie thought; probably used a knife.

Lotte's eyes were also brown, but with a yellow cast that made her look less like a mouse than a fox.

"Now," said Leonie, "take off your clothes."

Lotte slipped out of the skirt, which seemed to melt as the dirt washed down the drain.

"Good, but you must remove everything," Leonie said, pointing at her blouse.

She grumbled but turned her back and unbuttoned the filthy shirt. She slipped off one sleeve, but then stopped, keeping the other one wrapped around her arm.

"Many women here have the numbers," Leonie reassured her. "There is no shame in it."

Lotte glanced over her shoulder, winked at Leonie again, and then crouched down to urinate. In the moment Leonie turned her head away, Lotte removed the other sleeve and sat on the floor, leaning against the wall with her legs stretched out in front of her.

She sat with her head tipped back under the water, which

had warmed up enough to release some mist into the air. Lotte sighed and, for a moment, let her arms rest beside her, which is how Leonie caught sight of what looked like an oddly shaped bruise on the inside of her left bicep.

She turned off the water quickly, hoping for a clearer view of it before Lotte folded her arms.

"Here," Leonie whispered, holding out a towel and watching as Lotte pulled on a long-sleeved white shirt and a blue skirt that was too big around the waist.

"I'll get you a belt from the barrack," she added, "and a comb."

Tedi and Leonie walked on either side of Lotte, who kept her eyes on the ground and her shoulders pinched back. As soon as they crossed the threshold, she bolted to her bed and burrowed under a new, clean blanket.

Leonie took Tedi's arm and pulled her outside. "You have to tell me everything that you know about this woman."

"What's the matter?" Tedi said. "You're shaking."

"She has a tattoo."

"No, she doesn't," said Tedi. "I saw both her arms when I dragged her to the shower. There was nothing there."

"It's up here," Leonie said, pointing to the underside of her arm, near the armpit. "And it's not a number. She is SS."

"SS?" Tedi gasped. "That can't be possible, is it? Are you certain?"

"Not completely," Leonie said, suddenly not trusting herself. "What do you know about her?" she pressed.

"Shayndel said that she had been in Ravensbrück," said Tedi. "I heard that they did terrible medical experiments on the prisoners there, which explains her terror of Aliza. But she cannot be a Nazi; Shayndel told me that she has family here in Palestine. I'm going to go tell her about this right away."

"Not yet," said Leonie, gripping Tedi's arm. "Let me make sure. Don't tell anyone about this. If it turns out that I am wrong, the accusation would be too awful to forgive. I'll talk to Aliza, so she can stay in the barrack until I can get another look at her arm and make sure, one way or another."

Tedi groaned at the prospect of another night with Lotte beside her, but didn't argue; she could see that Leonie was set on getting her way. "But if you are right about her, why in the world would such a person come here? How could that happen?"

"I don't know," Leonie said slowly. "But there are times I do not know why I am here, either."

Tedi nodded. "I know what you mean. I look at the ones from the concentration camps and the ones who dreamed of coming here their whole lives, and I feel like a fraud." She glanced nervously at Leonie. "If she really turns out to be a Nazi, it might explain the way she . . . smells."

"I don't understand," said Leonie.

"I never told anyone this before because it makes me sound like a raving lunatic. But ever since I got here, I've been able to . . ." Tedi searched for a way to explain. "My nose, I mean my sense of smell—it became so strong, so keen. I can tell a lot about a person from the way she smells. Sometimes I think I can smell moods, states of mind, even something about the past."

"What do I smell like?" Leonie asked.

"Shame," Tedi blurted, but rushed to add, "Almost everyone here smells of shame, which is like fruit going rotten."

Leonie kept her face blank. "And what about Lotte? What do you smell on her?"

"I cannot describe it, but it's not shame. It's not fear, either. Everyone in Atlit smells of fear, except for the little babies. Guilt, too—I smell that on everyone. Guilt is sour," she wrinkled her nose, "like unwashed clothes.

"But on Lotte there is no shame. No fear or guilt, either. Even after the shower, she stinks of something like gasoline but stronger, and mixed with something animal and dark, not musk exactly. Whatever it is, being anywhere near her makes my throat close and my eyes burn."

Tedi stopped herself. "Now you think I'm crazy, don't you?"

"No," said Leonie. "I don't understand but I don't think you are crazy. Not at all."

Leonie paced around the outside of the barrack for the rest of the afternoon, waiting for it to empty so she could talk to Lotte alone.

"Fraülein Lotte?" she said to the shape under the blanket. "Am I pronouncing your name correctly? Or perhaps Lotte isn't your name at all?"

Peeling the cover down over her face, she stared hard at Leonie. "I have been lying here, wondering how Claudette Colbert learned to speak such elegant German. I thought, maybe she was married to one of my countrymen, or she might have worked for the Reich in France—a secretary typing the orders to deport her own family. And then it came to me: Claudette Colbert was perhaps a whore, opening her legs for the German boys who had no idea that she was a filthy Jew."

Leonie's eyes betrayed her and Lotte pounced. "I was right! You were a prostitute! A Yid bitch streetwalker. And you got away with it, too, didn't you? No one shaved your head and marched you out of town, naked, with the rest of the whores? But maybe that's what your friends here would do if I told them your secret."

Leonie made her face as vacant and pleasant as she had during the long, vicious anti-Jewish tirades she had heard in Madame Clos's apartment. Even Lucas would go on and on about the poisonous Jew when he was drunk.

Leonie had worked hard at charming Lieutenant Lucas and a few other young German officers who were clean and good-looking, who treated her a little more like a girl than just a cunt. She flattered them in bed with coos and moans and passionate thank-you's. When they brought her nylons and chocolate, she asked for books of German poetry. She improved her conversation and eventually they refused the other girls, which spared her from nights with men who never washed, and men who found pleasure in causing women pain.

When she was with one of "her" men, she emptied herself like a bowl and watched herself perform, permitting herself to feel nothing but pride in her own efficiency. Leonie listened to Lotte's rant with the same detachment.

"When they do find out about you, they will shame you in public. They will send you away. Maybe they will even stone you to death, which would be very biblical, don't you think? And so appropriate."

Lotte was enjoying herself. "I will tell you what is going to happen next, you little whore. You will tell that witch of a nurse that I am better now, that the water washed away all of my problems. And because you will say nothing about my past, I will say nothing of yours. We are in agreement, yes?"

Leonie lowered her chin.

"Now get out of here."

Leonie walked away, remembering the last time she had faced a question when "yes" would have meant death, and "no" meant life.

In the brothel, she would dose herself nightly with two sleeping pills washed down by a tumbler of cheap brandy. That was how she slept through until morning, and woke up feeling nothing but hunger and thirst. But one morning, a burst of gunfire roused her long before the amnesiac cocktail had worn off.

Leonie had opened a swollen eye and saw blood on the sheets. Her jaw ached, and her sex was bruised. Her legs were black and blue. It had been a horrible night, and worst of all, it had been Lucas.

He had staggered in drunk with two friends who demanded a turn with the girl he claimed was so talented, so willing—truly the best whore in Paris. She had wept and begged, but he'd slapped her and let his comrade turn her on her face and sodomize her. One of them had the SS tattoo on his upper arm and he made her kiss it before forcing her to her knees while Lucas watched, and smirked, and played with himself.

She closed her eyes and tried to sink back into sleep but a second burst of gunfire sent her flying to the window, where a flock of startled pigeons was flying around in tight circles in the deep, narrow courtyard. There, at the center of the flapping gray blur, Leonie saw a woman wearing a long gown. She floated midair, suspended among the birds, waving for her to follow. Leonie had opened the window and climbed onto the ledge when she heard a voice behind her say, "No."

She turned to see who had spoken, but there was no one in the room. And when she looked outside again, the pigeons were merely pigeons and the flying lady had vanished, a phantom of the drugs.

She crawled back to the bed and thought about the voice that had stopped her. It had been a woman's voice saying no to death, as peaceful as it might be. It had been her own voice, saying yes to life, as miserable as it was.

That night, as lights-out approached, Leonie told Shayndel that she wanted to sleep in the infirmary. "There's a girl with a fever in there, a timid thing from Lausanne who barely speaks. I thought I'd stay with her. Do you think I could get permission?"

"Oh, just go," said Shayndel, distracted and worn out after a long day of second-guessing and biting her tongue. "What are they going to do to us at this point? I'll see you in the morning."

"Good night," Leonie said and kissed her cheek, ashamed of how easy it was to lie to her friend. She held her breath, as though she were diving into deep water, as she ran across the shadows toward the infirmary. Knowing the clinic was empty, she took the key from beneath a loose floorboard, let herself in, and locked the door.

Feeling her way slowly through the dark, Leonie found Aliza's desk and opened the drawer where she hid the candy. She sank to the floor and let one of the sugar marbles dissolve in her mouth, savoring the solitude along with the sweet.

She could not remember the last time she had been completely alone. Madame had not permitted her to close the door to her room after they had found her with the razor blade; not that Leonie had been trying to kill herself. She knew exactly how deep to cut and when to stop. She glanced at the cabinet that held the needles and scalpels, but it was locked with a key that Aliza never left behind.

Leonie crawled to the space between two cots and ran her fingers around the hem of her skirt. By the time she opened the catch on the safety pin, she was sweating and breathing heavily. But she grew calmer after pressing the point against her fingertip. It was still sharp enough.

Leonie pulled off her shoes and socks and cradled her left foot in her hands and waited until her breathing slowed down, forcing herself to prolong the anticipation. Then, pressing her cheek against the inside of her knee, she pushed the tip of the pin into the space between her big toe and her second toe. She gasped quietly and welcomed the sensation, relaxing as pain took precedence over fear and memory.

It was only a few moments before the throbbing started to fade. Leonie removed the pin slowly, squeezing at the tiny wound, putting her pinky finger to the warm blood and placing the salty drop to her tongue, exactly as she had in the brothel. That was where she had created this small, silent ritual of punishment and purification.

She took her time, eight times in all, one foot after the other, ending with the worst jab, between the fourth and smallest toe. And then Leonie leaned back and closed her eyes, relishing a moment of respite, the closest she came to peace.

Aliza found her on the floor in the morning, sound asleep, her cheek against the floor, fully dressed, her shoes neatly tied, her hands pressed between her knees.

October 8, Monday

Early morning was Shayndel's favorite time of day. She savored the short walk from the barrack to the kitchen when the air was still and clear, free of the dust kicked up by hundreds of feet. She would look at the mountains, which changed color from one morning to the next, blue or gray or even gold, depending on the clouds and the angle of the sun.

But this morning, she saw nothing but the ground in front of her.

It had been a bad night, disturbed by dreams of running after things—first a train, then a child, then something she could not remember. She woke up worried about who was going to get out of Atlit and who was not, determined to pry the answer to that question out of Tirzah and Nathan. She would not let them dismiss her as they had yesterday. She would be immovable.

Nathan was already in the kitchen, leaning against the counter with a mug in his hands, watching Tirzah slice cucumbers.

"Good morning, comrade," he said. "Where have you been? We've been hard at work for hours."

Tirzah glared at him. There were dark circles under her eyes; clearly she hadn't slept well either.

"The breakout is tonight," she said.

"Tonight?" Shayndel said. "The Iraqis are getting out tonight?"

"Not just them," Nathan said. "Everyone is going. The whole camp."

"But there are," Shayndel calculated quickly, "two hundred, at least."

"Yes," Nathan said. "It will make for a dramatic story, don't you think? Of course, you are to be the captain for your barrack. We'll give you more instructions later today."

Tirzah said, "You should ask what she thinks about Myra in Barrack C and Regina in D."

Shayndel knew that she was grinning like an idiot, but she couldn't help herself.

"What do you think?" Nathan asked. "Can we depend on those two girls? Are they able to keep a secret? Will the others follow orders from them?"

"Both solid," Shayndel agreed. "But this won't be easy with the little ones, you know."

"Look at her, worrying and biting her lip," Nathan said. "I thought you'd be thrilled. I was even counting on a kiss."

"What's the plan?" Shayndel asked, ignoring his puckered lips. "How are you going to take out the guards? What kind of transport is coming? Where will we be going?"

"Relax, sweetheart. It's all taken care of," Nathan said. "Your job will be to help us to wake everyone up and get them dressed and out of the camp quickly and quietly. Come back before lunch and I will tell you everything you need to know."

"That's enough for now," Tirzah said, shoving platters of cheese and tomatoes into Shayndel's hands, sending her out into the mess hall.

Shayndel sat down, oblivious to her friends at the table. Her mind raced and wandered: swimming on the beach in Tel Aviv, picking kibbutz oranges, walking the narrow streets of Jerusalem.

Leonie waved a hand in front of Shayndel's eyes. "What are you thinking about?"

"Nothing."

"Don't tell me that. You look like the cat that caught the mouse. Are you in love?"

"Don't be ridiculous." Shayndel shrugged and scanned the room. Did Myra have enough Hebrew to communicate with the Palmach? Was Regina levelheaded enough to remain calm when things went wrong—as they were bound to?

If only she could talk this over with Malka, her beloved comrade-in-arms, and a great judge of character. Shayndel and Wolfe used to call her "the Psychologist." When Wolfe was planning a particularly nervy mission, he would ask Malka's advice about whom to bring along, whom they could trust. Wolfe admitted that he tended to believe the worst about people, though he probably could have talked the guards in Atlit into opening the gates for them in the name of the glorious Zionist future, or for the sake of Allah, or whatever they needed to hear. His nickname had been "the Politician."

And I was "the Old Lady," thought Shayndel. I brought up the rear and carried everybody's doubts, the one they could count on to argue in favor of getting more information before setting out on a dangerous operation. It was my job to keep them from forgetting that they could get killed, too.

Shayndel and Leonie chewed and swallowed in silence, lost in their own memories and worries. Everyone at the table noticed and Tedi asked, "Are you two having an argument?"

"Not at all. Nothing like that," Shayndel said, a little too brightly. "Time to clean up. I'll see you all later."

"And you?" Tedi said, sliding over and trying to read Leonie's mood. "I noticed you didn't sleep in the barrack last night. Were you in the infirmary?"

Leonie nodded.

"I wish I could have done that, too. I barely slept because, well, because of what I told you about my . . . about the stench on that . . . woman."

The mention of Lotte sent Leonie to her feet. "I should get to the clinic and talk to Aliza about her."

Tedi watched her hurry out and regretted having told Leonie about her heightened sense of smell. Maybe Leonie would tell the nurse that *she* was crazy and ought to be locked up. Or maybe she was overreacting. Everyone seemed a bit tense today, Tedi thought; probably because of those poor guys in the locked barrack. Still, she couldn't stop worrying about what Leonie might be thinking or saying about her, and decided to talk to her, even if that meant going to the infirmary, which she usually avoided. No amount of disinfectant, alcohol, or bleach could erase the acrid residue of terror and dread that accosted her even before she reached the door.

Two guards were posted outside; a young Arab well-known in the camp for his quick temper, and an avuncular Brit with a receding chin. As she reached the step, they lifted their guns to block her way.

Tedi pointed inside. "I have to visit my friend."

"First you have to smile," said the Englishman, shaking a finger and grinning so broadly that she had no choice but to obey.

"All right then," he said and waved her in.

Though it was still early, every surface in the clinic was littered with scraps of gauze, tubes of salves, needles and probes. The new arrivals had kept Aliza busy swabbing, dressing, and dosing their blisters, rashes, sprains, and pains. She had given away all of her candy, too.

When Tedi walked in, Leonie was standing beside the nurse, holding a metal basin as Aliza lanced an ugly-looking boil on the shoulder of one of the new men.

"What can I do for you?" Aliza asked.

"I . . . I came to talk to Leonie," Tedi stammered. "It can wait."

"Hmmm," said Aliza, assuming she'd come for a dose of penicillin. "Come back when it's quiet and we'll fix you right up. But on your way out, make yourself useful and take the sheets over there to the laundry."

Tedi had to pass between two young men who were lying on cots; one of them had a swollen knee, which was propped up on a pillow. The other sat up, leaning against the wall, his face flushed and his eyes glittering.

The man with the elevated leg said something in Arabic to Aliza, who laughed and translated, "He says you are too tall."

The feverish patient pointed at Tedi and said, "'*Ha Tikvah*'? Yes? You are the '*HaTikvah*' girl." He sang a few bars of the anthem and Tedi smiled and nodded.

"Ahh," he said, placed his hand over his heart, and began to sing. The words were incomprehensible but the melody ached with longing.

Tedi had never seen a more beautiful human being. His lashes were so thick, his eyes seemed ringed with kohl. His black curls lay in perfect rows across his damp forehead. He smelled of almonds.

As he finished singing, Aliza clapped her hands and said, "He was singing from Song of Songs. Love at first sight! Leonie, did you see this? Just like in the cinema."

Tedi clutched the laundry to her chest and ran out, flattered and aroused by the baritone quaver, the olive-brown skin, and the face that reached for her like an outstretched hand.

"Foolishness," she muttered, as she bent over to pick up a towel that had escaped from her arms. That was what her mother used to say, rolling her dark blue eyes, whenever anyone spoke about romance.

"Foolishness," her father would echo sadly. Tedi stood up quickly, struck by the thought that perhaps her mother had never loved her father that way at all. The idea that her parents' marriage had been loveless made her feel disloyal and lonely, and she pushed it away.

She also tried to shake off the sensation of that young man's voice vibrating in her own chest, and the mouthwatering smell of warm almonds. That really is foolishness, she scolded herself, starring down into the barrel of laundry.

"Are you all right?"

Tedi turned to see Shayndel's worried face. "What are you looking at in there?"

"Nothing," Tedi said. "I was a little dizzy."

"This is not a good time to be sick. Maybe you should have the nurse take a look at you."

"I'm fine, really," Tedi said.

They heard Nathan's voice in the distance. "Twenty more jumps and I will take off my pants."

"I think I'll go see what they're laughing about over there," said Tedi. "Will you come?"

Shayndel shook her head and went back to the barrack, where she sat on the bed and pared her nails as she told herself off.

In the ten weeks that she had been locked up in Atlit, she had grown comfortable, and even worse, proud of her status among the other prisoners. She had become complacent and docile. She knew that Malka and Wolfe would have made fun of her. They would have expected more of her. Shayndel wondered if those two would be looking over her shoulder for the rest of her life.

"Of course not," said the voice of Malka that resided inside her head. "You will get married and have children and life will crowd out everything else. I will become an old memory, me and Wolfe. And don't pull that face; you know I'm right."

Shayndel paced the barrack, trying to clear her mind and stay calm until it was time to get back to the kitchen. She found Tirzah sitting on the steps at the back door, smoking a cigarette. "Don't ask me," she said, before Shayndel could say a word. "I have nothing new to tell you."

Shayndel sank down on the step and stared out at the mountains. It might be nice to live up there, she thought, but she didn't much care where she was sent: mountains or desert, kibbutz or city, tent or bunker, as long as it was away from Atlit and these long empty days and Tirzah's unrelenting scowl.

Distracted, Shayndel scratched at her forearms until Tirzah slapped her hands. They sat together, disliking one another, until Nathan rounded the corner, dragging his feet and chewing his lower lip.

"What's the matter with you?" said Tirzah. "Did everybody stop laughing at your stupid jokes?"

"You have all the sensitivity of a cactus," he said.

"I had no idea you were such a delicate flower."

Nathan kicked at the dirt. "It's off for tonight."

Shayndel jumped up. Tirzah asked, "What happened?"

"They didn't say. Maybe they need another day to assemble the men."

"No, no, no!" shouted Shayndel.

"Calm down," said Nathan.

"Don't tell me what to do. I have to get out of here." She knew she should lower her voice, but she couldn't stop. "No more waiting. Now. Tonight."

Tirzah grabbed her. "What's gotten into you?"

"What's gotten into me? Sleeping on a plank, surrounded by barbwire, watching other people get out while I'm left behind? Why am I still here anyway? Answer me. Why am I still a prisoner in this shit hole?"

Tirzah lowered her voice. "If you don't stop yelling, I am going to slap you hard enough to loosen some teeth. Do you understand me?"

"Don't be such a bitch," Nathan said, putting his arm around Shayndel's shoulder.

"It's a twenty-four-hour postponement," he explained as they walked into the kitchen. "We go tomorrow night. The moon will still be dark, and if you think about it, the extra day is a blessing. We have more time to get ready."

"But what if they come and take these Iraqi men tomorrow morning?" Shayndel said. "Didn't you say they were being sent somewhere else?"

"You have to show a little trust," said Nathan. "My commanders know what they are doing, and the idea is to get them and everyone else out of here without any casualties. You yourself know this is not going to be easy. These people are not all strong or fit. Also we have the little matter of disarming the guards."

"That's no problem," said Shayndel.

Nathan laughed. "Do you plan to take them on yourself?"

"I know those guns," she said. "They're Italian. The firing pins are so badly made you can practically snap them off with your bare hands."

"Are you sure?" he said.

"She wouldn't say it if she wasn't sure," said Tirzah. "You can get Applebaum and Goldberg to fix them tonight."

Nathan put his hands around Shayndel's face. "When this is all over and done with, I am going to take you out to dinner in a wonderful little restaurant by the sea in Tel Aviv."

"What would your wife say about that?" Tirzah said.

Shayndel laughed.

The dining hall was louder than usual as the men teased each other and boasted about their performance in the morning exercise classes, but there was an undercurrent of anxiety beneath the bravado. Rumors were flying about spies in camp, and about the possibility that the Iraqis would be released before anyone else.

The Poles sitting at the table behind Zorah were complaining bitterly about that theory. "We've been here for weeks and they just arrived. It is intolerable. Where are our advocates? Where are all those heroic Jews who are supposed to rescue the remnants?"

"How can you tell that these guys are Jews at all?" someone asked with a smirk. "Did you see how dark they were? They look more like Hassan and Abdul than Moshe and Shmuel."

"Listen to that asshole. You want to check their foreskins? What about you? I heard those new calisthenics teachers are here looking for spies. Maybe you're a spy."

"Who the hell would I be spying for, idiot? You don't know what you're talking about."

"How naive can you be? If these people knew what they were doing, we wouldn't be stuck in this place. There wouldn't be a prison for Jews in Eretz Yisrael."

"No prisons? You don't think there are Jewish thieves?"

"Don't change the subject."

"The Yishuv knows what it is doing."

Zorah composed brilliant responses to their nonsense, even as she silently mocked the way they all talked past one another. My people, she thought, rude and arrogant as fishmongers. Or Talmud scholars.

It struck her that while the men were talking nonstop, the women sat in little groups or paired beside boyfriends, quietly sipping and chewing like domesticated animals. Even a heroine like Shayndel rarely spoke up in mixed company, she thought. And I am no better.

The debate around her stopped abruptly as the doors opened and four prisoners from the locked barrack walked in, accompanied by four armed guards.

The men seemed curious and eager as they searched the faces in the room, but the soldiers were nervous. "Hurry up," muttered one of the British soldiers, pointing at the platters that had been set aside for them. Tirzah appeared with a plate covered by a napkin, which the soldier ripped off.

"Biscuits," she said haughtily in English, then switching to Hebrew muttered, "Horse's ass." The room exploded into laughter and echoes of "horse's ass." The Poles behind Zorah stood up and started practicing their Hebrew obscenities.

After they were gone, everyone sat down and the room grew as quiet as an audience waiting for the curtain to rise on the second act. After a few minutes, people returned to eating and talking, and then drifted outside.

Zorah wanted to talk to Shayndel, but she had not sat down at all during lunch, so Zorah slipped into the kitchen and found her staring out the back door.

"You have to tell me what is going on," Zorah said. "I feel like a big storm is about to break over my head."

"Don't let your imagination get ahead of you," Shayndel said. "I think everyone is nervous because there are so many guards and guns in the compound."

"You are the worst liar I've ever seen," said Zorah.

"I have nothing to tell you."

"You can't even look me in the eye."

"Not now," Shayndel said, as the two of them went outside, drawn by the sound of a loud, angry argument rising from a tight circle of about twenty men. They had gathered around Uri, Bob, and Francek, who was poking Uri in the middle of his chest, one jab for every word. "We demand that you get us out of here before those other men."

"Look here, brothers," said Uri, who tried to take a step away from Francek's finger but was pressed forward by the crowd. "You have to be patient just a little bit longer, and then, I promise, you will all be free men in Eretz Yisrael."

"We are not children," Francek said, "and we do not acknowledge your authority, you asshole."

Uri's smile vanished and in a single deft move, he grabbed Francek's hand, twisted his arm behind his back, and dropped him to the ground with his boot at his throat. After one breathless, shocked moment, the other prisoners closed in. Bob tried to run for help but he was tackled from behind and fell to the ground face-first.

All of this took place so quickly and quietly, Zorah felt as though she were watching a silent movie.

Shayndel pushed her way into the middle of the lopsided tussle, as ten men struggled to keep the two Palmachniks from getting away. "What do you think you are doing?"

"We have to take matters into our own hands," Francek said, dabbing at his bloody nose. "Get them inside."

It was no simple matter moving the two flailing men without alerting the guards. On the way to the barrack, Uri and Bob landed several hard kicks to their kidnappers' shins and shoulders.

And then it was as if nothing had happened. A few men stood at the door, sharing a cigarette and calling out to some of the girls, who were strolling arm in arm.

Nathan and Tirzah came running toward Shayndel and Zorah. "What happened? Where is Uri?" Nathan asked. "And Bob? Where are they?"

Shayndel picked up one of Bob's shoes and pointed.

Nathan sprinted to the barrack door and started knocking. "Let me in there," he called. "This has to stop."

The noise started to attract attention. Esther and Jacob joined Zorah, who explained what was happening. A few minutes later, the sallow British sergeant known as Wilson-the-anti-Semite arrived. "What's going on here?" he barked. "What's going on?"

Wilson shoved Nathan aside and tried the latch. "Open up," he shouted. All of the windows were shut tight as well. "Open the door," he yelled and pounded on it with the butt of his gun. "That is an order."

"You have a little dick," came the reply in Hebrew, setting off a roar of laughter.

"What did he say?" Jacob asked.

"Shhhh," said Zorah.

Goldberg ran to the door and shouted to the men inside, in Yiddish, "What's going on?"

"Is that you, Goldberg?"

"Yes, it's me."

"We demand justice," Francek announced. "We demand our freedom. We will not release these two Yishuv stooges until every last man is out of Atlit. Go tell those fucking British assholes that, would you?"

Zorah watched Goldberg's craggy face register amusement, worry, and annoyance. He returned ten minutes later with Colonel Bryce, his aide, and four soldiers carrying bayonets through a crowd that included nearly every inmate in the camp.

Sergeant Gordon knocked at the door and announced, "Colonel Bryce will address you now."

"Gentlemen," said Bryce. "I have just spoken to a senior member of the Jewish Agency in Tel Aviv. A delegation is on its way to talk to you directly. The matter will be settled when they arrive."

He gave orders for two of the armed men to stay, and left, taking the hated Wilson with him.

The crowd kept a nervous watch. The mood was tense but not grim. A break in the routine boredom of a day in Atlit was always welcome, and as the hours passed, some of the children started kicking around a battered soccer ball. Esther tried to push Jacob to join the other boys, but he refused to budge. Zorah said, "Let him be."

"He needs to build up his strength," said Esther. "He must learn to join in with the others."

"I'm not sure that's in his nature," Zorah said.

"I know. All these other boys are so robust and it seems all they talk about is fighting and farming. I'm afraid Jacob is not built for that."

"There will be a place for him. Among Jews, there is always a place for the thoughtful ones." But Zorah frowned as soon as the words left her lips; she didn't know if that would hold true in Palestine. What if all of the pioneer propaganda turned out to be prophetic and Eretz Yisrael became a nation filled with new kinds of Jews: soldiers, farmers, and athletes living on communes, cheerfully following the rules, arguing about nothing but military tactics and crops and soccer?

What would happen to a dreamy child in such a world? What would happen to the solitary ones, with inward-facing souls? Where would Jacob fit in? Where would she go?

"Are you unwell?" Esther asked. "Perhaps you should sit down."

"I'm fine," Zorah said. "It's not too hot today."

"It is beautiful," said Esther in halting Hebrew. She raised her hand to shield her eyes and looked up at the sky. "This may be the most beautiful day I've seen since we got here."

Zorah followed her gaze up to the cloudless sky.

"It would be nice to walk by the sea today," Esther said wistfully.

"Or in the hills," said Zorah.

"Let us go into the open," said Esther, "among the henna shrubs. . . . And then, what is it? To the vineyards?"

"Where did you learn that?"

"Jacob has been taking lessons from that fellow from Grodno, the one who has so many books."

"Don't tell me you're letting him study with that fanatic?" Zorah said.

"He must become learned in the ways of the Torah," said Esther.

Zorah smiled. "You are already a better Jew than I am."

"Why don't you teach Jacob?" Esther said. "You are learned," she insisted, cutting off Zorah's objection. "Don't deny it. And you are not a fanatic. Most important, you care about him and he cares for you."

Zorah opened her mouth, but Esther stopped her again. "It doesn't matter what book you use."

The ball bounded out of play and landed at Jacob's feet. He smiled at his mother and booted it directly between two bricks that had been set up as a makeshift goal.

"Who did that?" cried the other boys. "It was Jacob? It was him? Hey, the baby can kick!"

Esther gave him a gentle push forward and he joined the game, which went on until the afternoon sun started to cool and an ancient Mercedes, coated with dust, roared up the road.

Two short, stocky men jumped out. They wore white shirts and jackets but no ties, and their hats were pulled down over their foreheads as they headed for the front gate. Goldberg met them and escorted them to the barrack where Bob and Uri were being held.

"Comrades," Goldberg called, "I have some gentlemen from the Yishuv to speak to you."

The door opened and all three of them disappeared inside. A few boys near the windows tried to hear what was going on, but everyone else settled in, anticipating a long wait.

Barely ten minutes later, the Yishuv men reappeared. Uri and Bob glared at the startled crowd as they marched behind their rescuers, arms stiff at their sides, fists clenched all the way to the car, which coughed and shuddered to life and raced out of sight.

By then, Francek and his friends had emerged from the barrack, packs of American cigarettes bulging in their shirt pockets.

"Look how our heroes were bought off for a carton of smokes," said Zorah, who pushed her way forward and put out her hand. "Not at all," Francek protested as he handed them out.

The mutineers would only smirk when asked about what they had gotten in return for the hostages. But Francek couldn't help boasting. "Those two guys you saw, they're big shots in the Jewish Agency. They were very sympathetic to our demands, and I could see, honestly, that I made quite an impression on them. When I get out of here, I am pretty sure there will be a commission in the army for me. Commensurate with my abilities—that's how they put it."

Zorah managed to keep from laughing at the double-edged message. "Good for you, Frankie," she said as she slipped an extra cigarette out of his packet. "Let's just hope your little stunt won't make problems for the rest of us."

With the breakout postponed for twenty-four hours, Tirzah had to inform Bryce about the change. Her head ached at the prospect of seeing him in his office, where everything they shared seemed distorted and dirty.

She walked through the gate, across the road, past Wilson-the-anti-Semite, and into the office, wishing she had thought to take an aspirin.

Private Gordon got to his feet. "Colonel Bryce is on a call at the moment," he said, "let me get you some water," pouring it before she could say no.

"Thank you," she said. She sat down, emptied the glass, looked up at the clock. "Where are you from?" she asked.

"I am from Scotland."

"Scotland is north of England, yes?"

"The British think of the Scots as peasants with odd accents."

"Your Hebrew gets better every day," Tirzah said.

"You are good to say so. And your son, is he healthy?" Gordon asked.

"Yes, thank you."

"The colonel speaks highly of him. He is, I think, most fond of your boy."

"He has been very kind to Danny."

"I have a brother also named Daniel," said Gordon as the phone rang.

"You may go in now," he said, hanging up. "And thank you, Mrs. Friedman, for letting me talk from you today."

"It was my pleasure," she said, adding, "but it is talk *with* you, not *from* you."

"I have trouble with that one. Many thanks."

Bryce did not meet Tirzah at the door, as he usually did. She found him sitting with his elbows on the desk, his hands pressed against his eyes.

"What happened?" she whispered. "What's wrong?"

He took a deep breath and pushed himself back against the chair, staring at her as though she were standing far away.

"I just had some news from home," he said, dropping his eyes to the top of the desk.

"Colonel Bryce?" she asked.

He sat up straight, as if called to attention, and asked, "Is Danny all right?"

"Yes," she said. "Although the reason I came to see you is because I must make a telephone call. The appointment must be changed. He cannot be seen until tomorrow."

"Tomorrow," Bryce repeated slowly. "I see."

"Tomorrow at exactly the same hour and in the same place," she said. "I hope that will not be a problem."

"I can't imagine why," he said, avoiding her eyes. "I'm sure that his visit will go as planned."

Tirzah lowered her voice. "Please tell me, what's wrong?"

A truck passed and the room filled with the engine's roar. Bryce closed his eyes. "My son is dead. My second boy, the younger one."

"Oh, no."

"Influenza. Three years in the RAF and not a scratch on him."

Tirzah's eyes filled with tears.

"I leave on Friday."

"I am so sorry," she whispered, wishing that she knew for which of the young men in the picture he was grieving. Though, of course, he was grieving for them both now.

"I will take care of Danny's appointment. Don't worry about that," he said as he reached for the phone again. She knew he could not look at her without breaking down.

"Shalom," she said.

He did not stand up. "Thank you, Mrs. Friedman. And to you."

She closed the door behind her softly.

In the outer office, Private Gordon rose to his feet.

"Your commander has had bad news from home," she said, walking over to face him. "You must do . . . you will take care of him, I know." She reached over to shake his hand. "Thank you."

Shayndel was flying around the kitchen—stirring, setting out platters, and swearing at Tirzah, who had not shown up to prepare dinner. She had waited as long as she dared before starting on her own, but once she settled down to work, she began to enjoy herself. She used to hate kitchen work as a girl at home; the endless cycle of cooking and cleaning always made her want to scream with boredom. But taking charge of feeding more than two hundred comrades made her feel like she had planned and directed a battle. Best of all, it kept her occupied.

When Nathan wandered in a few minutes before the meal, Shayndel nodded at him but didn't bother to ask if he knew where Tirzah was.

He watched her work for a few moments and said, "Applebaum and Goldberg will be taking care of those firing pins tonight. So all in all, it was a good thing we had the extra day."

"I am not so sure Uri and Bob would agree with that."

"Those two behaved like amateurs, letting themselves get ambushed like that."

"Aren't we in trouble without them?" Shayndel asked.

"Don't be so sure we will be without them. It will take everyone to pull this off. That includes you and your comrades, as well."

"As long as you don't involve Francek."

Nathan shrugged.

"Oh no. He's such a hothead," Shayndel said.

"Maybe, but he can get people to follow him—as we've seen."

"He could have screwed things up for everyone with that show he put on today."

"But he did not," said Nathan. "And of course you will be a great help, starting tomorrow night after dinner."

Shayndel put down the spoon and turned toward him. "Yes?"

"I'm not supposed to say more until tomorrow, but you are such a good girl, such an inspiration for your efforts during the war." He took her hand in his, tracing the lines on her palm with his finger. "I see a long life line and much romance."

Shayndel pulled away and crossed her arms.

Nathan shrugged. "You can't blame a man for trying. As for tomorrow, you will need to select three girls from your barrack to act as your lieutenants. I suppose you'll pick that pretty little French girl who is your friend. And the tall, good-looking blonde, yes? Your barrack has the prettiest girls, Shayndel."

"If I ever do meet your wife, I will be sure to tell her how friendly you have been."

Shayndel knew she was a bad liar and worried about keeping her new secret from Leonie and Zorah, both of whom saw through her easily. As she served lunch, she found reasons to keep running back into the kitchen. When she finally did sit down, she kept her mouth full and tried to imagine how the girls at her table would fare under the pressure of the escape.

"Tedi," Leonie said. "Tell Shayndel about your boyfriend."

Tedi blushed and shook her head, so Leonie took up the story. "In the infirmary today, one of the Iraqi boys took a look at our friend here and fell in love at first sight! He actually sang her a song. Aliza told me that his name is Nissim, which means 'miracles.' Isn't that lovely?"

"It's foolishness, that's what it is," Tedi sniffed and grabbed the pitcher. "I'm going to get some more water."

"He's very handsome, very dark," Leonie confided after she left. "But at least three inches shorter than her. They would make a strange couple." Shayndel nodded, suddenly ambushed by an image of Tedi in bed with Nissim, his legs wrapped around her hips, their contrasting skin and hair flashing black and gold, ivory and silver. She imagined their children; an entirely new species of Jew, with blue eyes in a brown face, or black eyes beneath a flaxen curtain. Not European, not Moorish; sturdy and graceful, tough and sentimental, and altogether beautiful.

When Tedi returned, Leonie said, "I'm sorry if I offended you. I used to hate it when the old ladies matched up boys and girls and talked about how lovely their children would be. Here I am doing the same thing and I'm not even twenty yet."

"Twenty," Tedi repeated. "Isn't it strange that twenty seems old to me?"

"That's because we've seen so much death," said Shayndel. "Usually, people are much older—fifty or sixty at least—before they know more dead people than living ones. To become young, we will have to have babies."

"I'm not the maternal type," said Tedi.

"Me neither," Leonie said. "I don't think I ever played with dolls."

"It doesn't matter," said Shayndel. "We'll marry and the babies will come and they change you. I've seen it. Even women with numbers on their arms, the ones who never used to smile, even for them, I see the light come back to their eyes when they hold a baby."

"That puts a terrible burden on the children," Tedi said.

"I don't think so. Kids don't understand," said Shayndel.

"Don't fool yourself," Leonie said. "They feel everything, even if they can't put it into words. It's not fair to make a child the source of its parents' happiness. Tedi is right. It is a heavy burden. And people only make it worse by naming their children after the dead."

Shayndel thought of her brother, Noah.

Tedi thought of Rachel, her sister.

"I like the new Hebrew names," Leonie said. "Ora, Ehud, Idit. They sound like a blank page, though really, I won't be having children. Not me."

"Don't be silly," said Tedi. "You'll be married and pregnant five minutes after you get out of here."

"We'll all marry. We'll all have children. That's life," said Shayndel. "But first, we have to wash the dishes. Tirzah never showed up, so you can help me clean up the mess I made."

Later that evening, after the lights were out, Shayndel lay in bed and tried to make herself believe that this would be her last night in Atlit. Tomorrow, everything would change forever, again.

She wished she could tell Leonie what was about to happen to them and stared at the rise and fall of her friend's back as she slept. Her throat grew tight as she realized that they might never see each other again. People without families in Palestine—people like them—were being sent to kibbutzim all over the country for "absorption," a word she found both funny and frightening. The idea of being soaked up like a spill in a towel made her smile. But it also seemed like an irrevocable disappearance.

Stop that, she scolded herself. The distances here are not so great. We might yet live close enough to visit one another. We could even end up raising families side by side, growing old together. Or not. In any case, we will go where we are sent.

Shayndel rolled over and closed her eyes, but before she had a chance to settle, she felt a hand on her shoulder.

Zorah was crouched beside her. "You said you would tell me what is going on."

"Not now," Shayndel pleaded.

"Now," said Zorah, making it clear that she was not going to budge.

"All right, but this must go no further."

Shayndel moved closer and whispered into Zorah's ear, "We are escaping tomorrow night. The Palmach is planning a breakout. Everyone is going."

Zorah's eyes narrowed. "Esther, too?"

"I suppose so. I don't really know."

"She is going, too. No matter what you really know."

"Is she even that boy's mother?"

"What difference does it make? She risked her life to bring him here."

"That is not the question," Shayndel said.

"There is no other question worth asking," Zorah said, choking back tears.

Shayndel was startled. Like almost everyone else, she had written Zorah off as bitter and unpleasant, sealed off from compassion. But Zorah's feeling for Esther and Jacob had transformed her intensity into something different—still fierce but no longer ferocious.

"So she *will* be coming with us?" Zorah whispered, insisting and begging in the same breath. "And Jacob, too."

"I will do everything I can," Shayndel promised.

"Swear it."

"Oh, for heaven's sake," Shayndel said. "You will be there to watch over them every step of the way. Now let me go to sleep."

October 9, Tuesday

Tedi tried to linger among the pine trees, so pungent and green, in her dream. She pulled the blanket over her head but after Lotte had stirred on the cot beside her, there was no scent but hers.

Tedi sat up and saw that Shayndel was already dressed, and waved for her to follow her outside.

They said nothing until they were inside the latrine and Shayndel turned on the tap. "What did you find out about the German?" she asked, splashing her face with cold water.

"Leonie thinks she might be a Nazi," said Tedi.

"What does Leonie have to do with it?"

"Her German is much better than mine, and it turns out that Lotte, or whoever she is, will talk only to Leonie. She calls her Claudette Colbert."

"Why does Leonie think she's a Nazi?"

"She says she saw an SS tattoo in the shower," said Tedi and pointed. "Here, under the armpit."

Shayndel frowned. "Did you see it?"

"No. She is trying to get another look to make sure," Tedi said. "What will happen if it's true?"

"I don't know."

"She cannot stay here with the very people who—"

"Of course not," Shayndel said. "I'll find out."

After she left, Tedi stood in front of the cloudy mirror that hung near the door. She loosened the string holding back her long hair, now white-blonde from the sun. Combing her fingers through the broken, knotted ends, she remembered a boar's hair brush with a silver handle, a crocheted drape on the nightstand, a goblet of water with the letter *P* etched onto it, her mother's hands rubbing rose-scented pomade into her scalp.

She went back to the sink and scrubbed her face with the merciless gray soap until her cheeks stung and her mind emptied and then headed back to the barrack to talk to Leonie.

She was still asleep. With her extraordinary eyes closed, she was just another girl, Tedi thought, unexceptional. She lay on her side with both arms thrust out in front of her, like a child. They were a child's arms, too, soft and pink. Her fingers were small and tapered to the pale ovals of her nails. It took Tedi a minute to decipher the meaning of the fine, white rows across her wrists, straight and intentional as lines printed on a piece of paper.

Tedi had once believed that anyone who tried to commit suicide was insane. But now she knew how easy it could be to give up and let go; to close your eyes and just fall asleep on the frozen ground, with the moonlight on your face, the tang of diesel and smoke in your nostrils. Why get up when everyone who ever loved you is gone?

Leonie opened her eyes, pale and smoky against the pillow, and smiled at Tedi. "What is it?"

"I told Shayndel what you said . . . about the German."

Leonie's smile disappeared. "What did she say?"

"Nothing. She ran straight to the kitchen. I guess she'll tell Tirzah."

Leonie sat up, wrapped her arms around her knees, and changed the subject. "What do you smell in the air today? Do I still smell of rotten fruit?"

Tedi flushed. "You're making fun of me. I shouldn't have told you."

"I'm not teasing. I'm really curious."

"Today I woke up smelling pine trees. A whole forest of them."

Leonie sniffed and grimaced. "Did it cover up the German?"

"No," Tedi said, embarrassed to be talking of this. "What do you think is going on with those Iraqi guys? And that drama with the exercise teachers yesterday? Then Tirzah doesn't show up to cook last night."

"And Shayndel is so jumpy," Leonie added. "Something must be happening. But for now, let's go see if Tirzah made it to the kitchen this morning. Shayndel may need us."

A few steps from the door, they nearly collided with Zorah, who was standing perfectly still and staring into the distance.

"Are you all right?" Tedi asked.

Zorah stared at them for a second before blurting, "I, uh, I have to go." She rushed around the corner of the barrack, pressing her back against the wall, frightened and furious at herself.

She had seen other survivors standing like statues right in the middle of the dining hall or on the parade ground, suddenly overwhelmed and paralyzed by memory. But Zorah considered herself the master of her past, immune to such displays. She had even started writing lists to keep her memories clear and orderly: names from the concentration camp, the deaths she had witnessed inside her barrack and on the parade ground, ingredients in the "soups" they had been starved with, the mind-numbing work they had been forced to do. Her register of misery, humiliation, and loss covered five pieces of paper, front and back, a hedge against forgetting and also a fence to keep the past in its place. She kept it folded within the pages of her Hebrew grammar, and ran her eyes over the columns every time she studied.

But she had no way of accounting for—or fencing off—the sensation of her own hair brushing against the back of her neck, which had, that morning, summoned the memory of her mother. She used to call Zorah's hair her "best feature" in a voice so heavy with consolation, it always made her wince.

Zorah shook herself and started for the dining hall. She would ask Leonie to take a scissors to her mop after breakfast. It would be cooler and lighter that way, and she would need all of her wits tonight.

As Zorah entered the noisy mess, Esther and Jacob waved for her to join them. "I got this for you," said the boy, pushing a plate in front of her.

Zorah bit into a roll and was stunned by the texture between her teeth, and the aroma of yeast. The soft cheese on her tongue was a tender revelation, a salty gift. The tea, which Jacob had mixed with too much milk and sugar, answered some long-denied craving. She bit into a slice of tomato and groaned.

"What's wrong?" asked Esther.

"Nothing," said Zorah, bewildered by the strange, overwhelming testimony of her mouth. "It's just that this food is . . . this tomato, I mean. It's all delicious today, isn't it?"

"Try the red pepper," Esther urged, passing another plate. "These are the best we've had. Let me cut one for you."

But Zorah was on her way out the door.

"Where are you going?" Esther called.

What is happening to me? Zorah wondered, hurrying toward the northern edge of the camp, where she could be alone. Why should I go mad now, after everything?

The answer came to her in a man's voice. *Life will not be denied.*

"Hah," Zorah roared and immediately clapped a hand over her mouth. She would not turn into one of the screamers or mutterers who caused people to turn away in pity or disgust. She started pacing, walking faster and faster, as she silently argued with herself.

Life most certainly can be denied, she thought. Life is unforgivably weak. Death is stronger than everything that breathes. I am an expert on the rottenness and hollowness of this world. Death is what cannot be denied. No one is going to tell me that life is a beautiful poem, filled with meaning, a God-given blessing.

And yet you nearly burst into tears over the miracle of a tomato.

Zorah recognized the voice. It was Meyer, who knew to woo her with cigarettes and who remained in her thoughts, no matter how often she tried to dismiss him.

I must have been hungrier than I realized. That's all.

You are sleeping better. You have gained a little weight.

Nothing but the fruits of boredom, she countered, wondering why she had turned Meyer into the straw man inside her head. She barely knew him. The only reason he is such a worthy opponent, she decided, is because he speaks with my words.

Worthy opponent or suitor?

Zorah blushed.

Your body is returning to life and so is your heart.

A small hand slipped into hers and stilled the voices in her head. "Are you ill?" Jacob asked. "Do you want me to fetch Mama? Or the nurse? Mama says we must take care of you because you are sick in the heart. I told her the doctors should give you medicine for your heart, and she started crying. Mama cries a lot. I have never seen you cry."

Zorah tried to smile away the worry that made him look even more like a little old man than usual. Jacob was far too small for his age, his face still thin and pinched despite a healthy appetite. Even so, Zorah was struck by the change in him; this was not the listless, silent child who had arrived in Atlit a few weeks ago.

As they walked back toward the mess hall, Jacob skipped beside her, a dervish of words and ideas. "Are you really going to be my teacher?" he asked. "That's what Mama says. She says that you are smarter than Mr. Rostenberger. I told her that your breath is much nicer than his and that you probably wouldn't pinch my hand if I make a mistake. When will we start, Miss Zorah? Will we continue with the page of Talmud about what time you're supposed to say the Sh'ma in the morning? That's where he started. Where is your book?"

"I have no Talmud," said Zorah. "We will begin with grammar. Hebrew is very dense, you know. Compact. Full of mysteries."

"What does that mean?"

She tried again. "Hebrew is a bit like hard candy."

He nodded seriously. "Does Hebrew melt when it's hot, too?"

It took Zorah a moment to realize that Jacob had made a

joke. "That was very funny," she said, again on the verge of tears. After tonight, he would become someone else's student, someone else's charge.

Zorah stroked his cheek gently. Now she knew that she wasn't going mad after all; she was mourning what she was about to lose.

"I'm sorry to bother you," said Leonie, rushing toward them. "Would you please come to the infirmary, Zorah?" she asked slowly, in her best Hebrew. "They need a translation."

"I'll be right there," Zorah said.

"How many languages do you know?" Jacob asked, taking her hand again as they walked toward the clinic.

"Four," she said, not counting the three she understood but had never spoken out loud. "Not so many."

"I think it's so many," he said, with such an emphatic shake of his head, Zorah couldn't help but pull him close and hug his bony shoulder against her hip. "Go find your mama, now."

She was met at the door by a skinny young man wearing a white coat. Volunteers cycled through Atlit so often, Zorah wasn't surprised that she had never seen this doctor before, but when he extended a hand that was calloused and not entirely clean, she looked into his pale green eyes with suspicion.

"You are Zorah, yes?" he said. "I am Avi Schechter. We have two men inside babbling to each other in some prehistoric jargon, pretending not to understand me or anyone else. I'm told you're a wonder with Polish dialects, so I'd like you to go in and find out what you can about them. They got off a boat last week and we already know they're not Jews; we need to find out how they got here and what they're up to and what they did during the war."

He talked like someone who was used to giving orders, and gave her no time to think or choose not to do what he wanted.

He opened the door and pointed at two thickset men, clearly brothers, sitting together on a cot. "I'll wait for you here."

Zorah heard one man tell the other to say nothing. "Can I get you some water?" she said, stumbling only a little over the Mazur dialect.

Their faces registered surprise and then suspicion. The older of the two asked, "You are from Danzig?"

"No, but I had cousins there," she said. "They lived on Mirchaer Street."

"By the synagogue," he said. "I know the neighborhood."

"Did you live nearby?"

He rubbed his hands over the dark stubble on his round face and asked, without hope or rancor, "So are they going to send us back or will they put us in prison?"

"I don't know," she said.

"I told you it was a stupid idea," said the other man, who looked even more like a bear than his brother. He turned to Zorah and pleaded, "Tell them we didn't hurt anybody. We didn't even turn anyone in to the police, and we didn't fight. We were cowards, my brother and I. We went to Denmark and waited it out," he said.

"Why did you come here, then?" she asked.

"There was no work in Danzig. There were a couple of Mossad guys in town after the armistice; we found out that they needed ironworkers here, shipbuilders. That's what we used to do. We had the documents, so I figured—"

"Where did you get Jewish papers?" But Zorah was unable to keep the edge out of her voice and the older brother said, "Forget it. No one's going to believe a word we say."

"I can't help you if you don't talk to me," she said, but they shook their heads and turned away.

Outside, the man in the white coat had changed into a worn leather jacket. "What did you find out?"

"Not much," said Zorah. "They're from Danzig. They say they were shipbuilders and ran away during the war. They are not going to tell me anything else. Not terribly bright, those two. I don't think they have any idea what they're doing here, actually. What happens to them now?"

"If it was up to me, I'd take them to the border and point them north and good riddance," he said. "The Yishuv may put them on a boat. I could care less."

"But tell me something," Zorah said. "Why are these guys in the clinic? They aren't sick. If you're rounding up Christians, why don't you bring over that Russian girl in A barrack who is more than happy to tell everyone that she's not a Jew?"

"And then there's the one in your barrack," he said.

"Who are you talking about?"

"That German creature, of course. Unbelievable story. A war criminal in Eretz Yisrael. You didn't know?" he said.

Zorah tried to look bewildered instead of relieved; he didn't seem to know about Esther.

"So maybe you aren't as smart as Hayyim said you were."

"Hayyim?"

"Hayyim Meyer. Surely you can see the resemblance," he said, turning his head to show off his profile. "Everyone tells us we look more like brothers than cousins." He took a half-empty pack of cigarettes out of his pocket and waved it in front of her. "He sent these for you. I hope you don't mind sharing," he said, handing it over. "Do you have a message for him, if I see him?"

"Tell him," Zorah said, trying to think of something clever, "tell him . . . thank you for the cigarettes."

"A real romantic, aren't you? Why don't I give him your love and tell him you're pining to see him again."

Zorah watched him walk off and stamped her foot. "His name *would* be Hayyim."

"What did you say?" asked Leonie, who had been waiting for her. "Hayyim means 'life,' doesn't it?"

Zorah held out the pack of cigarettes. "Do you want one?"

"Chesterfields? How nice, thank you." As Leonie extracted a cigarette, a slip of paper fell to the ground. "What's this?"

Zorah picked it up and unfolded it.

"There is only the letter *M,*" said Leonie. "Does it mean anything to you?"

"Sort of."

"Meyer." Leonie smiled. "*Non?*"

"Meyer, *oui,*" Zorah said, so plainly miserable that Leonie knew better than to tease.

"I'm going to the calisthenics class now," she said. "This Uri fellow is very entertaining. Will you join me?"

Before Zorah could say no, Leonie added, "Why not?"

She shrugged. "I don't know anymore."

Shayndel chopped the cucumbers in time with the internal metronome that had woken her early that morning. At first she thought there were real drums beating somewhere in the camp, but eventually she realized it was her own heartbeat urging, Let's *go,* let's *go*.

She tried to ignore it, but the beat grew louder and more insistent, crowding out everything, including her usual good humor. She had snapped at Tedi and growled at the two Arab guards who normally exchanged smiles and a thumbs-up with her. She was, she realized, behaving just like Tirzah, who had not even said good morning when she arrived.

"Ba-*dum,* ba-*dum,* ba-*dum,*" she muttered, bringing the blade down in time. Her hands were sweating so much, she had to stop and wipe them every few minutes to keep the knife from slipping.

The back door hit the wall with a sharp crack, announcing Nathan, who sailed into the kitchen, followed by Bob and Uri. "Look who's here," he bellowed.

"This is good news?" said Tirzah. "You two had better stay out of trouble today."

"They have plenty to do," Nathan said, stuffing a piece of bread into his mouth.

"Since Nathan figured out how to disarm the rifles, everyone is much more confident," said Uri.

Tirzah and Shayndel looked at each other, and then stared at Nathan.

"You really are a pig," said Tirzah. "I'll bet you didn't let on that it was Shayndel who told you how to fix those guns."

He ignored her completely. "Let's get out there," he said, grabbing a handful of olives and heading into the dining room. "I'll show you which men we've chosen as barrack leaders."

"What a schmuck," Shayndel sputtered.

"What do you expect?" said Tirzah. "At least he gets things done."

Shayndel pulled off her apron, muttering Yiddish curses under her breath. She was familiar with arrogant men; among her partisan comrades, self-importance had been a survival skill, as essential as the ability to sleep on the ground. Even so, in her outfit, the boys knew better than to pretend that they were tougher or smarter than the girls.

Nathan's conceit made her want to scream. She was so wound up she didn't even try to sit down for lunch but stayed in the kitchen, pacing and sipping a cup of tepid tea. Every few moments, her hand went to her left shoulder, searching for the strap of the small machine gun she had carried for nearly two years in the forest. The damned thing used to slip off a hundred times a day and she was forever pushing it back.

"Some women fuss with their scarves," Malka would tease, "but for Shayndel, it's her darling gun."

Shayndel assumed that the Palmach would not be handing her a weapon. We will be herded like prize livestock, she thought; they will take us out through the fence on the north side of camp, the emptiest, darkest, and least-defended flank. From there they will hurry us through those fields to trucks or buses, and then . . .

Thinking about what lay ahead set Shayndel's heart pounding again, as though she were already on her way, crawling through a gash in the fence, running after strangers into a moonless night. She knew something about escapes.

During the war, she had helped Jews through the shadowy forest, always in the worst kind of weather, it seemed. There was one family with seven-year-old twin boys who arrived during an ice storm, all of them frightened out of their senses. The only way to get them to cross a frozen river on their way to the campsite was for the partisans to drag them across on their coats.

Shayndel remembered talking down to them, as though they were stupid, as though she were above feeling the kind of fear that rose off them like steam.

Shayndel started scrubbing the stove, moving her arm back and forth, one-*two,* let's-*go,* ba-*dum,* so focused that she didn't notice when Goldberg came in.

"This kitchen doesn't deserve such devotion, I promise you," he said.

"It's just something to do," she replied. "I'm going a little crazy. The waiting is hard."

He took the brush out of her hand. "Go outside," he said. "Get some fresh air. It's a nice day."

She did as she was told, but once she got out into the sunshine, she didn't know what to do with herself. She headed back to the barrack to change her shirt, which was soaked.

She had only one other blouse, an ugly beige cast-off with a stain on the sleeve. At least I have good shoes, she thought, looking down fondly at the sturdy brown brogans she'd gotten from the Red Cross. She decided she would wear the short pants for the escape. They were her favorite item of clothing because of their deep pockets, front and back, and because they had once belonged to a boy named Marvin Ornish, whose mother had sewn a tag with his name into the waistband, securing it with a hundred tiny stitches.

She looked around, at the valises stuffed under the beds, the sacks hanging from rafters. She used to envy the others their rescued treasures, but not anymore. At least I don't have to worry about schlepping or leaving anything behind, she thought.

Shayndel had a few useful pieces of clothes and a leather rucksack, but the possessions that mattered most to her fit into the envelope tucked under her mattress. She withdrew the photographs, slowly, one at a time. There was Malka, smiling right into the lens, fully aware of how pretty she was, though the picture didn't do her justice. Her hair was much blonder than the black-and-white image suggested, and her brown eyes were flecked with green. She was curvy under the baggy jacket and wool trousers.

Wolfe never looked at the camera. He turned to gaze into the distance, showing off his impressive profile. It was an odd vanity in a man who seemed to care so little about his appearance. From the front, he was a garden-variety Jew, strange-looking, even, with his left eye a bit higher than the right. But from the side, with his dark brown hair, straight and heavy and hanging over that long, aquiline nose, he looked both intellectual and imposing. And he knew it.

Shayndel pulled out the picture of the three of them standing on cobblestones outside a church. Wolfe was in the middle, of course. I look like their little sister, she thought, which is why everyone thought that Malka and Wolfe were the couple and I was the third wheel. She put her finger on Wolfe's mouth.

Why was I smiling like that? Had he said something funny? Or was it Shmuley behind the camera who made me laugh?

Shmuley had been the company clown, and he had been in especially good spirits the day of this picture. He had just recovered from a horrible bout of diarrhea. They had been pinned down for a week, cut off by the icy roads and the threat of desperate, starving deserters, and Shmuley had been so sick that Malka had wanted to get a doctor for him. She had gotten into a big fight with Wolfe about it, but he said it was too dangerous and put his foot down.

Shmuley got well without a doctor. But he was killed just a month after the picture was taken. A sniper. Out of the blue. Shayndel had no photograph of him.

What was his last name? "Oh my God," she whispered, horrified that she could not remember.

She put the snapshots away carefully, placing them inside her scarred backpack. Her mother had scolded Papa when he gave it to her. "That is not feminine enough for a girl," she said. "Give it to Noah."

"It will keep her powder dry," said Papa, who loved to plague them with puns.

It was quiet in the barrack. The rhythmic drumming had become a dull throb just below her navel. Let's-*go,* let's-*go,* let's-*go*.

Shayndel walked to the clearing in front of the dining hall where Uri was holding his class. The day was perfectly clear, warm but no longer humid, and yet Tedi was sweating heavily as she stood before him, her face flushed and her fists clenched.

"This is not appropriate for girls," Uri shouted, at the end of his patience. "It's a kind of fighting that is too crude for you. Hand-to-hand. Brutal. When you reach the kibbutz, they'll teach you to handle a gun, but not this."

"Why shouldn't I know how to defend myself?" Tedi said. "I want to learn to do what you showed him." She pointed at one of the boys.

Shayndel slipped in beside Leonie and asked, "What's going on?"

"He was teaching them how to break away if someone grabs you from behind."

"There is no need for you to learn this. One of our men will take care of you," Uri argued.

"But what if I'm alone?"

"Someone as pretty as you?"

"Show her," said Shayndel, moving to Tedi's side.

"We don't have time for this," said Uri.

"You're full of shit," she said coolly and stepped closer to him. "Why don't you try it on me and I'll show them how easy it is to throw a man to the ground."

"Why don't you just go back to the kitchen?" he said.

"I'm finished in there," she said, "and if you're not willing to do your job, I'll teach Tedi myself. Leonie, come here, would you? I want you to stand directly behind me and grab me by the arms as tight as you can.

"Now, Tedi, the most important thing is to not think too much. Do not plan or hesitate. Just watch what I do."

As Leonie tightened her grip, Shayndel blew all the air out of her lungs and went limp, as though she had fainted. Her collapse startled Leonie, who let go just enough for Shayndel to turn quickly and jab her elbow back between Leonie's legs.

"You don't have to be big or strong to make this hurt," said Shayndel. "He will go down, I promise. Then you run as fast as you can."

No one said a word.

"Do you want to try?" Shayndel asked Tedi, whose face was white. "No," she said softly, "I understand."

Everyone was staring at Shayndel or trying not to. "Does anyone else want to try?" she asked. "No? All right," she said and marched away, one-*two,* one-*two,* one-*two*.

Leonie ran up behind her. "You were wonderful."

"I probably shouldn't have embarrassed Uri like that, even though he had it coming." Shayndel winced and grabbed at her abdomen.

"Is something wrong?"

"All day I've had this bellyache and it's getting worse."

"Do you have your period?" Leonie whispered.

"Oh, no! Not today."

Shayndel had been relieved when her cycle had stopped in the forest. It was miserable trying to manage that mess while they were moving from hovel to hole, rarely bathing or washing their clothes. Besides, it had given her the freedom to make love with Wolfe without worrying about a baby.

But Malka was afraid that she would never have children. "I want sons," she had said. "Girls are too much trouble."

Shayndel grinned and said, "Well, at least we can enjoy the sex for now. And since you can't guarantee boys, maybe it's better if your period never comes back."

Malka had flinched at that and refused to talk to her the rest of the day. But she wasn't the sort to stay mad, and the next morning it was as though the conversation had never happened.

Shayndel ran into the latrine and sat on the toilet, her head in her hands.

"*Chèrie?*" Leonie peeked around the partition and handed her a folded cotton napkin. "It's from the clinic; I took some extra ones, too."

"Thank you," said Shayndel.

"Does it hurt?" Leonie asked, as they walked back to the barrack, arm in arm.

"Not really. I just forgot what it felt like. There isn't much bleeding, thank goodness."

"But you seem upset."

"It's just, well, inconvenient," said Shayndel.

"I am still waiting," Leonie said. "I never had mine."

"Never?"

"No."

"How old are you?" Shayndel asked.

"I am seventeen. No, it's October, so I am eighteen. I think perhaps it will never happen to me."

"Don't worry. I was nearly sixteen when I got mine. Someone told me that it goes away when you don't eat right. With enough good food, we'll all get back to normal and have all the babies we want—I know you said you don't want any, but still . . ."

Leonie shrugged and smiled, as though it didn't matter. She could never tell Shayndel about the abortion that might have left her barren—or the doctor's disdain, or the way she could practically taste the steel of his probes and scalpel as they entered her, or the blood pooling on the floor beneath the kitchen table. If she confessed to even one detail of her disgrace, all the hard work of restraint and containment might come crashing down and she would never be able to regain her balance. Worse still, Shayndel would hate her.

"But I have to ask you about something," Shayndel said, in a hushed, urgent tone.

"Anything," Leonie said, pushing her hair off her forehead and resuming control of herself and her secrets.

"Tedi says that you think Lotte, the German girl, is SS. But why didn't you tell me yourself?"

"I'm sorry," said Leonie, "I wasn't sure and then I was afraid you'd think I was crazy. When she was in the shower, I saw what I thought was an SS tattoo on the inside of her upper arm. It might have been a bruise or a birthmark and the whole thing seems so impossible."

"You're perfectly sane, but that woman is a raving lunatic," said Shayndel, who knew that whatever Lotte's story might be, she posed a threat to the success of their escape. "We have to get her out of the barrack."

"No one will argue with you about that," said Leonie.

"I wanted to tell you how proud I was of you, standing up to Uri like that. And now I find out that you weren't feeling well, yet you were so strong, so powerful. I suppose you had to learn that sort of thing in the war." She looked over at her shyly. “It must have been terrible what you went through.”

“Some days were worse than others,” said Shayndel, remembering the worst day of all. They had underestimated the band of German deserters who had taken refuge in their forest. Wolfe and Malka had been cut off from the rest of their unit and were outflanked, outrun, and shot down like deer in a hunting party.

Leonie kept still as pain and loss played across her friend’s face.

“You don’t think ‘terrible’ when you’re in the middle of it,” Shayndel continued. “You don’t think much at all. We tried to kill Nazis and collaborators. We blew up some bridges. We helped some people escape. We tried to stay alive.”

“Staying alive is no small thing when you consider how many died.”

“You think surviving is a victory?” said Shayndel. “Merely surviving?”

“I don’t know,” Leonie said, her eyes growing large with tears.

“I’m sorry.”

“No, forgive me.” Leonie wiped her cheeks with the back of her hand. “But maybe it’s better not to think about it too much.”

“Maybe not,” said Shayndel. But just then, Shmuley’s surname floated into her mind, like a kind of peace offering from the past. It was Besser. Shmuley Besser. She would not forget it again.

IV

The Breakout

Through the Fence

It was nearly an hour after the end of dinner, but the dining hall was still full. People lingered as if they were sitting at a café, leaning on their elbows, passing cigarettes back and forth. Someone pulled out a deck of cards, adding a quiet shuffle and slap to the steady drone of conversation. Maybe it's the coffee keeping them here, Shayndel thought. It's rare that we have coffee in the evening.

In the whole room, only Nathan was on the move, going from table to table, making a big show of turning chairs backward, kicking a leg over them, and sitting like a cowboy in an American western. He made it look casual, but Shayndel knew that he was checking in with the men he'd chosen as leaders, who sat up, stiff and tall, while he leaned in to deliver last-minute instructions. She noticed that the two other female barrack captains were not in the room, and bit her lips to keep from ordering everyone else to clear out and get ready for bed. Her arms and legs felt itchy and tight, as though she were about to burst out of her skin.

Finally, she could not sit for another moment and started gathering the last of the cups. Backing out through the door into the kitchen, she was struck by the faces in the room. From where Shayndel was standing, all of the girls were lovely; Zorah as well as Leonie. Even Francek looked handsome. Her mother used to say that every bride was beautiful, and Shayndel had offered up chinless Luba Finkelstein as proof that she was wrong. But Mama said no, even Luba was a pretty bride. Tonight she understood.

Nathan followed her into the kitchen and got right down to business. "A few minutes after one o'clock, we'll send someone to your barrack," he said. "Then it's up to you. Each of your lieutenants should take charge of five girls: get them up, dressed, and ready to leave as quickly as possible. No one is to carry anything. No baggage, nothing. We have to move fast. Our guys will be in the camp by then and they will guide you out.

"One more thing," he said, opening a cabinet under the sink. He handed her an old pillowcase, lumpy and bound with a great deal of twine.

"You'll find a bottle of chloroform and cloth to use as a gag—enough for the two women."

Shayndel was furious. "You're just telling me now?" she protested. "My girls are going to be frightened enough without this going on," she warned him as sternly as she could, to hide her happiness at having Esther's fate in her hands.

"This is not a discussion," Nathan snapped. "The action begins in a few hours and you have your orders. There's a wristwatch in the bundle, too, so you can keep track of the time. Take care of our little problem after midnight. The most important thing is to keep everybody quiet and get them out fast.

"I'll see you later, Shayndel," he said, and kissed her hand before she had a chance to stop him. "Be strong."

As the men lined up for the roll call, Shayndel noticed that there were no jokes or games. Nathan's captains stepped up smartly and everyone else fell in behind them.

"Finally learning your p's and q's, eh?" smirked Wilson. After they were dismissed, however, the men took a very long time getting back to their barracks, stopping to chat or tie their shoes, and pretending not to hear the guards shouting at them to move along. The girls joined in, making a show of their independence, strolling oh-so-slowly on their way to bed.

Shayndel found Leonie and took her arm. "Tonight there is going to be a breakout from the camp," she said quietly.

"Tonight?" Leonie gasped. "You are leaving?"

Shayndel drew closer. "Everyone is leaving."

Leonie stopped. "Everyone? Surely not that German?"

"No, not her," said Shayndel, and explained how they would quiet and bind her.

"And what about me?" Leonie said, thinking about Lotte's threat to reveal her past.

"Of course you," said Shayndel. "Don't be afraid. I've taken people over much worse terrain than this, and in the winter. The Palmach knows the countryside."

Shayndel continued, "Your job is to help me get the other

girls in the barrack ready to go. Tedi and Zorah will be helping as well."

"I will try not to disappoint you."

"Disappoint? You underestimate yourself, Leonie. You are calm. You have courage. In a country like this, you cannot be so meek. You have to stand up for yourself." Shayndel stopped herself, but Leonie heard her words for what they were: parting advice.

When they reached the barrack, Shayndel brought Tedi and Zorah to her cot and told them the plan.

"I knew something was up," Tedi said, her eyes bright. "This is wonderful. Another week in this place and I would have been barking at the moon. What do you want from us? What do we do?"

"There will be a knock just after one o'clock. We must get everyone up, dressed, and ready to go as quickly as possible. They are to carry nothing. Quiet, light, and quick, that's our job. The Palmach will lead us out. I suppose they'll cut the fences, and then take us . . . I don't know where."

The door opened and Lotte fell into the barrack, pushed by two of the British guards, their faces flushed and angry. "Next time, we won't be so gentle," said one.

Lotte spit at them as they left, screaming, "Ass-lickers, idiots, weaklings." She wheeled around. "You are ass-lickers, too, all of you," she yelled.

After she got in her cot and pulled the blanket over her head, Zorah leaned over to Shayndel and asked, "Is everyone going?"

"All but that one," said Shayndel. "I have rope and chloroform for her."

"And Esther?"

Shayndel shrugged. "People make too many assumptions

about how much Hebrew I really understand. But the truth is, I don't want you mad at me."

Zorah smiled. "No, you don't."

As the time for lights-out approached, a kind of storm rolled through the barrack, with flashes of temper and tension breaking like thunder. Two girls got into a loud and stupid argument about a piece of fruit. Someone dropped a book and everyone jumped. Jacob started running up and down between the beds, like a wild kitten.

"Can't you control that little beast?" someone asked.

"Control your mouth or I'll fix it for you." Zorah glowered.

A loud knock startled everyone into silence. "Is everyone decent?" A moment later, Goldberg's head appeared in the door. "Everyone is present and accounted for, yes? Well then, sweet dreams, my little ones."

The lights went out, and the darkness bristled with a nervous thrum of throat clearing, coughing, nose blowing, pillow thumping, blanket smoothing, and sighing. It was an hour before the restlessness settled into the tidal whisper of steady breathing and light snoring, though not everyone slept.

Tedi lay facedown, her nose buried in the pillow as she tried to block the smell of Lotte beside her. Her arms hung over the sides of her cot, her hands pressed flat against the cool concrete floor. Her head buzzed with questions: Where will we be sleeping tomorrow night? What will happen if we're caught? She was proud that Shayndel had chosen her, but nervous. Would she have to fight? Was her Hebrew good enough?

This was bound to be very different from her escape from

the train: to begin with, it wasn't freezing outside and she wasn't starving. She was not afraid, either. She had faith in Shayndel's good sense, in Goldberg's kindness, in the passion of the Palmachniks, in the land itself.

She turned onto her cheek and as she closed her eyes, Tedi saw a letter sitting in a tray on top of the cluttered desk. The window beside it was open to the sound of lapping from the canal and voices from outside, amplified as they traveled over the water. Mr. Loederman examined the address and smiled to know that she was alive and well.

Tedi woke with a start, confused and angry. Why should her thoughts go to her father's business partner? Why should such a trivial detail from her past rear up just as the future was about to begin?

She clenched every muscle in her body, straining to erase the image of Loederman's craggy face, the mahogany sideboard, the brass letter opener, the leather pencil case. But it was all too vivid to wish or will away. Her memory was no more under her control than her sense of smell. She was connected to the past by love and grief, and that's how it would be until she died. I suppose I will have to learn to live with this, she thought. I wonder how long it will be before it stops hurting.

Zorah was keeping watch. After the lights were out, Esther had gotten down on her knees, her head bent over hands pressed together like a steeple. It was, thought Zorah, the most non-Jewish posture on earth. Esther appeared to be saying a rosary or asking for help from the Virgin Mary. Of course, she could just as well have been praying to Sarah, Rebecca, and Rachel or soundlessly reciting part of the Hebrew service, which she had taken to attending with Jacob, morning and evening, every day.

Zorah considered herself an authority on the futility of prayer. In the concentration camp, she had watched people beg for their lives or for an extra ounce of bread, as if God were a wizard or a rich uncle. She had known better from the time she was twelve years old.

As a little girl, she used to show off to the ladies in the synagogue balcony. They smiled and nodded their praise as she demonstrated her mastery of the prayer book, phrase by phrase, gesture by gesture, better than any bar mitzvah boy. That stopped after she had overheard them whispering about her; too bad that she was plain as a carp, with a father who didn't have two coins to rub together, not to mention the burden of that slow-witted brother. Too bad, they smirked, that piety made such a poor dowry.

After that, her letter-perfect performance of the liturgy was nothing more than a way to prove—to herself, since no one else seemed to care—that she was smarter than the stupid hens who went to shul only to gossip and brag about their sons. Let those who pitied her face and her fortune go to hell; she was determined that her life would never be as small as theirs.

And yet, as Zorah watched Esther pray to some imaginary uncle on high, she silently added an "amen." She had seen the broken and the doomed find consolation in their devotions, and a kind of peace. She knew that God had nothing to do with it. God was a pretext, or a metaphor, or a strategy. But sometimes that was enough.

Zorah found it easier to forgive Esther her naiveté than her own long habit of arrogance. "I'm sorry," she whispered, raising a clenched fist over her heart. "For the sins that I have sinned against you," she repented, once, twice, three times. "For conceit, for pride, for haughty condescension. Sorry, sorry, sorry."

Leonie stared up at the ceiling and thought about escape, a beautiful word, especially in French, *échapper,* which seems to whisper, "shhhh."

Her last escape had not been beautiful. Accidental and unplanned, she had been alone, half-conscious, and impossibly lucky.

After the brutal night with Lucas and his comrades and the early morning hallucination of an angel amid the birds, she had gone back to sleep and woken up on clean sheets. She was sore everywhere, torn and aching, but smelling of soap and antiseptic ointments. There was a soft, clean pad between her legs.

She reached up to the throbbing cut on her lip, but Madame Clos stopped her. "Don't touch," she whispered. "It's not so bad and there won't be a scar. You'll be fine in a few days; young flesh heals fast." She clucked her tongue and shook her head. "We're lucky this sort of thing hasn't happened more, given what animals the Germans are."

Leonie was allowed to sleep for what seemed like a week. The pills erased the hours along with the pain so she had no idea what day it was when she felt a hand on her shoulder, shaking her hard.

"Wake up." Madame Clos was angry. She was breathing heavily and her kohl was streaked all the way down her cheeks. "Get up. Enough slacking off," she said and stripped off the blankets. "I want you to go over to Freddy's bar and get me a bottle." She pulled Leonie to her feet and shoved her arms into the sleeves of a man's trench coat. At the front door, she put a gold coin into her hand. "If you aren't back in fifteen minutes, I'll get Simone's captain out of bed and send him after you."

Leonie clutched at the railing as she crept downstairs on unsteady legs. Out on the street, she was dizzy and lost. It had been months since she'd been outside; after one of the girls ran away, Madame had hidden everyone's clothes and shoes and done all the marketing herself.

She looked up and down the street and tried to get her bearings. She remembered that the bar was around the block and headed to the left. She was entirely alone. All of the windows were dark, the storefront shutters down and padlocked. Freddy's was locked up tight.

The taste of bile rose from the back of Leonie's throat into her mouth. The cobblestones were cold and slick under her naked feet and she was fully awake, facing the first real choice she'd had in nearly two years.

She could turn down the alley and go to the back door, where Freddy would certainly sell her the bottle, though she knew he would demand more than Madame's money. Leonie clenched her fist around the coin in the deep pocket of the coat. The wool reeked of cigar smoke. She turned and crossed the street, deciding that she would never get down on her knees like that again.

Stepping carefully to avoid the broken glass glittering on the pavement, she kept close to the buildings. She could not risk being caught as she was—barefoot, bareheaded, and wearing nothing but a cotton shift under a German officer's coat.

She moved quickly, without knowing where to go. Leonie had no family. She had not seen any of her friends or acquaintances for so long, she had no idea what they might say or do if she showed up as she was. When she rounded the corner and found herself in front of the bar again, a wave of fear erased the last bit of fog behind Leonie's eyes.

She started running. Nearly all of the streetlights were out and she had no idea where she was going as she sprinted, block after block, as fast as she could, over a bridge and past a long row of German trucks parked for the night. Leonie did not slow down until she had no choice but to stop and catch her breath. Hiding in the shadows of a deep doorway, she looked out over an unfamiliar little square with wooden benches, some empty flower beds, a dry fountain in the center. On the far side of the plaza stood a tall gray lady with her head tilted to one side, as though she were listening to a distant song from beneath her granite veil.

Leonie stared at the statue for a long time, shivering like a rabbit, until an engine backfired and sent her racing past the fountain and down the alley beside the convent. She tapped on the ancient kitchen door, quietly but steadily, until she heard a bolt click and slide open. A nun in a white habit caught her by the arm as she fell to the floor and begged for her life.

Shayndel's attention was fixed on the battered watch beside her ear. She held it up to a pale yellow patch of light, astonished that it had been only five minutes since she had last looked.

Leonie stirred on the cot beside her. Shayndel saw that her eyes were open and lifted the blanket, signaling her to come and join her. They held each other close, and the next time Shayndel held the watch to the light it was time.

She slipped her shoes on as she reached under the bed for

the bundle Nathan had given her. Leonie helped her untie the twine, unwrap the bottle of chloroform, and fold the cotton batting into a compress. Tedi and Zorah watched from either end of the barrack, waiting for Shayndel to move.

When she stood, the others rose, and the four of them tiptoed to Lotte's cot. Leonie poured the clear liquid onto the gag, releasing a cloying, confectionary-sweet aroma. Tedi held her breath and pulled back the blanket.

They found Lotte lying facedown, which complicated things. Shayndel pointed orders for Tedi to grab Lotte's shoulders and for Zorah to take her by the hip. She held up three fingers and when she dropped the third, they rolled her onto her back in one deft move while Leonie pressed the cloth over her nose and mouth. Lotte flailed for a moment but the chloroform took effect quickly, and Tedi and Leonie set to work lashing her wrists to the metal rail of the cot. Zorah and Shayndel tied her ankles down.

They glanced at each other across the body on the bed, nodding congratulations. But Lotte began to stir and within a few moments was thrashing from side to side so violently, she twisted her left leg free. Zorah and Shayndel struggled to hold her down and retie the knots, but the rope they had been given kept breaking.

Shayndel was furious. Did they really think kitchen twine would be strong enough to restrain anyone?

Leonie retrieved the compress from the floor and held it over Lotte's face, dousing the cloth until chloroform soaked through and began running down the sides of her neck. Tedi turned away to avoid the dizzying effect of the chemical, amazed that Leonie could be so close to the fumes and remain conscious.

After a few moments, the stuff took effect and Leonie set the bottle down, pushed up Lotte's sleeve, and twisted her limp arm to show them the double-thunderbolt tattoo of the SS.

Tedi whispered, "Impossible."

"Tell me, what is impossible anymore?" Zorah muttered as she pulled the pillow out from under Lotte's head and placed it over the wet compress covering her face. Zorah fixed her eyes on Shayndel, who met her gaze and nodded. Leonie and Tedi stepped closer, tight-lipped, and watched as Zorah pressed the pillow down and held it with all of her strength. Lotte's body reacted instantly and with astonishing force, rising an inch off the cot. The others added their hands and weight to the job as spasms rattled the bed.

Leonie imagined Lucas's face under her hands. Tedi throttled the men who had raped her. Zorah killed the neighbor who betrayed Jacob's mother. Shayndel felt the muscles in her arms shaking with exertion, avenging Wolfe, Malka, Noah, her mother and father, Shmuley, and far too many others.

Finally, Leonie, panting with effort and emotion, slid her hand under the pillow in search of a pulse. "We can stop," she whispered.

They stood up, avoiding one another's eyes as they arranged the body on its side and tied it in place. Tedi fussed with the blanket, trying to make it look as if Lotte were merely sleeping. "That's enough," said Shayndel. "No one is going to worry about why we're leaving her here."

The barrack door opened a few minutes later and the order was whispered: "Now."

Shayndel, Tedi, Leonie, and Zorah went from bed to bed, waking each girl as gently as they could, leaning down to whisper, "Wake up, shhhh. Don't be afraid. We are leaving, shhh. Tonight we escape from this place. Get dressed, hurry. Don't worry, but be quick. We are going with you, too. Bring nothing. Hurry."

The urgency and excitement in their voices turned everyone out of bed and the girls were on their feet before their eyes adjusted to the dimness. They bumped into the edges of beds as they dressed, while Shayndel walked up and down the center of the barrack, putting her finger to her lips and giving a thumbs-up. Zorah helped one woman hunt for her shoes. Leonie buttoned dresses.

Esther was the first one ready, waiting beside her cot, where the blanket had been neatly tucked in. She carried nothing in her hands, as she had been ordered. But she wore the heavy fur coat she had brought from Poland, a pair of silver candlesticks poking out of its bulging pockets. She had her hand on top of Jacob's head and kept his face turned toward the door.

No one looked at Lotte.

As soon as they were dressed, the women began jamming their belongings into sacks and suitcases.

"No, no," Tedi whispered to one girl stuffing a pillowcase with clothes. "We cannot bring anything with us."

Leonie tried to reason with another busy filling a bulky valise. "We are going to be running in the dark. Carrying this will be dangerous."

When Shayndel saw that no one was paying any attention to the order, she tried pulling things out of people's hands until one woman clasped a photograph album to her chest and said, "If I cannot take my family with me, I will stay here."

"I'm sorry," Shayndel said, and went to retrieve her rucksack, with her pictures inside.

The flutter of packing and preparation came to a halt as a loud, piercing scream rose from somewhere in the near distance.

No one moved. A minute passed and then another, but there was no alarm, no sound of boots on the ground, no orders shouted in English. Someone in the barrack started weeping softly but she was shushed from every corner.

Shayndel could barely breathe. She kept her eye on the wristwatch for four long minutes, until the door opened.

A silhouette of a man with a gun over his shoulder appeared. "Hurry up, children," said a familiar voice. "Come, my little ones," Goldberg said in Yiddish.

Shayndel was the first one outside, with Zorah, Esther, and Jacob right behind her. Leonie stopped at the foot of Lotte's cot, but Tedi put a hand on her shoulder. "It's over," she said, and gently guided her out the door.

The women found themselves surrounded by Palmachniks dressed in dark clothes and black caps. They carried guns, waved for them to follow, and started at a fast trot toward the back of the camp; their barrack was closest to the front, which meant they had the farthest to run.

The commandos shepherded them through the camp, avoiding the glare of the lights by zigzagging from one shadow to the next, around barracks and latrines. Crossing the parade ground, Zorah spotted four Palmach fighters dragging the two burly Poles she had talked to in the clinic—now gagged and bound at the wrists—in the opposite direction from everyone else. As she turned to watch them shoved through the back door of Delousing and out of her story forever, someone grabbed her arm and pulled her forward toward the back side of the dining hall. Esther and Jacob and the rest of the girls in their barrack pressed themselves flat against the wooden wall and listened to the sounds of footsteps moving into the distance, and then . . . nothing.

Zorah began to worry. They were certainly the last group to be released; perhaps they had been forgotten. Or maybe they were being used as decoys, to be discovered and sacrificed as a diversion so that the others could get away. It took Jacob three tugs on her sleeve before he got her attention and pointed to the wall where he had found "Esther" among the names and dates scratched into the wooden clapboard. Zorah touched his hair and thought, He will be all right. No matter what happens tonight, he must be all right.

A minute later, a man's head appeared around the corner of the building and they were on the move again. In single file, they made for a narrow gash that had been cut in the promenade fence. Zorah thought the women were amazingly fast considering what they were carrying. She followed Esther through the jagged hole, scratching her hands on the barbwire as she held it away from the fur coat.

When Zorah stepped into the corridor that had separated the men's and women's barracks, the fences, which were at least twenty feet apart, seemed to close in around her. She froze, confused and trapped, staring as the others ran toward the northern fence. They leaned into the effort, kicking their heels like athletes, racing toward an exit that she could not see. Some of the overhead lights had been extinguished, so that when people reached the shadows, it appeared that they vanished into the air.

The image overwhelmed Zorah with the need to join them on the other side—whatever that might mean. She made a dash for it, tearing past Jacob and Esther, weaving to avoid suitcases, brushing against Palmach gun barrels, flying with strength and speed she had never felt before. Running away.

She nearly laughed when she reached the opening in the fence, wide enough for a truck. She didn't stop running once she got through, savoring her momentum and the air on her face. She ran past a group of men, ignoring their hoarse whispers to "Stop. Stop!"

She would have run until daylight, but the thought of Esther and Jacob slowed her. They would be frantic if she disappeared, so she looped around and trotted back. Esther rushed into her arms. Jacob hugged her around the waist.

Once Shayndel saw Zorah, she knew that everyone in her barrack was safely out and her official duties were over. Still, she could not help but take stock of the situation, as though she were still responsible. She counted eighty refugees, including twenty women with children, standing in the dark in the middle of a chilly field. There were at least seventy Palmach rescuers as well, smoking and muttering among themselves.

Off to the east, she heard the faint whine of an engine and caught sight of a ragged line of people moving toward the road. There was another group, too—no more than ten—wandering due north. I hope these people know what they are doing, she thought, as time passed without a word of reassurance or a hint of where her group was headed.

Tedi stood beside Shayndel, shifting her weight from one foot to the other. She felt the muscles in her legs tense up, as though she were about to skate down a frozen canal. She leaned forward into a crouch, grabbed her thighs, and waited for the starting gun, for someone to give the order so she could go. She swayed side to side, faster and faster, mouthing the words, *ready, set, go.*

Shayndel saw her rocking and noticed Leonie shivering. She walked over to the Palmachniks. "Why aren't we going?"

A husky man glared and put a finger to his lips but one of the others leaned close and said, "One of our guys is still inside to make sure we won't be followed."

Shayndel nodded and returned to her friends, who were looking up toward the mountains, where a signal fire had been lit. She wondered how far away the bonfire was, and if that was where they were headed, and whether it wasn't a tip-off to the British. Her jaw ached with tension. If we don't go soon, I'm going to start walking and the hell with them all, she thought as her hand flew up to her shoulder, searching for the strap of her long-lost gun.

"Look," someone whispered. All heads turned as a man ran out of the camp. The Palmachniks immediately shouldered their packs and guns, fanned out among the escapees, and began directing them east toward the road and the mountains.

Tedi dashed over to one of the men in front and asked, "Where are we going?"

"Kibbutz Yagur," he said. "By the time we reach the road, the trucks should be there to pick us up."

It was a rough slog through the fields. Recently plowed, they were deeply rutted and surprisingly wet, and the children struggled in the furrows. People carrying heavy loads lost their balance and fell to their knees.

Leonie was having a hard time keeping her shoes on. After the mud sucked one of them off completely, she crouched down to search for it, but a Palmachnik grabbed her arm. "My shoe," she explained, but he pulled her to her feet and she had no choice but to limp after him. When the other shoe disappeared, she continued in her socks, which quickly became so wet and heavy, she peeled them off and walked barefoot.

By the time she reached the road, Leonie was in tears.

"Where were you?" Shayndel asked.

"I lost my shoes," she said, looking at her cold, aching feet. "I'm sorry."

"Don't apologize," Shayndel said. "We'll find you some others."

"Leave it to me," Tedi said, and began walking up and down the line, asking if anyone had an extra pair of shoes, filling her nose with the expectant smell of freshly turned earth, while keeping an eye out for Zorah, Esther, and Jacob.

They were still making their way through the field. Something about being out in the open had frightened Jacob badly. Esther and Zorah could only carry him for a few paces at a time, and they fell so far behind that a man was sent back to retrieve them.

"Give him to me," he said, swinging the boy over his head and onto his shoulders as though he were no heavier than a doll.

Esther put her hand on Jacob's leg and scrambled alongside. Zorah smiled at how much Jacob's mount looked like a gorilla, with his bandy legs and flatfooted gait. The little boy struggled and squirmed at first, but finally settled down and rested his chin on top of the man's head, wrapping his arms around the sides of his neck. In the darkness, they looked like a father and son on their way home from an afternoon in the park.

Will Jacob remember this? Zorah wondered. Will he someday make his grandchildren yawn with boredom as he repeats the story of how a soldier carried him away from captivity in Atlit? Zorah remembered how her mother used to carry her little brother on her hip when he was a baby, but she had no memory of being carried herself.

Zorah slipped her arm through Esther's as they approached the road, where Tedi embraced them as though they had been lost for months. When she noticed Jacob's sandals flopping against the Palmachnik's chest, she asked, "Does he have another pair of shoes? Leonie is barefoot. Those might fit her."

"Not for him," Esther whispered, "but wait." She plunged her hands into the seemingly bottomless pockets of her coat and pulled out a pair of pumps with ankle straps. "They're red," she apologized.

"I'm sure that won't be a problem." Tedi grinned and hurried back to where Leonie was sitting in the dirt, cradling her battered feet in her hands. Tedi got down on one knee and held out the shoes as though she were presenting them to a princess in a fairy tale. And, just as in a fairy tale, they fit.

Tedi tried to get Shayndel to come celebrate the miracle of the shoes, but she would not move away from her spot near the ranking Palmachniks, who were planning their next steps.

"Why isn't Sergey here?" someone asked.

"He said he wasn't going to wait for the trucks. He took a bunch straight up the mountain."

"That's crazy."

"Yeah, well, you know Sergey: ants in the pants."

"We can't pull that kind of stunt with all these kids here. We have to wait for the trucks to arrive."

"When the hell will that be, Yitzhak?"

"Shouldn't be too much longer now," said Yitzhak—who had been the last man out of Atlit.

"We waited for so long, some of us weren't sure we'd see you again tonight," someone teased.

"The inside team did a good job," he said, reaching for the cigarette that was being passed around. "But it was weird. The place was lit up like Tel Aviv on a Saturday night, but quiet as a cemetery. Not a soul in sight. The Brits were all in their beds, sound asleep. I could hear them snoring, so help me.

"Then, just as I was about to leave, I found myself face-to-face with a ginger-haired little guy in a British officer's uniform.

I was close enough to punch him, which I was about to do. But he blinked and walked past me, like I wasn't there. I didn't recognize him, but he had to be one of our guys."

"Must have been."

"What do we hear from the others?" Yitzhak asked. "Are you in touch with the walkie-talkie?"

"Worthless piece of shit," said one of the men, pointing at the boxy pack beside him. "I got nothing but static all night, and the damn thing weighs as much as my grandmother."

"That's no joke," someone snickered. "I've seen your grandmother."

The sound of engines somewhere in the dark silenced all conversation until two trucks and a small bus pulled up with their headlights switched off. The Palmachniks started helping people onto them almost before they came to a stop. Some of the men tried to talk the refugees out of bringing their belongings any further. "There is no room, sweetheart," someone said to a woman with a bulging satchel. But when he tried to pull the bag out of her hand, she slapped his face with enough force to be heard up and down the line.

"Enough," said Yitzhak, tossing the valise into the truck. "It's all they have, poor creatures."

Shayndel winced at hearing herself called a "creature" and ignored the hands extended to help her climb into the first truck, which she had chosen after seeing that the men in charge were crowding into the cab. Leonie, Tedi, Esther, and Zorah pushed their way up beside Shayndel and settled together on the floor, with Jacob squeezed among them.

The convoy crept along slowly until they turned left, away from Atlit and east into the mountains. After another hard turn that threw everyone off balance, the headlights came on, illuminating a narrow gravel road, and the driver put his foot down on the accelerator.

As they gained speed, the girls' hair flew up so that they almost looked like they were underwater. Zorah threw her head back and closed her eyes. Leonie held her hand out over the side, fondling the breeze. Shayndel had the urge to start singing.

As the truck started to climb the side of the mountain, Tedi inhaled the tang of pine and the mulch of fallen leaves and a dozen other scents: tree sap and resin, pollen from six kinds of dusty grasses going to seed. The soldiers up front added dark notes of leather, tobacco, onion, whiskey, sweat, and gunpowder. It was a wild mixture, the aroma of escape. She caught Leonie's eye and grinned. "It smells like heaven out here."

The roads became rougher and in the back of the truck, the refugees banged into one another and tried not to cry out. They slowed to a crawl as the incline grew steeper and the convoy negotiated one hairpin turn after another.

"It would be faster to walk," someone muttered as the initial giddiness began to subside. When the truck lurched to a sudden halt Shayndel jumped up and saw that they had come to a fork in the road.

The driver and two soldiers hurried out of the cab and immediately started arguing.

"Turn right," said Yitzhak, who was holding a flashlight.

"I don't think so," said the driver.

"What do you know?"

"More than you."

"Yes, but I'm in charge."

When they started out again, the driver turned right so sharply that everyone in back fell over.

They inched along what seemed like a footpath where overhanging branches raked the tops of their heads. Esther held Jacob's face to her chest to protect his eyes. After a few more minutes, the driver hit the brakes again. The other men in the cab swore at him and Yitzhak shouted, "Back up."

"Too dark," said the driver. "Too steep."

By now, men from the two other vehicles had arrived and joined the argument. The walkie-talkie crackled to life, but no amount of fiddling with the dials brought in a signal. Yitzhak finally switched off the machine. "Never mind that. I know where we are," he said. "Beit Oren is a couple of kilometers up this hill. It's a climb, but we're close enough to make it. Pass the word: we're walking."

"I hope you know what you're doing," muttered the driver.

There were no smiles as the refugees were helped from the trucks, but everyone felt the urgency of the situation and within minutes, all 150 of them—refugees and Palmach—were on their way.

As they headed into the forest, the darkness thickened, both shielding and thwarting them. A narrow path led through uneven, rocky ground that seemed to reach up and trip someone every few moments. No one spoke, but the sounds of panting and gasping grew louder as they climbed.

Shayndel stayed near the front of the line, close to Yitzhak and his flashlight. Leonie and Tedi scrambled to keep up with her, but Leonie's feet were on fire as the shoes rubbed through the blisters on her bruised heels and swollen toes. Tedi's lungs ached.

Zorah hated being separated from Shayndel, but she would

not leave Jacob and Esther, who lagged behind. Esther's fur coat, now heavy with moisture and mud, slowed her down, and Jacob stumbled beside her, dazed by exhaustion.

With the loud crack of a gun, the rescue turned into a hunt. The Palmachniks pushed everyone to the ground as another shot echoed through the trees over their heads.

No one moved or wept or breathed a word as they waited, pressed against the forest floor. The quiet that followed the second blast continued long enough so that Yitzhak picked up his head and gestured for a couple of his men to crawl forward and join him. "It's going to be daylight soon," he whispered. "I want you to go up ahead and see what kind of defense the Brits have mounted around Beit Oren. The order is to get these people to safety, not to fight. If there are too many of them, we may have to wait here until tomorrow night."

God forbid, thought Shayndel.

The two men ran out of sight and Yitzhak sent word back down the line: keep still.

People found places to sit and huddled together for warmth. Some rested their foreheads on their knees. Jacob slept with his head on Esther's lap, his legs draped over Zorah's. Leonie and Tedi looked up nervously as the night sky showed the first dim traces of morning. Shayndel crouched, eyes wide, listening for another gunshot.

It wasn't long before two dark silhouettes scrambled into view. "The western slope is damn near empty," Shayndel heard one of them say. "We have to stay as far from the road as possible, but we can enter safely on the far side of the kibbutz."

Kibbutz. The word echoed in her head, suddenly unfamiliar and unlike an ordinary noun like "pencil" or "soup." More like "justice," or even "unicorn." Not so much a thing you could put a hand on; a kind of fairy tale or dream—a nice idea, a noble goal, perhaps. Not a real place like the one these men were talking about—just out of view.

Yitzhak got to his feet. His men lifted children onto their shoulders, picked up suitcases, and set out at a brisk clip. Everyone felt the pressure of the coming dawn and walked quickly. Tedi caught the cold steel smell of anxiety around her. Zorah held branches back for those with bundles and babies in their arms. Leonie bit her lips as she hobbled on the outer edges of her feet. Shayndel shivered for the first time all night, suddenly aware of how cold she was.

"Look," someone whispered. A yellow glow, haloed in mist, blooming in the darkness, not sixty yards away.

Shayndel tried to remind herself that this was no miracle, merely the energy pulsing through wires. Just electricity, no different from the power that had lit her days and nights in Atlit. And yet, these wires and bulbs made her ache with the need to shout and laugh out loud and sing praises and simply say the word: kibbutz.

It was only a few dozen yards between the edge of the forest and the settlement fence, where people were waiting, holding lanterns aloft. The escapees raced across the clearing and were met with bear hugs and blankets. Leonie fell to her knees, weeping with relief. Esther covered a stranger's face with kisses. Tedi lifted Jacob and swung him around. Zorah panted and gasped, suddenly starved for air after a night of holding her breath.

The kibbutzniks and the Palmach rescuers cut the celebration short and led their guests over a dim gravel pathway and into a brightly lit dining hall. Mugs of hot tea were pressed into their hands. "Shalom and welcome," they were told, again and again. "Shalom and welcome."

Leonie sat down beside Tedi and asked, "Have you seen Shayndel?"

"The last I saw her, she was running through the fence. She must be here somewhere or maybe she's already talking to the kibbutz president; you know, giving him the full report and telling him what to do," Tedi said. "Now have some tea. You look frozen."

Leonie kept an eye on the door. After she drained her cup, she slipped outside and found her way back down to where they had entered the kibbutz. A man with a gun was on patrol near the fence, which showed no evidence of having been the scene of their arrival a few minutes ago.

She stepped off the path into a stand of tall pines, feeling that she had somehow found her way back in time, into a darker, chillier hour of the night.

"Shayndel?" she called softly. "Shayndel? Where are you? It's me."

Shayndel was barely twenty feet away from her, her forehead pressed against the trunk of a young tree, mourning her brother.

Noah had been in love with the idea of the kibbutz. He would stretch his arms over the backs of the chairs on either side of him—he had such long arms—and provoke silly arguments with his friends, just to prolong the conversation about what kibbutz life would be like. "You can pluck all the Hebrew-speaking chickens you want," he said. "I'm going to be an architect and create a beautiful kibbutz, not merely a utilitarian one."

He laughed when they called him bourgeois. "We're going to need buildings, right? And I see no reason why we shouldn't build cottages and classrooms and, hell, even chicken coops that will be the envy of the rest of the world."

Why not? thought Shayndel. But why aren't you here?

Leonie followed the sound of muffled weeping and put her hand on Shayndel's shoulder. "*Chérie,*" she said. "What's wrong?"

"I was never the brave one," Shayndel whispered. "In the forest, comrades were the heroes. I was a terrible shot, and after they died I was worthless. And my brother," Shayndel wailed. "My brother should be here." Leonie turned her around and held her tight. "We were supposed to be here together," Shayndel cried. "It was Noah's dream. I tagged along after him, and he was the best, the most wonderful . . ."

"You never told me about a brother," said Leonie, stroking her hair.

"He was so good, so smart. I'm sure you would have liked him," Shayndel said.

"I would have loved him," said Leonie. "How could I not?"

The light filtered through the pine needles around them. The dew drenched their feet. Shayndel pulled away gently and wiped the tears from her cheeks. "The worst thing is," she started, and turned to avoid Leonie's eyes. "I don't even know how to say this, but we lived for this, Noah and me. We were so sure we would be happy here, but now all I feel is afraid. He would have been ashamed of me, but the truth is, I have never been so afraid in my whole life."

"What are you afraid of?" Leonie asked.

"I'm not sure," said Shayndel, her eyes brimming again. "And that frightens me, too."

Leonie nodded. "Maybe you are just afraid of what is going to happen next."

"What do you think is going to happen?"

"That's just it. I don't know. No one knows. Even you, who

dreamed about life on a kibbutz in the land of Israel, even you can't know how it will turn out. Everything that has happened to you, to me, to everyone who came with us . . . it all proves that nothing is certain. That it's all a blank page."

"But surely all of our work will . . ." Shayndel began.

"Yes?" Leonie said.

"No, you're right," Shayndel said. "I don't know. I don't know anything."

"Well, I know that you are smart enough and brave enough to face whatever will happen, here or anywhere. That may be the only thing I am sure of." Leonie took Shayndel's face between her hands and kissed her on the right cheek and then on the left. "The sun is coming up. Let's go see."

"What are we going to see?"

"What happens next."

Beit Oren

Shayndel was grateful for the warm cup between her hands. In many ways, the kibbutz dining hall looked like the mess hall in Atlit, a bit smaller, perhaps, but the open-beamed ceiling was the same, as were the sticky tabletops, the loud scraping of chairs over bare floor. But the differences touched her deeply: these pine panels had been fitted, tongue in groove, and stained the color of honey. There were posters on the walls, too, displays of earnest pioneers wearing shorts and caps, like the ones that used to hang in her Zionist summer camp. She could almost hear the echoes of songs she had sung there, songs she imagined were sung in this room as well.

A girl with thick braids under a blue kerchief brought over a woolen shawl and wrapped it around Shayndel's shoulders. "My name is Nina," she said. "Welcome to Beit Oren. Welcome to Eretz Yisrael. Are you as cold as you look?"

"Cold and dirty. Is there somewhere to take a bath?"

The girl patted Shayndel on the back. "I don't think you have time for that," she said as she walked away.

"What did she mean by that?" Leonie asked. "Aren't we staying here tonight?"

Shayndel had no answer for her; she was as much in the dark as everyone else. She waved at Tedi as she walked in wearing a gingham blouse and a pair of too-big trousers tied around the waist with red ribbon—clothes that made her look like a leggy twelve-year-old.

Shayndel smiled at the transformation. "You fit right in."

"I think that's the plan," said Tedi. "The girl who gave me these clothes told me to go lend a hand in the kitchen, but when I went in there, they chased me out and told me to rest."

"Where is Zorah?" asked Leonie.

"She went with Esther and Jacob. I think they took all the kids to see the nurse. Jacob was too tired even to eat, poor thing. Not me. Pass the bread and whatever else is down there."

Three Palmachniks carrying rifles arrived; Shayndel recognized the man with the walkie-talkie, who raised his hands and announced, "Friends, comrades. The British are sending troops here and it has been determined that you will be safer at Kibbutz Yagur. It is not far and there are buses at the ready. We will be leaving in a few minutes, so gather your belongings and come to the front gate. Quickly, now."

Despite some grumbling, nearly all of the Atlit arrivals got to their feet, pocketing pieces of fruit. But Leonie crossed her arms and sat back in her chair. "I am not going anywhere else today."

"Don't be ridiculous," Shayndel said. "It's a matter of safety."

"I will take my chances here, *chérie*. I cannot walk another step." She took off her shoes and showed them her swollen, bloody feet.

"We must find you a doctor," Tedi exclaimed.

"All I need is soap, antiseptic, and some rest. But unless someone picks me up and carries me, I am not moving." She turned to Shayndel and said, "Don't worry about me. I know that you want to go. Please. You must."

Shayndel watched the others file out the door, and part of her longed to follow them. But one look at Tedi and Leonie decided it. "I'm staying," she said.

Zorah walked in, still wearing her own torn and filthy clothes. Her face was white with fatigue.

Leonie poured her a cup of tea, and Tedi buttered a slice of bread for her.

"Do you know they actually tried to wake up the children to take them God knows where?" Zorah said, between sips. "I told them that Jacob was not going anywhere; he was so tired, he was shuddering in his sleep. Esther was beside herself.

"How much can you expect of these children? The other mothers agreed with me," said Zorah. "We made a little mutiny, and none of them are leaving either."

"You were right to insist that they stay here," said Leonie. "I refused to go further, too."

"I'm staying as well," said Tedi.

"Me, too," Shayndel added.

Zorah bowed her head. The other three exchanged worried glances.

"Zorah?" said Leonie.

"I'm just tired," she whispered, overwhelmed by their concern for her, and by her feelings for them. "All of you must come to my barrack—though they don't call them barracks here; they're 'houses.' There is a little shower with hot water in the room. They have fresh clothes for us, too, though I'm not sure we're all going to turn out as well as Tedi."

Zorah led them to a good-sized room with six narrow beds. It was simply furnished but nothing like a barrack, with rugs on the floor and curtains at the windows, bureaus and night tables. Photographs of young people squinting into the sun were all over the walls.

Leonie insisted that Shayndel be the first to bathe in the little tin stall. "We command our commander to obey." Shayndel meant to hurry so the others could take their turns, but the lilac-scented soap and a bottle of real shampoo slowed her down. She lathered her hair twice, and nearly nodded off as the water washed the bubbles down the drain. It took all of her willpower to turn off the faucet.

Leonie was next. She sank down to the tile floor and ministered to her throbbing feet. The soap stung at first, but the warm water was soothing. She tilted her chin up and let it rain over her closed eyes and parted lips, feeling like she was a thousand miles away from Atlit, a million miles from Paris, and safe.

Zorah pulled her clothes off in a rush and started by washing her hair, thinking she would save a few moments by scrubbing her body while the shampoo rinsed off. But the soap got into her eyes and no amount of rubbing would get it out. Then the hot water ran out and suddenly her tears changed from irritation into grief. She leaned against the wall and sank slowly into a crouch, her arms folded over her head, as the icy stream stripped away the last of her defenses. Motherless, brotherless, and weary to the bone, she wept for the losses she had counted and remembered and for numberless, nameless injuries registered in her flesh.

Tedi reached in and turned off the tap. "Come," she said, wrapping Zorah in a towel and rubbing her arms and legs until she was warm as well as dry. "Cry as much as you like," she soothed, as she toweled off Zorah's hair, combed out the knots, and helped her into a soft flannel nightgown. Zorah submitted meekly, even taking Tedi's hand as she led her to a cot near Shayndel and Leonie, who were already fast asleep.

The four girls slept, undisturbed by the light or the quiet comings and goings of the kibbutz girls. They did not hear the roar and squeal of cars and trucks outside, or the shouts that followed. They woke up only when Nina, the girl with the braids, came to tell them that the British were at the gates, demanding that they surrender the escaped prisoners.

"You can stay inside if you like," she said. "If you do come outside, you must look and act like the rest of us. So if your Hebrew isn't good, keep your mouth shut and pretend to understand. Be strong."

Zorah went looking for Esther and Jacob, but Shayndel, Leonie, and Tedi followed the flow of kibbutzniks headed for the entrance to Kibbutz Beit Oren. The barbwire fence and the tall wire gate were all too familiar, but the evidence of everyday life—flower beds, bicycles, clotheslines—made it clear that this was not a prison but a home.

Shayndel took the lead, snaking her way right up to the fence beside Nina, where they could see what was going on. Four British military trucks were parked across from the entrance and the road bristled with soldiers in battle gear.

Inside the kibbutz, men concealed weapons under their

jackets. "I don't know why we're all standing around here," complained one of the men as he stared through the fence, taking stock of the enemy. "There should be people around the whole perimeter. We don't know where the Brits will try to break through."

The tension thickened as an official-looking staff car with its windows rolled tight arrived, followed by two open vans that added dozens of British Military Police to the regular army force already there. Inside the kibbutz, people stopped talking and stared. Those with guns glanced at one another. Shayndel crossed her arms to keep from reaching for her phantom rifle.

Nearly everyone seemed spellbound by the arrival of the police. But a small group of men went right on chatting and smoking, barely glancing at the growing threat a few dozen yards away. There were five of them, standing under a canopy of young pine trees on a knoll that gave them a clear view of the gate. Shayndel didn't recognize any of them from last night's escape. She guessed they were Palmach, but didn't want to break the silence to ask.

When the two English officers got out of the car and started toward the kibbutz, the men finished their cigarettes and headed down to meet them.

Shayndel was close enough to hear a little of their conversation. Her English was not good, but the British were clearly making demands. She made out the words "surrender" and something about the death of a constable.

Unlike the Englishmen, who stood at attention, the Palmachniks listened with their arms crossed or on their hips. They stepped back to confer briefly and a chuckle rose from their huddle. Four of them ambled back to their perch on the hill while one man delivered a short message to the Englishmen.

"What did he say?" Shayndel asked Nina.

"I couldn't hear, but I suspect he told the limeys to go screw themselves."

"I thought I heard one of them say something about a death. We heard shots last night," Shayndel said.

"It was just before you got here. One of their trucks pulled up in the dark and a gun went off, so our guys thought it was the beginning of a siege and fired. One of theirs died. None of ours, thank God."

The British soldiers had started arranging themselves in a row, their rifles across their chests, facing the kibbutz. They were so close that Shayndel could see their expressions clearly. Some of them scowled, others winced, but a few looked through the fence, curious about the people inside.

Tedi started to wave. "Yoo-hoo!" she called and blew a kiss.

Shayndel pulled her arm down. "What are you doing?"

"No, that's a good idea," said Nina, who had joined them. "The English may be pigs, but they usually follow the rules of the game, and shooting women—especially pretty ones—is decidedly against the rules. Come on," she said to Leonie. "You wave, too."

A few more girls joined in and when they saw some of the soldiers blush and look away, they cheered and laughed, lightening the mood on both sides.

Tedi stopped waving and touched the barbwire in front of her. She turned to Leonie and said, "Do you remember that woman in Atlit who screamed and went mad when she saw the fence? This stuff is so frightening, but here it is here for our protection. To keep us safe, like thorns on a rose."

"Thorns on a rose?" Leonie said. "I did not know you were a poet."

"Not me, I'm the down-to-earth one. My sister is the one who . . ." Tedi stopped. It was the first time she had invoked Rachel's memory out loud.

Leonie moved Tedi's finger away from the spike, and said, "You certainly have the nose of a poet."

"What do you mean by that?" Tedi bristled, but Leonie was giggling and pointing at her nose. "What does a joke smell like?" she asked.

Tedi couldn't help but smile. "It's not the joke so much as the joker, and then it depends whether it's dirty."

Leonie gasped. "Ooh, you're so naughty."

Tedi started laughing, too.

"Stop it," Shayndel said, afraid that the soldiers would think they were being mocked. She pushed them away from the fence, but as soon as Tedi's and Leonie's eyes met, they started again, covering their mouths to keep from howling.

"Barking mad, aren't they?" Nina smiled as they staggered away to collect themselves. She pointed at the soldiers who were grinning in their direction. "It's infectious."

Shayndel shrugged, too nervous to laugh.

"So what do you think of Beit Oren?" Nina asked.

"Beautiful," Shayndel said, gazing over the road at the valley of evergreens and the pale blue sky. "I've never been so high in the mountains before."

"We like to call it Little Switzerland," said Nina. "However, I must warn you that yodeling is strictly forbidden."

"I'll remember that," said Shayndel. She supposed there must be a reason for even a silly rule like that.

"Good heavens, I'm joking!" Nina poked her in the arm.

"Your friends haven't lost their sense of humor. You shouldn't either."

Shayndel blushed and stepped away to greet Zorah, Jacob, and Esther. Jacob held his mother's hand, pulling her forward and taking in the scene around him, bright-eyed and smiling. When he caught sight of a group of boys, he let go and ran toward them.

"Jacob looks wonderful," said Shayndel.

He ran back to them and demanded, "How do you say in Hebrew the place we were in? What do you call Atlit? What is it?"

Shayndel almost blurted the word for "prison," but thought better of it. "Tell them it was a welcome center for new immigrants."

"Okay," he said in English, showing off his new favorite word.

By late morning, the British soldiers and police officers were sweating in the sun. The kibbutzniks glared at them and muttered about what ought to be done next. Shayndel wondered why they hadn't at least moved the children out of the line of fire.

As the hours passed and the standoff continued, a sense of dread crept through the crowd. Even the Palmach leaders—now sitting on camp chairs on their hill—started to look uneasy. It felt like the quiet before a storm.

But instead of a storm, they heard someone singing "Don't Sit Under the Apple Tree with Anyone Else but Me." All heads turned as a teenage boy in a dusty school uniform appeared—seemingly out of thin air. "Hello, comrades!" he called.

The Palmachniks surrounded him. "Where the hell did you come from?"

"Haifa. The news about the siege of Beit Oren is all over town," he said. "When I heard what was going on, I ditched school and got a ride on a truck headed south. I jumped off, climbed up the hill, and slipped through the fence near the barns. But where are all the others? I figured there would be a big crowd by now. The schools are going to be empty, and the unions are sending busloads.

"Soon, there'll be so many of us here that those assholes won't be able to tell who's a refugee, who's a kibbutznik, and who's from town."

Shayndel watched the way his message erased the tension that had darkened their faces just a few moments before and wondered if the British had noticed the sudden rash of smiles and whispers of anticipation.

Within the half hour, thirty or forty students—girls as well as boys—emerged from within the kibbutz and joined the ranks lining the fence. Some arrived by foot, hiking the mountain, but most of them had crammed into cars and trucks that dropped them off in the woods nearby.

A factory crew in coveralls turned up and strolled through the compound as though they were on a coffee break, slapping kibbutzniks on the back and shouting greetings as even more of their comrades arrived from the city. Each new group was met with a louder and bolder welcome. When a shift of hospital nurses in white uniforms materialized like a mirage, they were met with a burst of applause.

At one o'clock, Shayndel counted at least five hundred

demonstrators, and more kept coming. The young men yelled through the fence at the soldiers and made rude hand gestures, daring them to try something. A group of students played soccer with the kibbutz children. Some of the men carried a table into the shade, where they played cards, passed a bottle, and argued.

"They won't do anything to us now," said a man wearing greasy overalls.

"Don't kid yourself. They're capable of anything," said a fellow who had taken off his jacket and tie and rolled up his sleeves. He shuffled the cards and said, "Look what they've done to our people, to these very immigrants—the tear gas and beatings on boats within sight of Eretz Yisrael. And then locking them up in a concentration camp? Don't talk to me about the British."

"Still, they don't want an incident here. There are too many civilians, too many women and children."

"You give them too much credit."

"Not at all. This is politics, pure and simple. They don't want to antagonize the Americans. They need the Yanks to help them rebuild London."

Tedi and Leonie could not follow the rapid-fire Hebrew, but Shayndel and Zorah listened intently.

"What do you think?" Zorah asked.

"I'm not sure," said Shayndel. "But if there was going to be a battle, I think it would have happened hours ago."

"I still think we should take the children inside," said Zorah.

Shayndel was about to agree with her when a busload of students and workers pulled up right to the front gate, singing "The Internationale" at the top of their lungs. They tumbled out of the door and arranged themselves in a line facing the English soldiers in a spectacular display of arrogance and courage.

"For now," Shayndel said, "I think we are safe."

The showdown ended quietly and without fanfare in the middle of the afternoon. Soldiers climbed back into their trucks and vans and pulled away, with the officers in their car right behind them. Their departure was met with a roar of catcalls and insults so loud, a flock of startled birds added their own screech of "good riddance" as they drove off.

As soon as the last vehicle disappeared around the bend, the gates were pushed open, and everyone rushed out into the dusty clearing, stamping their feet to reclaim the ground, cheering, "Victory!" Shouting, "The Jewish people live!"

The men shook each other's hands, hugged, slapped each other on the back and pinched each other's cheeks. The girls kissed and laughed. Hats were thrown into the air. It was D-day, New Year's Eve, and the coming of the Messiah.

Someone started to sing, "A new day is dawning, come brothers, join the circle." Raucous, almost tuneless, the song swept everyone into a circle and no one was permitted to stand apart. Tedi and Leonie dragged Zorah into the giddy vortex, and Jacob pulled Esther, who danced her first hora, laughing and crying and kicking as high as anyone.

Shayndel threw her head back and looked up at the sky as she was carried along by strong arms on either side. Her heart beat time in Hebrew, I am *here*. I am *here*.

They danced until they were dizzy and sang until their throats hurt, and they did not stop until the Palmachniks started waving and pointing toward the gate, where a line of empty trucks and buses was pulling up.

"Time to go back," they called, "before it gets dark."

Some of the students walked past the vehicles, their arms around each other's shoulders. "We'll hike it," they cried, drunk with success and unwilling to let go of the moment. Others crammed into the vehicles, eager to return home and brag about how they had faced down the British Empire. From the windows they shouted, "Shalom, good luck, *B'hatzlacha*."

Among the last people waving them off were the twenty refugees from Atlit who had stayed in Beit Oren. The mothers with little ones lifted their toddlers high and shouted their thanks. "*Todah rabah,*" they cried. Zorah was the loudest of all.

When she caught Tedi watching her, Zorah dropped her hand and said, "You know, *Todah rabah* does not just mean thank you. It means *great* thanks. Big thanks. Many thanks. Thanks of rabbinic proportions and of all-encompassing magnitudes."

Tedi put a hand on her shoulder and said, "Thank you, *professora*."

Shayndel and Leonie decided to explore the kibbutz grounds before dinner. They walked slowly, careful of Leonie's sore feet.

"We're like a couple of old ladies," Leonie said, remembering the story Shayndel used to tell about their lives lived side by side in Palestine.

"I know," said Shayndel, wondering if they would ever stroll the Tel Aviv boulevards together.

A short bleat disturbed their thoughts. "Did you hear that?" Shayndel asked and pointed. "It sounds like it came from over there. Come on." She dropped Leonie's arm and raced ahead.

When Leonie caught up with her, she was inside a pen, scratching a small white goat between the ears.

Leonie said, "I've never seen you look so happy."

"I don't know what it is about goats." Shayndel laughed. "I like them better than dogs. Do you want to come inside and pet her?" Leonie wrinkled her nose. "I'm sure she's very nice, but no."

Shayndel kissed the goat on the nose and latched the gate behind her.

"I do feel much better," Shayndel said shyly, as they started back. "When you found me in the woods this morning, I was exhausted. But today, after what just happened, I have hope again. How can I help but hope among such people? And what about you? Aren't you glad we finally got out of that miserable Atlit?"

"Of course," said Leonie. "But unlike you, I did not grow up thinking of myself as part of this project, this Palestine. I have so much to learn, it's a little—"

"There you are," Tedi cried, running toward them, breathless and beaming. "They've put out a lovely meal for us. And oh, my dear, dear friends, there is ice cream!"

In the dining hall, a tall girl brought over a platter of bread and hard-boiled eggs. "I'm sorry," she said, "but it seems that the salad is gone."

Tedi and Leonie burst out laughing.

"Forgive them," said Shayndel. "Some of us are amused about the local passion for chopped salads morning, noon, and night."

Nina came to their table with a bowl of vanilla ice cream. They each took a spoonful, but passed it along so that Jacob could have the lion's share.

He sniffed it cautiously and asked Esther, "Will I like this?"

"Don't tell me you have never had ice cream before," Tedi gasped.

After one tentative spoonful, he smiled at the five watching women and said, "This is good."

He inhaled the rest while they interrupted one another debating the merits of flavors he had yet to taste: chocolate, strawberry, coffee, caramel.

But after he licked the bowl clean, Jacob declared, "This is my favorite, forever."

They sat in the dining hall long after everyone else had finished eating, until there was no one left but the people mopping the floors. Jacob fell asleep with his head on Esther's lap. Their conversation meandered from ice cream to the beauty of the mountains to the courage of the people who had filled the kibbutz that afternoon. They worried about Leonie's feet, but they said nothing about what might happen tomorrow, and eventually they stopped talking and fell to sighing.

"I can't believe I woke up here this morning," said Tedi. "It feels like a week ago."

"Last week we were in Atlit," said Shayndel.

"That was yesterday," Zorah said. "We were in Atlit yesterday. Last night, in fact."

They stared at each other, shaking their heads in disbelief.

"I wonder if we will ever be together like this again," Tedi said sadly.

"Maybe," said Leonie. "Do you remember Aliza, the nurse in the clinic? She was always telling me what a small country this is. She says that she runs into people from her childhood all the time, even people she hasn't seen in years."

"It's possible," Shayndel said.

"Who knows," said Zorah.

Esther, too tired to sit up any longer, rested her head on the table.

"That's it, my friends," said Shayndel. "Time for bed."

They walked outside to say good night.

Leonie kissed them all, cheek after cheek. When she got to Tedi, she whispered, "What do you smell?"

Tedi held her close and said, "Pine trees and lavender."

Tedi lifted Zorah off the ground in a bear hug.

Esther put her forehead to Shayndel's and said, "Bless you."

Shayndel hugged her and said, "Enough, already. We will see each other in the morning."

Esther led Jacob away, serenaded by a melancholy chorus of "Good night."

Shayndel and Leonie, Tedi and Zorah walked back to their room and dropped into bed like leaves falling from the same tree. Even Zorah slept like a child, soundly and deeply throughout the night. And each of them saw wild and dappled visions in her dreams.

Shayndel floated on a wooden raft in the middle of a lake surrounded by willow trees and birches. She dipped her finger in the sweet water and brought it to her lips.

Zorah soared in a white winter sky, like a hawk, weightless on the wind. Then, suddenly, she was on the ground watching as a great bird flew into the distance.

Tedi sat at a table piled high with fruit that glistened like polished stones, far too beautiful to touch, much less eat. She saw a loaf of brown bread and bowed her head.

Leonie walked into a quiet room with a child-sized bed. Her name was carved on the headboard, and when she lay down, she found it fit her perfectly and fell into a second dream of open windows and sunlight.

Farewell

Shayndel smiled blankly at the handsome young woman who sat down across from her. It took her a few seconds before she recognized the girl in the dark green blouse. "Is that really you?"

Zorah's hair had been smoothed into a chic little bun that revealed a pair of high, round cheekbones. Her eyes, the circles and shadows erased by a good night's sleep, shone like polished onyx. "I look ridiculous, I know," said Zorah, "but this girl pulled me into her room and refused to let me out until she, well, until this." She waved her hands around her head as though she were shooing gnats.

"You look beautiful," said Tedi, as she and Leonie joined them.

"Don't be silly," said Zorah.

"Not at all," Leonie exclaimed. "Did you see yourself in a

mirror? Whoever chose that blouse for you is an artist. From now on, you must wear only that color."

Esther shrieked when she saw Zorah. "I knew it."

As they settled down to eat, Shayndel asked, "Did you sleep well?"

Esther answered, pronouncing the Hebrew words as precisely as she could, "I do not remember so good a sleeping."

"Me as well," Zorah said. "Better than ever."

"Yes," they all agreed and filled their mouths with bread and salad to avoid talking about the rest of the day.

A thin man with powerful forearms stepped into the dining hall waving a newspaper over his head. "Seligman," cried the people at the other tables. "What does it say?"

"Comrades," he announced, "we are on the front page in the *Palestine Post,* so that even the English know what's up. And here, my friends, is what *Ha'Aretz* has to say.

"Two hundred and eight Maapilim Were Freed by Force from Atlit," he read.

Cheers erupted. Seligman—the kibbutz administrator who was rarely seen without his clipboard—pursed his lips and waited until they settled down.

"'Wednesday, close to midnight, the interned refugees at the Atlit camp broke out with the help of forces from the Jewish settlement. One hundred and eighty-two immigrants who went through the horrors of the concentration camps were imprisoned in Atlit; in addition, there were thirty-seven refugees from Iraq and Syria, who had received deportation orders, leading to high tension in the camp.

"'A Christian woman died from suffocation while she was tied up.'"

Zorah glanced over at Leonie, Tedi, and Shayndel, who stared intently at their plates.

"'Toward morning, large police forces surrounded Kibbutz Beit Oren and Kibbutz Yagur. When the news reached Haifa many workers and youth left work and school and rushed to assist the besieged farms. Thousands of people returned to Haifa from the Carmel.'"

"Thousands?" someone shouted. "There were maybe six hundred people here. You can't believe anything you read in the newspapers."

"'A crowd of four thousand people gathered on He'-Halutz Street. Speeches were made emphasizing that the workers of Eretz Yisrael and the Settlement are ready for a long battle with any decree against immigration.

"'All of the factions expressed sorrow at the losses suffered by the police. The British officer Gordon Hill was killed. Twenty-two years old from Avedon, with a master's degree in law from Aberdeen University, he attended an officers' course before joining the police force of the British Mandate.'"

"Gordon?" Tedi whispered to Shayndel. "Was he the young sergeant from Atlit who worked in the commandant's office? The blonde boy who spoke Hebrew?"

"I don't know."

After the kibbutzniks headed off to work, Leonie moved closer to the others and whispered, "They made her death sound like an accident."

"So be it," said Tedi. "No name was given, did you notice? It has already been forgotten."

Zorah shrugged. "I don't know what you are talking about."

Seligman approached their table, rifling through the papers on his clipboard. "Eskenazi, Shayndel?" he asked.

Shayndel raised her hand.

"Do you know someone named Besser?"

"I knew a Shmuley Besser," she said, remembering how he used to hold the camera as though it were made of glass. "But he is dead."

"This is from a Yeheskiel Besser," he said and handed her an envelope.

She took the letter, which had been opened and carelessly refolded. "It's from Shmuley's uncle," she said. "He writes that I am to join him at Kibbutz Alonim. Is that far from here?"

"Not far," Seligman said. "Close to Haifa. I have many friends there. They will be sending someone for you tomorrow."

"What do you know about my friends here?" Shayndel asked.

"Names?"

"Dubinski," Leonie said.

"Dubinski, Leonie. You are going to Kibbutz Dalia."

"That is also near Haifa, isn't it?"

"How did you know that?" Tedi asked, impressed.

"I think that is where Aliza's uncle Ofer lives. I wonder if she had anything to do with this. Is that possible, Monsieur Seligman? I worked in the infirmary with Mrs. Gilad. Nurse Aliza Gilad?"

"I have no idea how these assignments were made."

"What about me?" said Tedi. "Pastore."

"You are going to Kibbutz Negba. That's in the south," he said. "And you should go and pack your things. They're coming for you this afternoon. You may have to stop overnight somewhere; Tel Aviv if you're lucky."

"Negba," Tedi repeated, trying to get used to the sound of her new home.

"Do you have any letters for Weitz?" said Zorah, trying to sound as though it didn't matter.

"You are Weitz, Zorah? No letter." He consulted his list again. "But you are going to Kibbutz Ma'barot. I hope you speak Romanian."

"Why?"

"They're all Romanians down there," he said, and made a circle with his finger beside his ear. "A little crazy, you know?"

"What about Esther Zalinsky? She's my cousin. Also her little boy, Jacob. The name is Zalinsky."

He ran his finger down a list. "Kibbutz Elon."

"Where is that?" Zorah said.

"That's up in the north. Mostly Poles, so your cousin will be fine. You can tell her," he said. "Pastore leaves today but the rest of you have until tomorrow. Enjoy Beit Oren while you can. Good morning."

Zorah turned to Shayndel. "This is a disaster," Zorah said. "Esther is a terrible liar and the minute she opens her mouth they'll know she's a peasant. If she winds up among a bunch of doctrinaire Poles, they'll throw her out. You have to do something. You have to get it changed so I go to the same place."

"I can't do anything about this," Shayndel said.

"Don't be stupid," Zorah said. "Tell them who you are, what you did in the war. They'll all shit in their pants and do whatever you ask."

"I don't think so," Shayndel objected. "The whole idea of the kibbutz is that everyone is treated the same."

"That is not the way the world works," Zorah said. "Not even in a kibbutz, my Zionist friend. And listen to me, Shayndel, I will not permit those two to suffer anymore. You can fix this, I know it. And I am not going to leave you alone until you say you will."

"You might as well do what she says," Leonie said. "She won't let go. You know perfectly well that our Zorah is like a tick."

Shayndel pulled away from Zorah's grasp. "All right, I'll try," she relented, and chased after Seligman.

Zorah trailed behind and watched as Shayndel caught up with him. Seligman turned around with the bemused, tolerant smile of an adult responding to someone else's annoying child. After Shayndel made her request, he put the clipboard under his arm and actually lifted his finger to deliver a lecture about procedure or fairness or some other principle. But she interrupted, saying something that made him stand up straight and look her in the eye.

He lowered his chin and asked a question.

As Shayndel answered, her eyes narrowed and her jaw tightened, and in that moment the immigrant girl turned into a battle-tested commander. At one point, she reached up to her shoulder as though she were searching for something. She leaned close and pointed at the clipboard.

Seligman bit his lip as he flipped through the papers, pretending to look for something, taking a long time to prove that he was the one who wielded the power. Then he made an offer, screwing up his face like he was biting into a slice of lemon.

Shayndel nodded her thanks primly and walked away with the hint of a swagger in her step.

"So where are we going?" Zorah asked.

"Nowhere yet," Shayndel said. "You'll all be staying here until they come up with a place that will take the three of you. It may take a few more days. But you have to understand that this may be temporary. You could be split up again at any time."

"I just want to get them settled," Zorah said, and raised an eyebrow. "And wherever we go, I will let it be known that we have a friend in very high places."

"You are relentless," said Shayndel. "Go tell Esther and Jacob."

Zorah took Shayndel's hand. "Thank you, my friend."

Tedi had nothing to pack, so she wandered around the kibbutz, inhaling the comforting aroma of baking potatoes, the happy stink of the goats, the dry-kindling smell of fallen pine needles. A few kibbutzniks asked where she was going, but none of them had been to Negba. They wished her good luck and safe journey and invited her back for a longer visit.

By midmorning, she was sitting on a bench near the front gate, where Esther and Jacob found her. Tedi hugged the boy so tightly that he pushed away and said, "You are strong," and ran back toward the children's house. Esther kissed her on the forehead and scurried after him.

A little while later, Leonie, Zorah, and Shayndel sat down with Tedi, but nobody felt much like talking.

After a while, Leonie said, "Too bad that Nissim fellow isn't going to the same place as you."

"I heard they took all the Iraqis straight to Yagur," said Shayndel. "By now, they're probably scattered around the country, where no one can find them." The others nodded.

They ate a quiet lunch and returned to the bench, moving closer together as the afternoon wore on. Esther and Jacob came by again, but Jacob could not sit still and Esther promised to return. Shayndel took Tedi's hand. Leonie put her head on Tedi's shoulder.

Tedi was grateful for the silence, sure she would break into pieces if anyone asked her a question.

At three o'clock, another woman from Atlit joined them on the bench. She was carrying a one-year-old baby and a basket full of pink and white clothes, gifts from the kibbutz nursery. "I hear it's hot in Negba," said the young mother. "But it's close to the seashore. That will be nice, don't you think?"

It was nearly five when the jeep pulled up to the gate. The moment she saw it, Tedi jumped to her feet. "Does anyone have a camera?" she demanded. "I want a picture of us together—Shayndel, Leonie, Zorah, and me."

The woman with the baby got into the jeep, but Tedi refused to budge. "I cannot go without a photograph," she said, her voice suddenly high and shrill. "Surely someone has a camera."

Seligman walked over. "You lot again? What's the problem now?"

"All I want in the world is a photograph," said Tedi. She showed him the small paper bag that held all of her worldly possessions, but it was her brimming blue eyes that undid him.

He offered her his handkerchief and said, "There's an old Brownie in the office."

The driver honked his horn. Leonie went over to ask him for a little patience, and Seligman returned with the boxy black camera.

"Get ready," he called as he ran toward them.

The girls stood in line as he peered through the lens. "Everyone smile. One-two-three. That's it. Good. Good luck. Goodbye."

Tedi hugged him. "Promise you'll send it to me: Tedi Pastore, Kibbutz Negba. Write it down."

He chucked her under the chin. "How could I forget anyone as pretty as you?"

"No, no," she insisted. "You must write it down. I will not go if you don't." She grabbed his pen and clipboard and scribbled her name and the kibbutz on a piece of paper, and stuffed it into his shirt pocket.

Her friends surrounded her. The four of them held each other, weeping and whispering salty oaths.

"See you again," said Zorah. "This is not good-bye."

The driver leaned on the horn and gunned the ignition.

Tedi sobbed as she ran through the gate. She kneeled on the seat as the jeep pulled away and shouted, "Write to me! Shayndel, Leonie, Zorah! Remember: Kibbutz Negba. Tell Esther good-bye. Give Jacob a kiss. We will see one another again."

Epilogue

The Photograph

Seligman forgot to empty his shirt pocket that night and Tedi's address went into the laundry, where the ink washed away and the paper melted to lint.

It was a full year before the roll of film was developed and returned to the kibbutz. The pictures were laid out on a table in the dining hall, but no one recognized the four young women standing by the gate. Seligman had left Beit Oren and even if he had been there, he would have been hard-pressed to remember the name of the girl who had begged him to take the picture, much less where she had been sent.

The other pictures in that batch were group shots of one sort or another. There were weddings and holiday meals, parties and dances. The snapshots were all meant to go into a kibbutz archive, but they had a habit of disappearing. Wedding photos were taken almost immediately, purloined by brides for family albums. The photos of birthday parties vanished over time, claimed, far too often, by young widows who had no other pictures to show their fatherless sons and daughters.

Because no one could identify Tedi or her friends, their picture was consigned to an envelope with blurred images of crowded Seder tables and out-of-focus horas. Over the years, the leftover photos were moved into a cardboard folder, which yellowed as it was transferred from desk drawer to filing cabinet.

From time to time, one of the more enterprising Beit Oren children would discover the cache of old pictures and use them for projects about early kibbutz life, until finally there was barely anything left from the 1940s.

In 1987, the Beit Oren kibbutz went bankrupt, ceased being a collective, and reorganized as a spa and mountain hotel for tourists. Some of the old-timers stayed on as part-owners, but only a handful of them remembered what it had been like in the days before statehood.

For now, the Kibbutz Beit Oren archive—a few letters and some first-person accounts, as well as a handful of orphaned pictures—resides in a battered gunmetal gray cabinet inside a tiny, damp, cinder-block building within sight of the swimming pool.

The visitor from America walked through the chill of an overcast March morning, up the winding pathway surrounded by enormous hosta plants, sheltered by graceful pines. She had taken a tour of Atlit, now an education center at the site of the old internment camp—a museum surrounded by a barbwire fence. The story of the heroic rescue and the perilous climb up the mountains had moved her to learn more.

Leafing through a fly-specked folder in the one-room hut,

she picked up a photograph of four young women. "Could these girls have been among the ones who were rescued?"

"I couldn't tell you," said Gershon, Beit Oren's unofficial historian, an unbowed, still-handsome elderly man whose recent illness had not dimmed his smile or the light in his blue eyes.

"I was not here at that particular time," he said. "I was back in Romania, helping to bring more of our people to Israel. It is possible that these girls could have been among the group from Atlit, but there are only a few of us left from those days, and I'm sorry to say that I've got the best memory of the bunch." He smiled. "Perhaps someone at the museum can tell you. They have computers there, you know."

Gershon cleaned his glasses and took another look at the picture.

Shayndel and Leonie stand at the center, hip to hip, arms around each other's shoulders. Their heads are tilted, almost touching. They are the same height and wear similar white, short-sleeved blouses; even their smiles seem to match, except for the fact that Leonie's eyes are open so wide, she seems haunted.

Leonie hated having her picture taken. Her husband—a doctor she met in '46—would beg and tease to get her to smile for the camera, but she would always turn away. After ten childless years, they divorced, and Leonie never remarried. For forty years, she worked as a clerk in a Tel Aviv hospital; when the staff was assembled for its annual portrait, Leonie hid in the last row.

Shayndel gazes straight into the lens. Her grin leaps off the paper, still infectious even after forty years.

It is the same forthright expression she wore in the early pictures of her with Malka and Wolfe in Europe. The same in the later family snapshots, sitting between her son, Noah, and her daughter, Tedi.

Tedi stands to Leonie's right. She is a full head taller than the others, a blonde beacon with a tentative smile. She blinked just as the shutter closed. Her hand is raised as if to wave.

Shayndel was pregnant when she found out that Tedi had been killed in the Egyptian attack on Negba.

At Shayndel's left, Zorah seems to be moving toward the camera, her right shoulder ahead of the left. Although her lips are pressed together, not quite smiling, her eyes are dancing. She looks younger and more carefree than anyone else in the picture.

Meyer was killed in '48, weeks after the declaration of Israel's statehood, and Zorah married a Polish survivor. They raised two sons in a cramped, three-room Jerusalem apartment, and she worked in the library at Hebrew University until her death. At the memorial service, students and professors recalled her infallible memory, her green raincoat, and the way she pressed candied dates on anyone who walked into her cubicle. Shayndel read the obituary, which reported that the distinguished cardiologist, Dr. Jacob Zalinksy, delivered a moving eulogy about her abiding friendship with his mother.

Gershon pointed at Zorah. "See how this one hides her arm behind her back? She must have been a survivor from the camps."

"But she looks so happy," said the American.

"Why not?" he asked. "She was alive. She had made it to the land of Israel. From the look of this picture, she had friends. She was young, pretty."

"That sounds like a happy ending."

"I hope she was happy. I hope all of them were," said Gershon as he slid the picture back into the folder. "But that wasn't the end.

"That was just the beginning."

Acknowledgments

Thanks to many teachers, friends, guides, and supporters in Israel, beginning with Baruch Kraus, principal of the NFTY-EIE High School, from whom I first heard the story of the rescue from Atlit. Elisheva Benstein was an indispensable translator, researcher, reader, driver, and ally through the whole process. Alon Badihi, in his role as Executive Vice Chairman of the Society for Preservation of Israel Heritage Sites, enthusiastically aided and guided my research, arranged visits to the Atlit Illegal Immigrant Detention Camp, and organized meetings with site director Zehavit Rotenberg, and historian/archivist Neomi Izhar, who were gracious hosts and generous resources. Thanks also to Hagit Krik, Atlit Camp Guide; to Kibbutz Yagur and Kibbutz Beit Oren for use of their archives; and to Moshe Triwaks of Matar Publishing for his kindness and encouragement.

It was a privilege to meet with Tzvi Carmi of Kibbutz Beit Oren, and Haifa resident Osnat Blechman, both of whom experienced Atlit firsthand. Thanks also to Sara Emanuel, Haya Harari, Ruth Gorney, Murray Greenfield, Dr. Gershon Yelin, and Dr. Naftali Hadas, who shared their stories of Atlit, the war, and the years before the founding of the state of Israel.

My friends and teachers, Lorel Zar-Kessler, cantor of Congregation Beth El of the Sudbury River Valley, and Rabbi Tara Feldman accompanied me on visits to Atlit and helped me understand what I saw and heard there.

For their advice, comments, and various forms of encouragement, I am indebted to Eleanor Epstein, Laurie Gervis, Marcia Leifer, Ben Loeterman, Rabbi Barbara Penzner, Sondra Stein, Sebastian Stuart, and Ande Zellman. Thanks to Amanda Urban at ICM and everyone at Scribner, especially Nan Graham, Samantha Martin, Susan Moldow, and Paul Whitlatch.

I was cheered on by my family—daughter Emilia, mother Helene, and brother Harry. Jim Ball, my husband, was a rock—as always.

Amy Hoffman and Stephen McCauley have been strong, wise, and patient writing group partners/coaches/nursemaids every step of the way. I am glad to be in their debt, forever.